**Eden couldn't remem~~ber~~
been more frightened by a stranger…**

…and more intrigued.

If Ashur had told her the truth, she was in deep
trouble. How did she dare escape an angel
with supernatural abilities? Her only choice
was to trust this man who called himself an
angel slayer. What was that exactly? Was he
even human?

But what she craved now was something entirely
different than she was accustomed to dating.
Like the sexy, rock-hard abs of her slayer—
whatever he was.

Ashur was the opposite of everything she'd ever
found sexy in a man. Pure muscle and might.
Commanding. And a bit arrogant, too.

And she wanted it all.

Books by Michele Hauf

Harlequin Nocturne

*From the Dark #3
Familiar Stranger #21
*Kiss Me Deadly #24
*His Forgotten Forever #44
*The Devil to Pay #55
†The Highwayman #68
†Moon Kissed #72
**Angel Slayer #90

*Bewitching the Dark
†Wicked Games
**Of Angels and Demons

HQN Books

Her Vampire Husband

MICHELE HAUF

has been writing for more than a decade and has published historical, fantasy and paranormal romance. A good strong heroine, action and adventure, and a touch of romance make for her favorite kind of story. (And if it's set in France, all the better.) She lives with her family in Minnesota, and loves the four seasons, even if one of them lasts six months and can be colder than a deep freeze. You can find out more about her at www.michelehauf.com.

ANGEL SLAYER
MICHELE HAUF

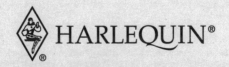

HARLEQUIN®

TORONTO • NEW YORK • LONDON
AMSTERDAM • PARIS • SYDNEY • HAMBURG
STOCKHOLM • ATHENS • TOKYO • MILAN • MADRID
PRAGUE • WARSAW • BUDAPEST • AUCKLAND

Recycling programs
for this product may
not exist in your area.

ISBN-13: 978-0-373-61837-8

ANGEL SLAYER

Copyright © 2010 by Michele Hauf

This edition published by arrangement with Harlequin Books S.A.

For questions and comments about the quality of this book
please contact us at Customer_eCare@Harlequin.ca.

® and TM are trademarks of the publisher. Trademarks indicated with
® are registered in the United States Patent and Trademark Office, the
Canadian Trade Marks Office and in other countries.

www.eHarlequin.com

Printed in U.S.A.

Dear Reader,

I've done a few series for the Nocturne line, including Bewitching the Dark, Wicked Games and now Of Angels and Demons. Even though they are placed into different "series," all these stories take place in the same world. I always know that anything can exist in my world, be it vampires and werewolves, or faeries, golems and witches—even the devil Himself. It was time to explore truly vast opposites.

So set aside all you know and believe about angels and demons. I'm going to twist things up a bit. You think all angels are benevolent and good? And demons are bad, right? Well, not in this story. I based some of my mythology on the *Book of Enoch*, a pseudepigraphic work ascribed to Enoch, the great-grandfather of Noah. But that was merely a starting point. It's all my crazy thinking in this series, so you can blame me when your guardian angel shoots you a sexy grin or even a malevolent sneer.

Michele

The Internet makes it possible to "meet" and "know" so many people. As a writer I am always thrilled to hear from fans and readers. One reader, in particular, Anna Dougherty, hung around a bit on a blog I participate in with a group of writers. I didn't know Anna at all, but sensed from her comments she liked paranormal romance. So when I began my vampire book club project, Bite Club, I e-mailed her to see if she would have an interest in heading it up. She agreed, but I don't think she realized it would become such a "huge" project. Bite Club takes a lot of time and dedication, and Anna has it in spades. She dove into the project and made it her own, and Bite Club simply would not exist without her devotion, organization and vamp-smarts.

So, here's to you, Anna! Many thanks!

Prologue

An obsidian sea roiled behind a black titanium throne. The throne grew up from the sea at the tongue of a dark steel island, its surface intermittently visible through the wavering liquid surface.

A demon sat upon the throne, his horned head bowed. A crown of bone and feathers tilted upon his skull. His powerful forearms relaxed upon the throne arms. Taloned fingers of muscled black flesh tapped resolutely.

He had been tapping for centuries. It meant nothing. It passed the time.

A silver cloud, thick as mercury, dusted across the sea. The commotion behind him made no noise.

Noise did not exist here—Beneath. At times he attempted to sense his own heartbeat. He had a heart. It was black, forged from the same ineffable substance of which he'd been forged. But he had never heard it beat. Never.

He did not require that confirmation of life. He knew

he existed on a level forbidden to most, and unreachable by mere mortals. Feared by all others.

He was Ashuriel the Black, Stealer of Souls, Master of Dethnyht. Only he wore the crown. Not a mortal or paranormal creature in any of the realms—no matter how twisted and black—should like to claim the same.

Time did not exist here, though he knew he had once grasped the hours and days and even years that some valued to order their lives. He had no need. He had lost memory of time, of physicality and sensation, and emotion.

Save the one emotion he yet clung to as if a screaming soul seeking escape—but he would not think on it, for to do so would render excruciating pain throughout his being.

When a brilliant burst shimmered across the jet surface of the sea it startled him. He had not been aware such light could exist Beneath.

Ashuriel lifted his head. The black armor he wore— fashioned from demonic metal mined from the depths of his realm—clanked, but the noise was only imagined, not real.

He waited for the light to form into shape, a recognizable creature, something that would remind him of what he'd once known in another time, another place. It did not.

Instead the light brightened until he had to close his eyes, and yet the intensity seared a bold flash across the inside of his metallic lids. Strange warmth welled inside him, but he could not touch the meaning or properly label it.

"You are summoned, Sinistari," the light intoned in a voice so deep it vibrated inside Ashuriel's metal chest.

And then the light vanished, leaving only a fading silver resonance behind his eyelids.

Reaching for the crown of bone and feathers upon his head, the Sinistari demon removed it. He stroked a talon over the thirteen feathers of all colors and design that marked a kill, each of them.

The Sinistari were summoned for only one reason. He'd thought the threat was controlled and swept away with the great flood. A time long ago, or perhaps only moments had passed.

But he would not question a summons.

Cracking his neck from side to side, he stood from the throne and stretched out his arms, thrust out his chest and sucked in the airless nothing about him.

Ashuriel let out a roar. The noise was audible, and it shuddered waves across the obsidian sea. It pleased him. Dangling the crown on one long finger, he flicked it over a shoulder to land upon the throne.

The master slayer was back in business.

Chapter 1

Eden Campbell worked the small corner art gallery across the street from Chelsea Park like a pro. Though she cautioned herself not to break into song or shout, "Hey! This is my first gallery showing and it means the world to me, and it's going well!"

No, that would be crass. Beyond the occasional eccentricity, she was known for her calm, collected demeanor—and her killer legs, which she'd decided to showcase as well as her artwork this afternoon.

She was happiest in sweats and a T-shirt when painting, but she could do the sexy businesswoman look, too. A black leather skirt skimmed her thighs. A white long-sleeved silk blouse boasted a deep V-neckline and ruffles at wrist and waist. Diamond chandelier earrings added a necessary touch of romance. She'd pulled her waist-length wavy hair into a loose ponytail to keep it from tangling in her earrings. Sexy violet suede stilettos finished the look with a promise of things Eden usually only whispered, and only to men.

She unbuttoned her left sleeve because her forearm tingled weirdly, much like getting hit in the funny bone. The thought to scratch it was put off when she caught the eye of a woman in black horn-rims who thrust her a discerning nod.

"Act professional," she coached inwardly. "You want them to take your work seriously."

As seriously as a woman with preternatural knowledge of the heavenly ranks could be taken. That was a detail she kept close to the cuff.

The people milling about were all like her—rich, stylish, entitled—but not like her. Eden wondered if they had heartbreaks, dreams and obsessions. Or did they simply exist on the surface, decorating themselves to catch an approving nod from the right kind and class of person?

Eden didn't require approval. She wanted to exist in her world, even if it wasn't like their world beneath the surface. She tried to fit in, and succeeded. Most saw her as a privileged society woman who attended charity balls and had once been a common fixture on Page Six.

But this artistic side of her was the real Eden, no fake smiles allowed. This showing was her attempt to show them she needed to breathe her own air, as different as that may be.

It was easier for her to walk behind people and listen in on conversations about her work than to boldly approach a visitor face-to-face. *Control the urge to tell them what you know. It's all there on the canvas; they can figure it out for themselves.* Sure, a few friends were in the mix for support, but Todd, who worked part-time at the gallery, and Cammie, a friend since prep school, lingered somewhere off near the wine and cheese.

Eden caught the middle of a conversation and frowned.

"But angels are heavenly beings. Innately good," the critic argued with a friend. "What the heck is that?"

That was one of her favorite pieces.

Eden painted only angels, but their variety was as vast as her imagination. Rarely did she paint a winged angel descending on a beam of light from the clouds. That image had been overdone.

And really, she knew fluffy wings and white robes were all wrong.

Hence, her titanium angel with steampunk-geared wings of binary code. Its face was hollow, exposing honeycomb bone, and silver filaments sprouted on the skull. A halo spun like the rings of Saturn at the back of its head. The angel's grin was more seductive than some of the expressions Eden had seen on her lackluster dates of late.

"It's blasphemous," the critic decided.

Eden shrugged and walked on. Definitely not her sales base. Didn't matter. She wasn't showing her work to make a profit; she simply wanted to hear what others thought. And so far most of the feedback had been awesome.

A particular man caught her eye. He stood before The Fall, her depiction of an angel falling from the heavens. The angel wore a devious smile on its glass face and its redwood wings blazed with blue fire. Steel rain extinguished some of the flame. Its halo, detached, cut through the rain, spattering it like oil stains. A single crystal tear dripped from the angel's eye and stained the ground it had yet to touch.

Though he was unusual in appearance, the man who studied her work didn't shock Eden. All sorts crowded Manhattan; she loved the exercise in individuality. Silver-white hair punked about his head. He wore a black eye patch over his left eye, and a tight white T-shirt enhanced considerable abs. Gleaming silver hardware hung from his ears, nose, eyebrows and chin. Leather pants hugged his lanky legs like plastic wrap, rendering the belts buckled about his thighs and hips unnecessary. The entire look screamed anarchist raging for a fire to fan.

Paralleling him, Eden waited to see if he would make the first comment. She didn't like to influence her viewers one way or another.

A familiar scent emanated from him. Sweet and subtle like fruit. He smelled enticing, which baffled her because she was not attracted to his type—it was Wall Street business suits all the way for her.

Her forearm tingled again, like the pins and needles sensation she got when her arm or leg fell asleep. What could it be from? She hadn't challenged Cammie to a match of tennis for weeks. She shrugged up her sleeve to scratch, then reminded herself to be cool.

When finally the punk jerked a shoulder back and looked at her it was as if she had materialized beside him out of the blue.

"Sorry," Eden offered politely. "Didn't mean to surprise you."

"My fault. I was lost in the painting. It's interesting. You are very…" His one pale gold eye squinted as he studied her face. Rather, gold was the prominent color. Many colors glittered like a kaleidoscope in that single eye. A trace of blue curled out the bottom of the eye patch. Must be a tattoo.

"Unremarkable," he finally announced. "Your voice is green," he continued. "Square. And your scent…" He sniffed. "Smooth. But those shoes. Violet. Yes. Nice. Short leather skirt. Hair…chestnut."

His weird inventory unsettled Eden. She didn't judge people by their clothing choices, personal habits or even religion. Hell, she'd been judged far too many times.

Intuition, on the other hand, had a tendency to knock a little too late on her skull.

"Who are you?" He tilted his head and looked her up and down. It was the most uncomfortable dressing down Eden had ever experienced. She should politely dismiss herself.

Yet what was with her arm? Eden's divided attention pestered her. Something strange was going on beneath the silk sleeve. That was the last time she took her shirts to the dry cleaners on Fifth. She suspected they weren't as green as their ads claimed to be.

"I'm the artist," she offered and thrust out her hand. The punk looked at it a few moments before shaking it. "Eden Campbell."

"Eden. How…sardonic. Means nothing. What I want to know is how you know all…this."

"This?"

"That!" He gestured angrily toward the painting. "You've quite the talent. One could call it a preternatural talent."

"You think?" Heartbeats skipping, Eden beamed at the painting. No one had ever labeled her work that way. She was the only one who believed she had—

Stop it, Eden. He hasn't a clue. Do not make a fool of yourself.

"If I were of the mind to purchase I'd buy them all," he remarked, "but unfortunately I've no permanent residence. Bit of a world traveler."

"That must be exciting."

"There is something about you, Eden." He leaned in close and his fruity scent enticed her to remain in place, despite the creepy stranger signals he was sparking out at her. "Do you by chance," he whispered, "wear a sigil on your body?"

"A sigil?" That was a weird question, but oddly intuitive.

Could he also know what she knew?

The man glanced about the crowded gallery, not appearing too interested in her response.

No. What Eden knew about her paintings was private, personal. He hadn't a clue, and she didn't dare discuss it because she had a healthy fear for mental wards.

Compelled to get away from the man, Eden slipped away while he studied the painting, insinuating herself behind a few tall men in business suits.

Todd appeared and slipped a goblet of pinot noir into her grasp. "I thought you were taking off before six, Eden? I can close up shop and handle the stragglers." He tugged at his pink tie; it clashed brilliantly with his purple shirt and his soft emerald eyes.

"Thanks, Todd. Did you talk to the guy with the white hair and all the nose rings?"

"Not yet. He just wandered in. Creepy?"

"To the tenth degree. He makes me feel uncomfortable." And yet, intrigued. Could a person be compelled and repelled at the same time?

"Want me to go punch him for you?"

She hugged Todd across the shoulders. "No. Save those valuable fingers for your IT work. I think I'm going to sneak out, though. I've been here six hours. Need to sit and put my feet up. See you tomorrow evening for part deux of Eden Campbell's fabulous debut."

"I'll be here. But it'll be a close call. I've a shift at Cloud Nine until five." He kissed her check. "Talk to you later, sweetie."

Eden tilted down the wine and claimed her purse from the office before deftly making her way toward the front door.

Rolling up her left sleeve as she gained the door, she spied the top of the strange man's white hair. He still stood before The Fall. His attention was rapt, so she was able to slip out without his notice.

After hobnobbing in the stuffy gallery for hours, Eden welcomed the refreshing summer rain. She lifted her face to catch the light mist. She should have utilized her father's limo, always at her disposal, but the driver's son turned twelve today, so she'd given him the day off. She wasn't one of those trust-fund babies who thought they were entitled to everything. At least, she tried not to be.

The July sun peeked through the clouds and glinted high on the windows of another trendy little gallery across the street. She examined her forearm. It had stopped tingling and the skin wasn't red so it couldn't be a rash.

Tapping the birthmark below her inner elbow, she wondered at what the punk had asked her.

Do you wear a sigil on your body?

"How could he know?" Was it possible he knew things like she did?

"No." He must have seen her tug up her sleeve. Talk about a cheap pickup line at its strangest.

Waving her arm, she sought a cab. The sidewalk was cluttered with people en route to the subway for the supper rush. Toeing the curb, Eden was distracted by the sudden appearance of the white-haired man charging toward her.

A cab pulled up with a squeal.

Startled by the man's intent path toward her, Eden rushed for the cab's back door and managed to open it just as the punk grabbed her by the wrist.

"You were holding out on me, Eden."

The wild look in his eye cautioned her. His crooked grin freaked her. "Let go of me!"

He stroked his fingers over her forearm. "A number. That's an interesting one. Six," he pronounced with a hiss.

She struggled, but his grip pinched her skin.

Then he did something so bizarre Eden could but stand, frozen like a scared alley cat, and watch. He licked her forearm, right below the weird birthmark that looked like a Roman numeral six. As if from a cat's tongue, the contact abraded her skin.

His exposed eye now glowed a brilliant blue as he drew his gaze up to hers.

Survival impulse kicked in. Eden leaned against the cab and kicked high. The spike of her heel sunk into his gut. The man staggered backward with a yowl of pain.

Eden bent and landed in the backseat of the cab butt-first. "Go!" she yelled. "There's a creep after me." She slammed the door shut as the cab spun away from the curb.

"Fight with the boyfriend?" the cabbie asked in a Texan accent.

"What?" She was so flustered, she sat sprawled across the backseat, arms groping for hold and one leg still poised for another kick against the door. "Boyfriend? No, he dumped me after the— No! I've never seen the guy before."

"They're all a bunch of crazies. Where to?"

"Just drive!"

She shuffled upright on the seat and looked out the rear window. The punk's arms pumped vigorously.

"He's running after us!" He couldn't possibly catch a car on foot, could he? "Take the next left turn. Don't slow down or let him catch up."

"Yes, ma'am. A car chase. Haven't done one of those in a while."

"Yeah? There's a big tip in it for you if you lose the guy."

"He's on foot." The cabbie gunned the engine. "No problem."

Shaking the rain from her hair and tugging up her sleeve, Eden stroked her forearm. It was pink.

"He licked me," she said in horror.

"What did you say?"

"That man, he licked me. Why do you think he'd do that? Oh my God, I wonder if he has AIDS? No, I couldn't get it that way. What are you doing? I said don't stop!"

"Sorry, ma'am, red light."

Eden twisted up onto her knees and scanned the sidewalk. No sight of the punk. He was thin and she hadn't nailed him for being overly strong. That she'd been able to kick him away impressed her inner kick-ass chick. He must have given up. Though it was likely a man on foot could catch a cab in this rush-hour traffic—

Thunk.

The man landed on the trunk of the car on all fours, as if an animal had dropped from above.

"Holy crap," the cabbie said, and rolled through the green light. "That is a mite dangerous."

"Shake him off," Eden warbled nervously. She slid her hand along her thigh, feeling for the small blade she kept strapped there. "He's climbing onto the top of the cab."

"I don't want anyone to get hurt," the cabbie protested.

A sudden right turn resulted in a clatter across the top of the vehicle. Eden saw the punk land on the asphalt— on two feet. Not like he'd been whipped off the car and couldn't catch his bearings. He was agile and determined. One glowing blue eye remained focused on the cab.

"Unbelievable," the cabbie said. "There's a short tunnel ahead. We'll lose him in there."

"Go for it!"

The punk stood in the middle of the road, right on the

yellow no-pass center line. Arms curved out in a fierce stance, he stomped one booted foot and snarled.

Eden couldn't comprehend this.

He must be on drugs to have survived being thrown from the top of the car, and then to stand as if nothing had happened. Now he ran after the cab like some indestructible robot from a sci-fi movie.

"Drive faster!"

The cab interior went dark. The red lights lining the inner walls of the tunnel flashed intermittently. The cab slowed.

"What are you doing? Traffic is going faster than this. Keep up!"

"It's…an…angel…" the cabbie said in a wondrous tone.

"What?" Eden leaned over the front seat, dodging her head down to see around the rearview mirror. "I'm the only nut who ever thinks she sees an— I don't see anything. You have a clear lane. Keep driving!"

She snapped her fingers next to the cabbie's ear. He shook his head as if snapping out of a trance.

Daylight burst into the cab as the car cruised out of the tunnel. Ahead, a four-way stop did not slow the cab. Eden gripped the driver's-seat headrest and twisted her body to scan out the side and rear windows. No sign of the punk.

Then the cab turned left—into oncoming traffic—and Eden's body was thrown from the back of the cab into the front. Her head plunged toward the passenger side floor. Impact thudded her shoulder. Metallic blood trickled across her tongue.

The vehicle's tires left the tarmac. The cab flipped and landed upside-down, spinning twice before slamming into a street signal pole. Glass shattered. Iron bent.

Eden blacked out.

* * *

Her eyelids fluttered.

The smell of gasoline mixed with the sweet odor of blood. Her chin was shoved down to her chest and her legs felt higher than her shoulders.

Trapped.

Blinking rapidly, Eden grasped for what had happened. The accident. They'd run a stop sign. Because the punk with the eye patch had tracked them across the city—on foot!

She eased herself out through the open door and landed on the street on her knees. Safety glass littered the ground, but she avoided it. Peering into the taxi, she spied the cabbie, his head on the steering wheel. There was no visible blood, and he was groaning.

"Not dead, thank goodness."

A constant honking car horn effectively cleared her foggy brain. Other vehicles had been involved in the crash—two more, she saw from her kneeling position.

Fore in Eden's mind remained the strange man. He'd literally been hell-bent on getting to her. Was he still in pursuit? Had he been hit by one of the cars that had collided in the accident?

She slid shaky fingers along her forearm. It itched where he had licked her. She scratched, but a drop of blood on the seat distracted her. Where had that—? She touched her head. A gash across her eyebrow bled. Didn't feel deep. It didn't hurt at all, which could be a good thing, or very bad.

A slide of fingers under her skirt and along her thigh verified the small blade still there. She could have been poked with it. She'd been fortunate.

"Have to…" If the punk found her what would he do? Heart racing toward a cliff, she couldn't think beyond the insanity her pursuer had instilled in her. "Hide."

Shuffling backward, Eden scrambled along the curb until she stopped at a spinning tire attached to a battered SUV. The radio inside the car blasted a Jimmy Hendrix tune.

Bent over, she crept-walked around the front of the SUV and spied a magazine stand on the sidewalk. She dove to the ground behind the wooden rack, her position hidden from the accident scene.

The sound of a new crash, like rubber-soled boots landing on a trunk, set her rigid. Already her heart beat maniacally. She couldn't get more alert or tense.

"Here, pretty, pretty."

It was the punk. Clasping her arms about her legs, she winced when her forearm crushed another cut below her knee. She would not cry. She must not make noise.

What would a man who had followed her through traffic, been thrown off a moving vehicle and was sorting through the scene of a wreckage want with her? No answer was good.

And any answer tested the boundaries of what was real and what could only be supernatural. Eden believed in beings not like herself. She had to, because she believed in angels.

The boots stomped the sidewalk not twenty feet from where Eden hid. She heard a snorting noise, like some kind of animal. He was…sniffing. It was as if he were a wild cat stalking its prey.

She didn't like thinking that word—*prey*. Her gut clenched and she tried to stifle the uncontrollable need to sob.

Boot steps slowly approached. They paused and she heard a sniffing sound, as if he were testing the air. Then the boots jumped onto a vehicle and she heard metal crunch beneath them.

In the distance an ambulance siren wailed. Eden realized people from nearby shops had begun to step out and were gathering near the crashed cars.

"Not here," the punk growled under his breath. "Bitch got away." He landed on the asphalt. It sounded like he was walking away.

The back of Eden's head fell against the boards behind her. She could be injured but she didn't care. It was a relief to know the creep had given up. Finally.

She scratched the itch on her forearm. As if a wasp sting, it burned worse than any of her cuts.

The crowd exhaled a collective gasp, as if they'd witnessed something strange or horrible.

A pair of heavy leather biker boots landed on the sidewalk right next to Eden.

Chapter 2

The punk leaned over Eden, extending his hand for her to grasp. She fixated on the shiny steel bar pierced through his nose as if a bullring waiting for tether. His smile was wrinkled. It didn't meet his kaleidoscope eye. Nothing on his face was cohesive.

He did not speak, yet the eye not covered with the patch screamed at her. The promise of something vast and unfamiliar shouted from that eye. It frightened her.

And it compelled her.

She'd almost touched that feeling once. A year ago. *Joy*.

The crowd again gasped in unison as rubber peeled across the asphalt. Out of the corner of her eye, Eden saw a motorcycle do a one-eighty. The rumbling steel bike approached the accident too quickly. Surely it would crash—

The rear tire stopped two feet from her legs.

The white-haired punk snarled and leaped away from

her. It was a physically impossible move, because he soared straight up through the air, flipped in a backward somersault and landed on the other side of the crashed cab.

"My lady, take my hand," commanded the black-leather-clad motorcyclist. "If you want to be safe."

Too much happening. So much to register. But Eden heard *safe* and scrambled to her feet.

Yet she looked to the punk, standing poised to leap upon the hood of a stalled car. Still, his eye beckoned.

I can give you what you seek. If you dare to take it.

"Now, my lady!" the rider insisted.

Shaking from shoulders to legs, wanting to scream, and wondering why she could not physically make a sound, Eden was tugged onto the motorcycle behind the imposing man.

She recorded sensations only. The rough slide of leather under her palms as she groped to wrap her arms about his waist. The burn of the exhaust cylinder when she initially put her shoeless foot right on it.

The intense realization that the man was solid, hard and all muscle. Yes, safe.

The rider gripped her by the ankle and pulled her foot higher to hook behind his booted foot. She sucked in a gasp as his fingers clasped about her bare flesh. At this frantic moment it was too strange to feel desire, yet she did.

The command he projected with the protective move melted her resistance. The world wobbled and skinned her face with brisk air as the motorcycle sped away from the scene of the crash. She clung desperately, crushing her cheek to the supple plane of his leather-clad back.

She didn't know who this man was, but he'd taken her away from the other man who had looked like a junkie. A man whose hand she had almost taken because the un-spoken promise in his gaze had reached inside and touched a part of her she'd thought buried.

Had she heard him say, "I can give you what you seek"?

How could he know what she wanted? Half the time she didn't know what she wanted.

Safety was fore on that unknown list, and she grasped it, if only for the moment.

"Stop ahead on Eleventh Avenue," she yelled. Eden could barely hear her voice. She doubted he could hear her over the roar of the motor. "Please!"

He reached back to slide a hand along her thigh. Her skirt road up high and his palm burnished her flesh. It wasn't a suggestive move, but more to ensure she was still there. Safe. The tingling desire she'd felt when he'd touched her ankle returned. The touch ignited beneath her skin, shimmying adrenaline and a frenzy of want to her belly.

So this was what the damsel felt like when rescued by the knight?

She'd take it.

Guilt reared up too quickly. They'd ridden away from those injured at the scene. But she'd heard the ambulance. The driver, and any others who may be injured, would be taken to the hospital.

And what of her? Beyond a few cuts she hadn't a more serious injury. What hurt was that damned spot on her arm where the man had licked her. If she were not clinging for life to her rescuer, she'd be scratching.

The motorcycle veered right sharply. Squeezing her thighs against his to hang on, Eden recognized the Chelsea Piers. The area boasted a lot of new developments, but as well, many unoccupied warehouses and storage facilities were badly in need of restoration.

They drove through a narrow warehouse door and into a dark, empty storage room three stories high.

The motorcycle stopped and tilted left as the driver let down the kickstand. Eden slid off. Before the man could speak, she rushed him, threading her arms about his chest and squeezing.

"Thank you," she said. She pushed away and stepped back, sliding her palms down her hips. "Sorry."

"No need for apologies, my lady."

"It was a reaction to being rescued. I don't normally hug strangers. I'm just so thankful."

"This is not a rescue."

"Seriously? What is it? You got me away from that freaky guy."

"He will come to you. I will be waiting."

She scratched her forearm. Cautious to keep the man in view, she scanned her surroundings. The door they'd rolled through was her only way out.

She noticed his curiosity as she scratched. Eden tugged down her sleeve, embarrassed when she should only be thankful she was safe. But was she? He'd said this wasn't a rescue. So what did he intend to do with her, alone in this abandoned building?

She wasn't about to stick around to find out. Reaching up under her skirt, she claimed the blade tucked against her thigh.

Eden dashed toward the open doorway bursting with a shock of orange from the setting sun.

Just as she slapped a palm against the rough wood door frame, a huge body slid before her. Eden's entire body slammed into the unmoving force of man. He was a head taller than she, and twice as wide.

"I prefer you remain in here, my lady."

"Yeah? That's what scares me."

Pushing from his solid chest, Eden stepped away, knife held before her in warning. She'd taken a self-defense course and was prepared to stab if necessary.

But how big could a man be? He filled the doorway.

The low sun behind him glowed about his figure, giving him a remarkable aura, almost heavenly. Black tousled hair shimmered blue and swept low near a square jaw. A line of dark beard, trimmed thin, framed his jaw and lips. A sexy soul patch marked a smudge from his thick lower lip down his chin. His flesh was pale—no sun-worshipper, he—yet his eyes and everything else were so dark. The contrast was exquisite. Handsome was an insufficient term for his beauty.

Yes, she actually thought the man beautiful, like a rock star or an actor pumped up for the role of warrior. Yet she also sensed danger from him.

"My lady." He shook his head at her in pity. "I wouldn't use that little stick to pick my teeth."

Suddenly the knife jerked from her fingers and flew toward his. He caught it and tucked it in the waistband of his pants.

"Who— What? How did you do that?" Eden asked.

She took another step back and clasped her arms across her chest. "You ripped me away from the scene of an accident. I thought you were rescuing me. And who was that man? The punk guy. He chased me through the city on foot! He ran so fast it was like he wasn't human. And he flew away from me when you arrived."

"That was Zaqiel, and he's come for you."

Eden didn't know how to respond to that statement. The name was weird, but the second part of what he'd said was weirder.

"Come for me? Who are you?"

"I am…Ashur." He glanced toward the motorcycle and added, "Ashur Man… Yes, Manning. I won't harm you. I require you to draw Zaqiel here so I can slay him."

"Slay?"

Nausea wavered through Eden. She spread out her

hands in the event she toppled, which was looking probable. But she had to stay strong and keep a clear head. All her instincts screamed danger. And the rescuing knight was beginning to sound more villainous. He had made up the name he'd given her, surely.

"A Fallen one is on your trail," the man—Ashur—said.

"Fallen?"

"Or Grigori, if you prefer."

The oddness of recognition straightened her posture and she found a clear thought. For someone who had been painting angels since she was a teenager, she'd spent a lot of time sorting through books about them. She'd read parts of the Hebrew bible and the pseudepigraphal book of Enoch.

"Do you know what a Grigori is?" she asked, hoping he'd grabbed the wrong term.

"I do." He bowed closer to her, his massive frame shadowing her and making her feel so small. "And you, my lady, do you know what a Grigori is?"

"I most certainly do." She squeezed her forearm because if she scratched any more she'd tear skin. "Next you'll be telling me you carry a flaming sword and—"

Glass crackled from above. A row of windows along the second story shattered. A rain of glass shards poured downward.

Ashur slammed into Eden. Her breath gasped out. He shoved her into the darkness near the far wall, away from the falling slivers of deadly glass.

"He's here. Stay put," he said in a low command. "Don't get in the way."

If he was speaking about the punk being here, Eden didn't see him.

"Where is he?" she called nervously. "How could he have possibly followed us?"

Ashur tilted his head aside and lifted a hand to silence

her. She could sense his anxious alertness. But he wasn't half as tense as her muscles were. They felt ready to snap.

She scratched her forearm.

Suddenly Ashur approached her. He gripped her wrist and looked at the red skin right below the birthmark. "This is how he follows. The angelkiss. It is a beacon. Scratch again, my lady. Lure him to me."

"But he just—" A beacon? Scratching where he had licked her lured the crazy druggie to her? No way was she going to continue. "No, I—"

What sounded like wings, yet sharp and cutting as if metal, sliced the air. Eden searched the broken window frames overhead. She could only huff and try futilely to settle her frantic heartbeat.

"This is not proving successful. He will not approach when he knows I am guarding you." Ashur twisted to look at her. "I must lead him to believe I've left you to your own devices."

"No! Don't leave me alone."

Her outburst caused him to pause. Had he intended to leave her here? Obviously he was weighing it in his mind right now. And had she just asked for help from a man who scared the crap out of her?

All her life she'd wondered about things like angels and the fallen and what they might look like, and now… This could not be happening.

Finally Ashur nodded. "I will not leave you. But my intentions cannot be fulfilled here and now. Give me your hand."

She tucked her hands behind her hips.

Ashur lunged and gripped her wrist, roughly forcing her hand forward. And then he bent and dragged his tongue over her skin, right over the itchy spot where Zaqiel had licked her.

"What the hell?"

"It counteracts the angelkiss," he said. "For a while. Don't scratch until I tell you to do so."

He grabbed her, sweeping her into his arms as effortlessly as if she were a doll. He deposited her on the back of the motorcycle again. Tears rolled down Eden's face as he kicked the bike into gear and they rolled over the litter of glass.

"Tell me where you live. I want the angel to think you are alone and waiting."

"Oh, hell. An angel? A real…? This can't be happening."

"Your address, my lady."

If she had known the address for the police station, Eden would have rambled that one off. Yet the idea of being dropped off at home, where she felt most safe and could lock the doors and keep out all the crazy men after her, sounded too good to be true.

She gave him her address, and the motorcycle picked up speed.

He'd spoken of Fallen angels, and kisses from angels, which made her think he was talking about *real* angels. She believed in angels. They weren't all glowy and peaceful and full of grace as modern media would have a person believe. Some were positively evil—the fallen ones.

Something the cabbie had said returned to her. When they were in the tunnel, the cab had slowed and he said he saw an angel.

Had Zaqiel been that angel?

But why would an angel be after her? Had it something to do with the dreams she'd been having all her life?

As they sped down the pier, Eden glanced over her shoulder and saw Zaqiel keeping track with them on foot.

Chapter 3

Bruce speed-dialed Antonio in Paris, then checked his watch only after he'd done so. It was 6:00 p.m. in New York. That made it something like midnight in Paris.

The receiver clicked. "What?"

"Er, sir, hey. I'm here in New York."

"Obviously. What do you have for me, Bruce?"

"I tracked the Fallen to an art gallery."

"You tag him?"

The GPS injection gun Bruce wore in a holster was still loaded with a cartridge. "No. But I did discover something very interesting." He turned and eyed the gallery, still swarming with mortals oohing and aahing over its contents.

"No tagged vamp? What the hell are you doing? Traipsing through Times Square?"

"Listen, Antonio, I found some paintings you'll want to see."

"Paintings?"

"Yes, they were painted by a chick named Eden Campbell. They are all of angels. I think she knows something. They are remarkable."

"You've never seen an angel, Bruce, what the hell makes you think some woman painting fluffy-winged angels knows something? I'm very disappointed—"

"In each painting the angel wears a sigil," Bruce hastened out. "And I know I've never seen an angel, but I have seen those symbols in that ancient book you used to summon Zaqiel and the other. They are the same. I know it."

He heard shuffling. Antonio must be sitting behind his desk in the cavern. Bruce called the guy's home a cavern because seventy percent of it was located underground. Five hundred years old and sunlight had never touched his skin. Holy water burned him and he seriously could not see his reflection in a mirror. He was old world all the way.

"You swear this is serious?" Antonio asked.

"I'm sure of it, boss."

"Who is the woman? How does she know this?"

"I have no idea. Some society chick. I missed her. I guess she left before I got here. The gallery closes in a few minutes."

"Buy them all," Antonio ordered. "Ship them to me overnight."

"Will do, boss."

A thousand years sitting Beneath, doing nothing more than contemplating emptiness, tends to steal a demon's energy, if not his sense of what is.

What *is*, is the world had changed, Ashur told himself. Drastically. He hadn't afforded the time to look at his surroundings upon arrival here on earth. Immediately he focused on tracking Zaqiel. It was what he did; nothing else concerned him.

So why was he cruising through an overcrowded city on a strange two-wheeled vehicle with a muse clinging to his back?

He never got involved with the muse. The woman was merely bait, a necessary lure to bring the Fallen into its half angel/half human form—the only form in which it could be killed. As well, the form it assumed to impregnate the muse.

Generally Ashur arrived just as the Fallen was going to attempt the muse. Then he slayed the angel.

His timing was irritatingly off. He should not have been summoned until the very moment of the attempt. Had the rules been altered? And why were the Fallen walking earth again? Hadn't their ranks been swept away with the great flood?

He had no concept of how much time had passed since the flood, or since he'd been banished Beneath. Millennia, surely, for the world had changed drastically.

"Take a left!" the woman yelled over the roar of the motor.

Ashur liked the noise of the engine as he revved it, but he did not care to take directions from a female. However, he did turn because he had not navigated this city before, and her directions had given Zaqiel the slip many city blocks earlier.

So long as Zaqiel knew a Sinistari was with the muse, the angel would not approach her. But it was in the angel's interest to keep his muse in sight, for he could not track her by scent but only by the identifying mark. Though the angelkiss made all senses unnecessary.

If the muse irritated the angelkiss, it acted like a beacon.

Ashur did not want to use the angelkiss until he had the woman in a space he could control.

Slender fingers gripped him tightly about the waist, clinging to the front of his shirt. He'd gained a mortal's raiments after surfacing from Beneath. Upon arrival following his summons, Ashur had taken a look around, seen what the mortal men were wearing and had assimilated the trousers, shirt, jacket and boots.

A few minutes observing the men and their motored bikes, and he had learned the driving technique. He'd stolen a bike, leaving behind a crew of leathered bikers shouting at him as they struggled to start their own vehicles. Only one had managed to follow him, but he'd given him the slip.

He'd sacrificed valuable time gathering a few essential tools of this realm, and because of his delay the Fallen was still alive. Yet the angel would have never attempted the woman out in the open with witnesses. Or would he?

The world had changed. Ashur expected everything else—including the Fallen—had changed, as well.

"Drive under there," she said, pointing toward a slope in the street that lunged beneath a towering cement building. "It's my building. You can park underneath in the garage."

Ashur took in the rows of shiny metal vehicles as he rolled slowly down into the cool, lighted garage. Man had come a long way from the horse-drawn carts he recalled. The improvement was unnecessary to judge from the huge, dense city where he suspected most could walk to and from their destinations.

And yet the motorized vehicles were bright and loud. He must get one of those if he were to spend any amount of time here. He slowed and read the words on the back of a vehicle that appealed—Ferrari.

Concentrate, Ashuriel. Do you fall to the old sins so quickly?

Heh. Sins? He'd mastered them all. And with ease.

Mortal sins were not considered evil or wrong to his kind. In fact, indulgence was a way of life.

Theft had come easily, without thought. Vanity, well, he wasn't sure if the clothing he wore was the finest, but he was clothed.

Lust? Well, that suited him fine. He vaguely recalled that particular mortal sin now as the woman's fingers impressed upon his chest. Though the particular elements that designed the sin had been lost to him over years of desolation. He knew it had involved touch and emotion and intense physicality. It would come to him, surely.

Violence would be granted when he shoved Dethnyht into the angel's glass heart.

Parking the motorbike, he pulled out the key, sensing he'd need it to restart the thing. He waited for the muse to slide off behind him. He could feel her head pressed against his back and her fingers didn't so much dig into his chest as affix themselves to it.

Touch. He pressed a palm over her narrow fingers. Yes, he'd forgotten the pressure of another person's flesh against his own. So odd how he could feel her warmth even through the shirt. It shimmered through him and— He must stop regarding the sensation.

"We're here," he said. "It is safe now."

An easy lie. One thing he did remember was the muse was always frantic and inconsolable upon learning her fate—which was usually seconds before the Fallen attempted her. "My lady?"

"Huh? Oh." She slid off and tugged at her torn skirt. It revealed so much of her fine, long legs, Ashur had to steel the sudden desire to stroke his thumb along her thigh. "Sorry. You were…nice to hold on to."

Ashur lingered on her smile, knowing it was a distraction, but unable to resist.

He slid from the bike and tugged off the heavy leather jacket to offer to her. "Here. Your skirt is torn. This will cover your legs." And keep his eyes from straying.

"It's not torn." She dashed a finger along the hem, which upon closer inspection didn't look torn, rather straight, but it was above her knees. "You've never seen a miniskirt before?" She smirked. Somewhere she'd lost her shoes and she stepped on the balls of her feet. "Would you, um, give me back my blade?"

"Why?"

"It's mine. And if you don't, I'm going to scream."

She sought a show of trust. Ashur handed her the blade, and she clasped it to her chest, yet not in defense. Foolish woman.

"Thank you. So, that man… He's a real angel?"

Ashur detected a lightness in her tone that didn't seem right after what she'd been through.

"I mean…" She absolutely beamed at him. "I've always wanted to see one. And everyone has always made me think I'm a nut for believing in them. But if he was the real thing I really need to know because that would mean I'm not crazy, and—"

"Yes," Ashur blurted out, mostly to stop her from rambling. "Zaqiel is a real angel. A Fallen one."

She sucked in the corner of her lip and her eyes flashed brightly. The shadows and shades of gray the world offered him shimmered about her and expanded into a brilliant aura of white. Something inside her wanted to explode, Ashur felt, yet she restrained it by tensing her muscles, and then she did a strange move by bending her arm up and pumping it once. A triumphant gesture?

"Come on," she said, turning and rushing away from the parked motorbike. "I suppose I at least owe you a drink for saving my life. If you could call that a save. You coming?"

He followed her into a small box with doors that closed automatically behind him. The interior was lined with mirrors and a panel of blinking buttons. He recognized the numbers and assumed she knew what she was doing.

"You called this an angelkiss," she said, stretching out her forearm.

"Yes, and don't scratch it." Not yet.

"And why did *you* lick it? Is that some kind of new pickup move I'm not keen on?"

"My saliva counteracts the angelkiss for a while, but it's obviously wearing off if you are feeling the need to scratch. Whatever you do, Six, don't scratch it. It acts as a beacon to Zaqiel. It is the only way he can track you and I'm not yet prepared to face him. I want you in a secure place first."

"Right."

He could sense her fear, but he also sensed her strange fascination. It put out a sweet odor that intrigued him. It had been so long since he had experienced the mortal condition. She was still traumatized. Her fingers shook minutely and she worried her lower lip. A pretty, thick lip that held his attention until the doors opened with an alarming ding.

"Did you call me Six?" she asked as she strode down a white marble hallway carved with elaborate designs. Steps bouncing, she appeared giddy. "What's that about? I do have a name."

"I don't want to know your name."

She glanced over her shoulder. Deep, dark eyes dusted by long lashes took him in. Ashur couldn't determine if they had color; the world—which he knew should be in color—was revealed only in black, white and shades of gray to him. For now.

"Sounds kinky to me," she said.

"Kinky?"

"Yeah, you— Sorry. It's not every day I'm chased by an angel. Will we see him again?"

"Soon. Surely." Ashur quickened his steps to join her before a door where she tapped in some numbers on a lighted panel. "Six." He took her arm gently and turned it up to display the mark. The Roman numeral six sat on the surface of her skin, the color dark like her hair. "That is your sigil."

"It's a birthmark. It does kind of look like a six. But seriously, I'm not going to answer to a stupid number—"

He gripped the door as she pushed it in, stopping her abruptly. "Do not give me your birth name. Please. It is easier this way."

"No commitment with fake names?" she asked. "Easier to walk away?"

"Trust me."

"That's a loaded statement. I distinctly recall you telling me to scratch this puppy to lure that man to us. How does using a woman to lure in a maniacal angel involve trust?"

She scanned his eyes for so long, Ashur had to look away, over her head and into the foyer. He'd never felt so noticed before. Easy enough when he'd just come from a long stint Beneath. It was as if she clutched her fingers about his black heart and actually squeezed the hard steel organ that kept myriads stolen souls locked away for eternity.

He was not accustomed to conversation or even the presence of another, yet he adjusted quickly. Acclimating to his surroundings was necessary to his task. But this closeness between them stirred something inside of him he'd long thought tortured out of him.

Women are dangerous.

He knew that, and yet he could not recall why. Were they not simply fine bed mates?

Tapping her lower lip with the blade, she captured Ashur's attention, but he sensed her favor toward him had dissipated. "Maybe I don't want you coming in."

"But I must."

"Must?"

"I find the day's course of events has exceeded my grasp and you are…in need of protection." She'd buy that one. "To be honest, it is new to me. Protection. But it is a task I will not refuse. The Fallen will not relent in his pursuit of you. And I need time to form a plan."

"You don't have a plan?"

"I should have already slain the Fallen. I've never before had to track one after they've made contact with the muse. As well, this world, and your need for me, is new."

"My need for you?" she said on a nervous, chuckly tone. "Please. I don't need any man."

Quite a unique woman, then. What had become of the subservient, faithful and devoted women who answered to their husbands and cared for the children?

"Can you fend off the Fallen when next he shows?" he countered.

"I…" Diverting her eyes from his face, she looked away and sighed. She stepped inside the home, leaving him to follow, which he did. "Maybe I don't want to fight him off. Maybe I want to talk to him. It's not every day a girl gets to meet an angel."

She may think she was strong, but he sensed her lacking confidence. Yet the tiny bit of gumption she did possess intrigued him. She had thought to defend herself with that little blade against a man twice her size and possessed of supernatural abilities.

Everything about her was different from the women he had known so long ago.

Ashur had been in fine palaces of marble and stone. This

one was similarly luxurious, though on a smaller scale. The decorations were elaborate and resembled flowers and curved leaves. The style pleased him. Lights on the walls were not torches, but contained within fine glass. Remarkable.

He must not question the changes in the world since he'd been Beneath. To do so would surely drive him mad. So he would simply accept them. Easy enough when he had greater things with which to concern himself.

Six opened a steel container lighted inside and which boasted an array of vegetables. The food storage box, he guessed. She took out a clear container and offered one to him, which he accepted. He watched her twist off the cover and drink from it.

Ashur tried it. Water in a bottle. Convenient.

"I know a thing or two about angels," she said. And then as a challenge, she offered, "Does that disturb you?"

Ashur strolled through the room he labeled the galley and into a vast room with plush divans and chairs. Huge ferns and small decorative trees in pots gushed from every corner. The walls were floor-to-ceiling windows. The view of the city was remarkable, and he walked up to scan the buildings and tiny spots of people below.

"No," he replied. Because whatever she thought she knew was wrong.

"Then you're the first who is not troubled by it," she said, joining him. "I've been dreaming about angels all my life."

He turned to find her gazing out the window, a small smile curving her lips.

"I've been waiting for something like this to happen," she said. "To finally have proof. To know that what I know is not delusional."

Ashur sighed. Though he'd no protocol on how to

interact with the muse, he did not think lying or avoiding the situation wisest. She needed to know the facts—which were undoubtedly far from her idea of the truth.

"Proof? Is that so?"

"Yes," she said on a wondrous hush.

"Well, let me tell you about the Fallen. They once walked the earth, yet were removed many millennia ago, during Noah's flood. Recently, though, Fallen ones have been conjured by ceremonial magic. Others are investigating who is behind the conjuring. That is not my concern. So now Fallen walk the earth, their mission renewed as they seek their muse."

"I've read the book of Enoch. It's about the angels called the Watchers, or Grigori, falling."

"Was that book chosen to be included in the Bible? I've not been around since Constantine's time."

Fascination brightened her eyes. Ashur wondered briefly if they had color.

"No," she answered, "that book was suppressed in the middle ages, and ruled fantasy. Pseudepigraphal. You've been alive that long?"

"Yes. But back to the Fallen. And you. You wear the sigil he seeks."

"Seriously?" She stroked the skin near the mark on her forearm. "Numbers? What wiseass thought that one up?"

"Yours is the first number I've seen. They are symbols unique to the angelic dominions. It is a good means to locating a match."

"And I'm that angel dude's match?"

"You are a muse. Whether or not you are a match is something I do not know."

"Well, if I'm not a match…"

"If the Fallen has already claimed his match, he can then seek other muses."

"A muse. I thought muses were gorgeous women who inspired artists, and all that."

"You inspire the Fallen to seek you."

She leaned in the archway between the two rooms, tall and slender. The thin fabric shirt did little to conceal the gorgeous curves beneath. Curves Ashur assumed would feel exquisite to touch.

Touch? It teased at his memory. Her hand against his chest, clinging as they rode through the city. There was that want again.

And yet the desire was accompanied by a twinge across his back. Flesh-stripping ghosts of violence. A violence so dark and rending it had brought him, the Stealer of Souls, to his knees.

Inspecting the gash above her eyebrow with a finger, Six winced. That was enough to distract Ashur from his fall into wicked memory.

"I can heal that for you," he offered.

"Really?"

He approached her, holding out his hand in offering. Surprisingly lacking in concern, she nodded and he placed it above her eye, not touching the flesh. The intense wave of her body heat pulsed against his palm. Mortal warmth. Another experience he had forgotten. An experience he'd had tortured out of him. Now he used that connection and focused his own inner healing salve to emanate outward. Within moments the cut healed.

She smoothed a finger over her brow. "Wow. You actually did it. And when you took the blade from me, and it flew through the air... You have powers. What are you?"

As new as the world was to him, he did know to keep some things to his chest. "If it is important to label me, then you may call me angel slayer."

She lifted a beautifully arched brow. Ashur turned

toward the view again. He should not waste time admiring her beauty.

"A slayer. Of angels?" She exhaled, and her breath touched Ashur's black heart. He suppressed a shiver. "That's sort of sad."

He tilted a curious look to her. No, her breath hadn't touched his heart. That organ was hard and black and impervious to everything.

"I mean, well, first reaction is it's sad," she said, unaware of his struggles. "But like I said, I know about angels. They're not all fluffy and full of grace. The fallen ones are downright evil. I suppose someone has to take care of the bad ones."

"The Fallen are lacking in grace and compassion. It's dangerous to have a soulless angel walking the earth," he said. "They have little concern for their actions, and are focused only on finding their muse. I am surprised you say you wish to speak to one."

"That might have been my excitement talking. He really wants to find me? What for?"

"Now that the Fallen one has been conjured, it resumes its original intention upon falling. I am not familiar with how many millennia have passed since the original fall. Then, two hundred angels fell to earth to mate with human females."

"I'm familiar with that story."

"It seeks its muse."

"That's the part I'm not familiar with."

"Once the Fallen finds his muse, he will mate with her in hopes of creating a nephilim. They are carnivorous, blood-hungry giants. It's the beginning to a plague of dark divinity. You, Six, are to give birth to the end of the world as you know it."

"Is that all?" She forced a chuckle, but he sensed it was

just that: a constructed means to temper the shock. He was quickly learning her emotions. He wasn't sure if it was because he'd spent so much time with her already, or if he were taking on the world's feelings.

"Have an angel's baby?" Six's eyelids fluttered. "I, uh, I think I need to sit down."

Halfway to the plush, cushioned chair placed before a marble hearth, she wobbled. Ashur crossed the room and caught her as she fainted.

Standing with her fey weight draping his arms, he again felt the tap at his black heart. It was more than a squeeze. This time it felt as though the hardened muscle actually pulsed.

That wasn't supposed to happen. Had to be the souls trapped within his heart. On occasion they made their presence known to him.

He should ditch the muse and seek the Fallen one. Thing was, keeping her close to him was the best way to lure Zaqiel to him. But no Fallen would approach a Sinistari willingly.

How to bait this trap?

Chapter 4

Eden came to with a start. She sat up on a delicately crocheted bedspread. Her bed. The iron lamp curved to resemble a lotus flower on the nightstand glowed over her stack of artist's color charts. "How'd I get here? Who—?"

Reality rushed upon her like a tsunami wave and she toppled against the pillow, but this time she didn't faint—because a man stood in her bedroom doorway. Tall, dark and confused, he was the most appealing thing she'd seen in months.

"You fainted," he offered.

"No kidding? Whew!" Eden sat up and smoothed down her shirt. "It's been a day, hasn't it?" She glanced toward the floor-to-ceiling window, which looked out over Central Park. It was dark, yet the city's innate glow beamed upward. The clock verified it was almost eleven. "How long have I been out?"

"A few hours. I didn't want to wake you."

"That was kind of you. After what I've been through—"

"It gave me time to walk the layout of your home."

"Oh. So it wasn't concern. You needed to case the joint. Find anything you want?"

"I have no intent to steal from you, my lady. Though I did find this in a kitchen drawer." He waved a small stack of one-hundred-dollar bills before him. "I may need some cash while I'm here on earth. Mind if I take it?"

"You just said you don't steal."

"I'm asking. Thieves do not ask."

"Yes, whatever. Take it if you need it. It's the petty cash I leave for my maid, Rosalie, to pick up things. I'll replenish it tomorrow."

Eden reached to scratch her forearm and Ashur dove onto the bed, grabbing her hand and trapping it against his chest. His body so close to hers had her heartbeat tripping. She couldn't remember a time when she'd been more frightened by a stranger's presence—and more intrigued.

Looking away, he released her arm and slid off the bed. "Don't scratch," he said. "Not until I give you the go-ahead. Forgive me, my impropriety overwhelms the need for your protection."

"I understand." Actually she didn't understand a thing. Exhaustion had tapped her neurons to the core.

Shoving her forearm between her thighs didn't quell the need to scratch. "I think I'll take a shower. I feel like crap after today's adventure. Maybe the water will relieve the itch. Is that okay? You're not going to stand guard outside the bathroom, are you?"

"I dare not. I will wait for you out in the main quarters."

"That would be the living room."

"Appropriately named. Please come find me when you feel ready. We have much to discuss."

Soon as the door closed, Eden stripped off her blouse and skirt and made a beeline for the bathroom. The glass-walled shower was her favorite place to escape the real world. Sound was muffled in here and the only sensation was the pressure of water upon her skin.

She always headed straight to the shower after a day spent at a charity event or amongst a crowd. Most people thought she had it all being rich. She wouldn't knock it, but having it all did not imply material wealth to her. *All* was something ineffable that could only fit into her heart.

The hot water rinsed away the dirt and shivers but it didn't chase away the subtle tingling where the angel had licked her.

"An angelkiss," Eden muttered as she dried herself off with a thick terry-cloth towel, being careful to avoid the mark. "And he's after me because he wants to get busy with me? I don't want to have sex with a bad angel and become the mother of the apocalypse."

Resting her palms on the marble vanity, she took a couple of deep yoga breaths to settle her growing tension. Water from her hair dripped down her arms and puddled on the floor. Her reflection echoed how tired she was. Rarely did she get shadows under her eyes like tonight.

But it was more than that.

If Ashur had told her the truth, she was in deep trouble. How did she dare escape an *angel*? Zaqiel possessed supernatural abilities, as she'd already seen. She was no match. And her only choice was to trust the man who called himself an angel slayer. What was that exactly? Was he human?

Had she garnered her own personal guardian angel?

"I hope so." Because she didn't want the white-haired guy getting close enough to lick her again. And if he had his way, he'd get close enough to have sex with her.

It had been over a year since she'd shared her body with a man. That had ended disastrously. And yet she had been able to put that event on a shelf only recently, and had begun dating again. Dating, but still no sex. Not that she didn't want it.

But what she craved now was something entirely different than she was accustomed to dating.

Like a sexy, rock-hard-abs guardian angel.

He was the opposite of everything she'd ever found sexy in a man. Pure muscle and might. Commanding. And a bit arrogant, too. And she wanted it all.

Damn.

Dressing in black silk pajama bottoms and top, Eden wanted to crawl between the sheets and lose herself in her dreams, but she didn't think Ashur had left. She slipped on her marabou slippers and clicked out to the living room.

He sat on the couch, back straight and body tight as if he didn't dare relax. A potted aloe vera plant sat on his lap. She almost laughed, until he sprang up and his eagerness startled her.

"Aloe Barbadensis," he said, thrusting the pot toward her. "It is an ancient plant for healing. I marvel you have such. It is good the plant has survived the ages. You can put it on the angelkiss."

The plant was used to relieve itching and rashes, but Eden had never had the need to try it. Todd had given it to her. Despite the lush acreage of plants she kept in the apartment she had furnished in the Art Nouveau style, he'd decided she needed something more functional, and with spines. Todd was always trying to get her to reveal her inner vixen. He'd certainly growl over Ashur.

"Try it," Ashur prompted. He broke off the tip of a thick leaf, and set down the pot. Squeezing the cool liquid from inside the plant, he stroked it across her flesh and spoke quietly. "The women wear trousers now."

"Pants, yes." He'd said he was new to this world.

"I intend to learn all tonight. While you sleep I will walk the world and assimilate its speech, customs and ways."

"The whole world? You'd better have some comfortable shoes."

He tilted his head, wondering at her.

"A joke."

"That word is not in my knowledge."

"You'll understand after you've assimilated, I'm sure." She inspected the glob of clear aloe on her arm. It did quell the desire to scratch.

"So I really do need to sleep. I thought I was exhausted after worrying about the gallery showing for a week, but being chased by an angel tops that. Will I be okay all alone? If the angel found me earlier, why can't he find me now?"

"You haven't scratched the angelkiss?"

"No."

"Then you should be safe. The beacon is only activated with irritation. When you scratch you send out a signal only the Fallen can track."

"Like pheromones?"

"I do not know that word, either."

She nodded. "It's an attraction thing innate in all of us." And, man, was she feeling it right now.

"Attraction. Like lust?"

"Exactly." The corner of his mouth curled. Eden had to consciously warn herself against touching the crease. Damn, they were making rescuing knights attractive these days. "So, you don't know things? I suppose not, if you've been out of touch for so long."

"I knew things, and then that knowledge was taken

from me through time and— It is not important. Perhaps you should wrap a bandage about your forearm to keep it from brushing against the bed linens. Would you like me to stay and watch over you while you sleep?"

"No, uh…no. I'm a big girl." A handsome man leaning over her while she slept? Talk about a fantasy! "No, that's not a good idea. I don't know you. You staying the night would be major awkward."

He shrugged. Obviously he didn't know. "I will return in the morning. Sleep well, Six."

He strode toward the front door, leaving Eden wishing she could call him back, but not daring to speak the words.

Big girls didn't invite strange men to watch over them while they slept. They could invite them to snuggle, though. But Eden suspected her knight wasn't the snuggly sort. And she wasn't in the right mindset to make decisions regarding sex right now.

Or maybe, just maybe, she was in the best frame of mind she'd been in for years.

Angels?

Finally.

The night moved swiftly through his brain, the world even faster. Ashur walked in a hurried pace innate to the Sinistari—they termed it flashing—from New York to California and then on to Japan, Russia, France, Africa and all the countries in between.

He listened to voices speaking, observed the customs, tasted the food, watched the transportation and analyzed the education. Knowledge permeated the costume of mortal flesh he wore and insinuated into his steel marrow.

The palette of sin the world offered had grown immeasurably since his last stay on earth.

In Las Vegas Ashur learned the pleasures of gambling.

He stole a fine pair of sunglasses out of an Aston Martin in Madrid then took the car for a joyride. He inhaled opium in a dark, musty cave in Andalusia with the locals, and learned to fire an AK-47 at a wall of broken bottles outside a Palestinian army base.

Fast food in Berlin awakened his palate to the strangely tasty idea of processed food. Gluttony led him to a Chipotle restaurant three times during the night, each time in a different state. Man, did he love tacos.

He followed a diamond thief in Milan and snatched the prize for himself, then scattered the five-carat stones in the Atlantic Ocean as he crossed to Iceland.

He was Sinistari. Sin ran through his black blood.

He held the world within him now. He knew all.

By all that was sacrilege in the dark sea Beneath, the world had changed vastly. And that parts of it frightened even him was not a good feeling. The weapons were fascinating, but he could not condone putting them in the hands of children. And lust was always entertaining, but it became a sickness when viewed obsessively on the computer.

Among the evil though, yet walked goodness and integrity. Ashur was no creature of prayer, but a wish for world sanity came to his lips before he could question the unnatural concern.

He'd also gained the ability to form emotion. It wasn't necessarily a boon to his mission, but it was unavoidable as he imbued his being with the human experience.

Ashur now saw some things in color instead of the bland grays he'd been experiencing. Not all of it, mostly the food (which he devoured) and the women's clothing (which he desired; the women, not the clothing) and the material objects that fascinated him, such as sports cars and yachts and those fancy little iPods.

Music! How it had changed over the centuries. It was

now a literal world compacted into each song. He enjoyed it all but especially the orchestral pieces and the stuff called heavy metal. Though how the little device worked puzzled him. He hadn't the time to take one apart, but soon.

He'd acquired a pair of worn black jeans from a street seller in Paris because he liked the snug, comfortable fit. A woven long-sleeved shirt appealed to his burgeoning need for touch and to experience all the sensations of texture, weight and temperature against his skin. He retained the biker boots and black leather jacket.

Back at Six's building, he approached her door and slid his palm over the carved wood surface. He recognized the artistic style of the carvings now: Art Nouveau. It had flourished at the end of the nineteenth century, as had absinthe, can-can and opium. Six's entire apartment was decorated in the style. He admired craftsmanship.

Prepared to knock, he noticed the door was open a crack. He had learned mortals in the twenty-first century did not leave their doors open or unlocked. Something must be wrong.

He pushed the door inside and entered stealthily, pressing a shoulder to the wall as he scanned down the hallway. He didn't sense Six, but something inside had a pulse.

Could Zaqiel be here? Angels and demons had no pulse, but Ashur could sense the Fallen's presence in the vibrations that shuddered his rib cage when close to an angel, yes, even one fallen from His grace.

"Let him be here," he muttered lowly. "Attempting his muse."

Reaching behind his hip, he unclasped the leather sheath and drew out Dethnyht.

Chapter 5

Slinking along the hallway wall, Ashur quickened his pace toward the bedroom.

Dethnyht was the only dagger capable of piercing an angel's impermeable flesh. He would never brandish it against a mortal—too cataclysmic. The mere strength he wielded with his bare hands could overwhelm any human.

Kicking the bedroom door open, Ashur sprang inside, Dethnyht raised to strike.

A woman screamed and dropped a stack of bed linens from her arms. She pleaded with him in Spanish not to hurt her. She had a family. Dogs. Three children under the age of ten.

Quickly assessing her attire, Ashur decided she was the chambermaid.

He sheathed Dethnyht. "Is Six home? Er, the lady of the house?" She didn't understand English, so he switched to Spanish, a language he had assimilated only hours earlier.

The maid clapped a palm over her rapidly rising and falling chest and nodded , explaining her mistress was at Starbucks.

"Starbucks?" He searched his newly gained knowledge. "Coffee?"

"Yes, she will return soon," she said. Then her tone changed remarkably, shedding the fear and taking on a curious edge. "You are her lover?"

"Does she have many?" he asked before he realized curiosity was not his mien. And yet, he waited for the answer with something he associated with anticipation.

The maid shrugged. "Not my business. You are the biggest, though." Admiration beamed in her brown eyes. "Scared me. You must work out. You go out to the kitchen to wait. I need to finish this room."

"Yes, the kitchen." He was hungry again.

He closed the door behind him. No angel on the premises. Damn. He'd been itching to kill something.

Just as well. He'd not seen Six yet. And why all of a sudden did that matter? Did he want to spend time with her before slaughtering the Fallen and then dashing off to the next kill?

Ashur scuffed a palm over his short hair, which hadn't seen a comb, and hallelujah for that. Drawing his fingers down his face, he shook his head. Gotta get his act together, as they said nowadays. Learning the world had put so many new things into his brain. He had to set his priorities straight.

Priority one: Lure Zaqiel to the muse.

Priority two: Kill the Fallen.

Priority three… There was no need for further tasks. As soon as Zaqiel was dispatched, Ashur would await further command.

Six stepped inside the front door and Ashur bounded

up to meet her. He gripped her wrist and slammed her against the wall.

"Whoa, dude! I have hot coffee in my other hand."

"I did not give you permission to leave."

"I don't need permission. I'm a big girl. Let me go."

He followed her into the kitchen and pressed his palms onto the granite countertop. The cool stone beneath his flesh managed to chill his annoyance. And so did the white gadget near the sink, which he picked up to study.

She took out two paper cups from the bag. "You purchased coffee for me?" he asked her. "Why would you do that?"

"I knew you'd be back this morning, and it is the nice thing to do, isn't it? Sharing."

"Taking is much easier."

She flashed him a death stare. "You're not big on simple kindnesses are you, Mr. Slam-Them-Around?"

"I have little concern for niceties." One twist and the gadget broke in two pieces.

"No kidding," she said, taking the pieces from him with a curt tug. "I never could figure why Rosalie needed two garlic presses. But this one was her favorite." She handed him the coffee but he refused.

"I don't favor those commercially manufactured brews."

"Seriously? You're gone one night and all of a sudden you've become a connoisseur?"

"Apparently so."

"I see." She sipped the hot brew, and Ashur decided he did not like the smell of it. He preferred the freshly ground coffee beans from Peru he'd experienced while walking the world. "You look different. More…modern. Did you get a haircut?"

"No, but I did get it wet in the Peruvian rain forest, then the deserts of Egypt dried it out."

"I like it. Spiky and tousled. Nice shades, too."

He took the Ray-Bans from the top of his head and set them on the counter. "I acquired fine things while I was out."

"Goody for you."

"Do you not appreciate them? You are rich. Are not fine things your mien?"

She smirked, but no mirth traced the curves of her lips. "Material things are stupid. They mean nothing. That's why I can toss a three-hundred-dollar garlic press without a blink. But if it makes you feel good…" She sighed. "I have some things to do this morning. I want to prepare another piece for the gallery this afternoon. I'm doing a show over in Chelsea. It's my debut."

"You are an artist?"

"Yep, been at it for over ten years. But Todd set me up with this killer computer system a few years ago, and my whole style changed. Oh man, I have to show you. Then you'll understand why I was so excited about seeing the angel last night."

The phone rang. Six put up her palm to signal him to wait. "Hi, Emily."

Ashur studied the small screw mechanism on the sunglasses frames as he folded it back and forth, back and forth. So small, it fascinated him.

"What?" Six said into the phone. "All of them? You're not— Seriously? That is so freaking cool. Yes, give me the phone number, I'll be happy to call him." She scribbled a few numbers and a name on a yellow Post-it note.

The sunglass arm broke off in Ashur's grip. He glanced at Six and when she turned to see what he was doing, he shoved the broken glasses aside next to the garlic press.

"Thanks, Emily. I don't have any replacements. You can do that? Take orders? Cool. I'll see if I can print up some examples and have them delivered later this afternoon."

She hung up, her face aglow. "That was the gallery owner. Someone bought all my paintings after I left the gallery last night." She tucked the phone number in her purse.

"You must be very talented."

"And you must be very curious." She tapped the broken glasses.

He shrugged. "I like to see how things work."

"Yes, well, just leave all major appliances alone, will you? And don't lay a hand on my computer, if you know what's good for you."

"Computers are remarkable."

"Oh, I was going to show you. Come on. I will now reveal the deep, dark secrets of my insane little mind to you. I've been waiting so long for someone who understands."

Attracted to her infectious enthusiasm, Ashur followed Six down a hallway. The silk pants she wore clung to her hips and flared out at the feet to reveal pointed-toe shoes with super-high heels. They made her legs look long enough to wrap around him twice. The feel of the fabric might push him over some precipice on which he was beginning to balance. He'd remembered lust last night, yet hadn't time to indulge it, thinking it wise to hold off until the task of slaying Zaqiel was completed. But how could he when the muse wore a clingy top, and the faint line of her brassiere strap teased him to slip it down her arm?

"Ashur?"

"Huh?"

"I asked if you liked art. Are you okay? You seem distracted." She stopped at a door and paused to sip her coffee. "Were you looking at my ass just now?"

"No," he said, too quickly. "Yes."

Her smile was wicked.

Ashur fixated on her mouth, those thick lips softened

with some sort of clear polish. Her teeth were so white as to sparkle. And straight. He'd never seen that before. Nowadays, he knew, it was all an illusion. Mortals spent millions on altering their appearances in an attempt to look more attractive.

Thing is, one man's attractive may be another man's ugly. Everything about Six fell into the attractive category.

"Are you all natural?" he asked.

She quirked a gracefully arched brow. "You mean organic? I recycle along with the rest of them, but I will never give up my Starbucks habit."

"No, I mean, you, your body and face. You have not altered your appearance?"

"You mean like cosmetic surgery?"

"Yes, I learned about that last night."

"Do you *think* I've altered myself?"

He sensed an underlying challenge—which he would never refuse. "Perhaps. Your teeth are too white."

"I've had them whitened."

"And your lips are so lush."

"They're all mine. Everything on this body is as is, the way God intended, except my teeth."

"Yes, you're like an earth mother meets sex kitten, all curves and lushness."

She bowed her head and glanced aside. He'd made her blush, which only increased her sensual appeal.

"What about you, big boy? If you're not human, is that the way you usually look? Like a human man? A man with incredible muscles and a killer smile?"

"These muscles are lesser than my normal appearance. And yes, this is a costume."

"Did you steal it from some real mortal man?"

"No. For all that I enjoy the sins of the flesh, and the world, I do not harm mortals. This costume is as I would appear should I have been created mortal. You do not like it?"

"Like it? I love it. Bet it's hard as steel and…well…" She sighed. "You said you enjoy sin?"

"Devour it. Need it, actually."

"Oh?"

"It is what makes me tick, as they say."

"That's weird."

"Your opinion means little to me."

"I realize that. Yet my appearance interests you to no end."

"I could look all day. What about there? Are they real?" Ashur pointed to her chest and she looked down and stroked between her breasts where he imagined it would be soft.

"My breasts are real," she said.

"Nice. And soft?"

A lift of her brow tweaked Ashur's smile. "My God, you don't have much of a moral compass, do you?"

"It isn't necessary to my survival."

She tilted her head. Soft dark curls as tight as a spring bounced over her shoulders and down to her elbows. He wanted to crush them between his fingers. "Soft? You want to touch and see?"

She was right on about his lacking moral compass.

Tracing his finger down from the base of her throat, Ashur closed his eyes as the softness of female skin tendered at his expectations. All things in his life were hard, impermeable, adamant. Yet beneath his skin glided something like fine silk. He remembered silk, slipping beneath his touch, waving in the breeze, gliding over his mouth…

"I think that's enough."

Six's voice brought him up from the dive into lust. Ashur retracted from the one place he should not go until Zaqiel was dispatched. "Very soft."

"Thanks. I didn't expect you'd be so…well, forward."

"You did invite the touch."

"Yes, I did. Something about you… Anyway!"

Dismissing the intimate interlude, Six opened the door and strode into a vast room done in white marble. Floor-to-ceiling windows faced the far side of the blindingly white room.

"This is my workroom," she explained, setting the coffee on a clear Lucite desk and pushing a button on the Macintosh computer.

"It's different from the rest of the place," he said. "It's as if another person's living in here."

"Kind of. My artistic self is opposite from my chumming-around-with-friends self. I don't want any distractions when I'm painting so I made it as neutral in here as possible. No music, either."

He tilted his head, wondering.

"It's an artist thing. Sort of like you explained the angels hearing in colors is an angel thing."

"So what is all this stuff? I don't see any canvas or paints."

"CG painting is my method of choice to create. I use a spatial operating environment."

He only understood half of what she'd said. But he wasn't about to let on to that fact. He touched the smooth white exterior of the computer.

"Don't touch," she admonished sweetly. "No taking apart my computer, big boy."

Ashur offered her a surrendering shrug, then strolled about the room, thumbs shoved in his front pockets, taking it all in.

A huge plasma screen flickered awake on one wall and he approached it, waiting to see what would appear.

Behind him, Six sat before the desk clicking away at the keyboard. Twisting at the waist, his eyes lingered where he had touched her between the curves of her breasts. Softness bound up and waiting release, or a dash of his tongue. If only the angelkiss had been placed there, and he would have had to lick it to grant her temporary relief.

Nice. Thinking about the carnal pleasures was almost as good as doing them. And when his erection tightened against his pants, he grinned. The old demon still had it. Some things were never forgotten, no matter how much torture.

Six typed rapidly. The sleeve bulged on her forearm. "Did you bandage the angelkiss?" he asked.

"I put some aloe on it again this morning, and tied a scarf around it. Seems to do the trick. You ever hear of CG art?"

"Sure."

"You like it?"

He spread out his arms and swaggered toward her. "Doesn't everyone?"

She sighed. "You have no idea what it is."

He approached the desk and caught his palms on the edge. "Very well, what is CG?"

"You didn't assimilate that last night?"

"I feel it somewhere in my knowledge, but it's difficult to understand. It is to do with technology and much as I hate to admit it, that is beyond my comprehension."

"It's beyond every normal person's comprehension, believe me."

Yes, but he wasn't normal. And how easy would it be to take this computer apart? It appeared to have a removable back—

"CG is computer-generated art," she said. "I paint with pixels. The screen is my canvas. I'll show you my latest. Look."

Ashur turned around. The screen, which was as high as

he and three feet wide, filled with grays and silver and shades of black and blue. Spreading his hands over it, he marveled at the screen's give. It wasn't glass but some soft surface that gave with his touch. Marvelous.

"Put your hands down," Six said. "I'm turning on the spatial controls."

He stepped back to take in the image that appeared on the screen. It startled him. He hissed lowly.

"My friend Todd had the same reaction when he built it," Six said as she joined his side. She raised her hand and tapped her fingers in the air before her. The screen zoomed out to display the whole painting. "Spatial operation," she said. "It's all done by recognizing my hand movements. Pretty cool, huh? The technology is so new it's still in beta form for home use."

The technology did not concern him; it was the image she had constructed on the screen.

"It's my latest angel. I only paint angels. I call this one my indigo savior."

The figure on the screen was forged of blue metal and gears that glistened with white. Bulging steel muscles rippled down its arms and thighs. At its back a spread of wings stretched straight out five times as long as the body, and the wing tips curled, thanks to moving gears on each of the mercurylike appendages.

"How do you have this knowledge?" Ashur asked fiercely. "How can you know?"

"Zaqiel said the same thing to me in the same accusing tone. Of course, you've seen angels. And me? I have, too." She tapped her head. "In my dreams."

Coaxing his breathing to a steady pace, Ashur exhaled. "In your dreams? Are you a seer?"

"I don't know. Maybe. I once thought I might be an angel because of this." She tapped the sigil on her forearm.

"But it never quite matched any of the sigils I've seen in books on angels. I've had dreams about angels since after my mother died. I've tried to tell people about them, but they always think I'm a nut. My father threatened to put me in a psych ward when I was eighteen."

"The place where they put those out of their minds?" He looked her over again. She seemed quite sane. But then madness often cloaked itself in beauty.

"It was a stupid threat, but it brought me down from a weird place," she said. "I was just so tired of people not believing me that I flipped out. And well, you know how teenagers can be." She sighed. "Probably you don't. So now here you are, a man who actually slays angels. You believe me, right?"

"That you've seen them in your dreams?" He glanced at the painting. She'd seen something, that was for sure. Parts of the figure were not exactly right, but other parts were right on. "Where did you learn this?" He pointed to the sigil she had painted on the angel's shoulder, a wavy line with one dot beneath the middle wave. "In your dreams, as well?"

"Sort of. Not really. That's the last thing I put on a project before I call it finished. It's not like I see what the symbol looks like, but more that I touch my fingers before the screen and just follow my heart. I know it sounds weird. Delusional. But heck, maybe I am a little crazy. I mean, how many girls actually have an angel chasing after them to get them pregnant? You ask me, a person would have to be insane to accept something like that."

He didn't know what to say. Six had somehow created this image by drawing from a greater collective consciousness. Yet she was unaware how close her depiction was, or that the sigils were dead-on.

Was it possible an angel had visited her previously?

"You going to recommend a nice quiet place with strait-jackets now?" she wondered.

"No, I want to know more."

Chapter 6

Eden liked to study the reaction on people's faces when they viewed her work. She especially liked the extremes of joy or disgust. Ashur had looked at the painting and hissed.

Had she actually created an angel he recognized? It was self-indulgent to think she could depict an angel accurately. But she had painted exactly what she'd seen in her dreams. The angels she painted were like her friends; she felt comforted by them.

Angels who didn't want to have sex with her, that is.

Ashur's gaze soared out the window and across Central Park. She'd touched some part of him, and that surprised him more than it did her, she suspected.

"Just dreams?" he asked.

"As I said, they started after my mother's death." She joined his side and said, "At first, I thought they were a message from her. But there were so many. I'd see a new one every night, it seemed. If I painted a different angel every day, I don't think I'd ever put them all to canvas. They are innate to me, and yet, I can't tell others about it if I want them to think I'm sane."

"Mortals have a difficult time with the supernatural."

"Yep. I started sketching in my teens, but I really became passionate about recreating my dreams after I found my first halo."

Ashur's eyes flashed. They were so colorful, fathomless, with pinpoints of light centered in each. It was as if a piece of a Maxfield Parrish painting abided on his face.

"You found a halo?"

"Yes, an angel's halo. You must be familiar with them."

"I am," he said cautiously, "but mortals are not. The only time the halo is separated from an angel is when they fall to earth. It falls away and is lost to the angel ever after. If they should ever find their original halo, it can be wielded as a weapon no man or demon can defeat."

"Cool. I was never sure how the halo ended up here on earth."

"It also holds their earthbound soul," he said. "If an angel reunites with its halo it can take the soul and become human, but I can't imagine a Fallen choosing to do so, to become merely human."

"What about you? Would you take a soul?"

"You know nothing about me, mortal. Do not pretend you do."

Duly chastised, Eden strode across the room to the freestanding coatrack that held three circular disks on its curved hooks. "I found the first one at a flea market my father took me to when I was twelve—that was two years after my mother's death. Dug it out of a box full of scrap tin. I knew immediately what it was. It didn't bother me the seller thought it was nothing. I knew."

"More dreams?"

"No, just an innate knowing," she offered casually.

She removed the first find from one of the coat hooks. It was dented and yes, it did look like tin, but she couldn't bend it, nor had her father been able to. She displayed it to Ashur. "See?"

He took the circle. It was exactly a foot in diameter and the metal was two inches wide all around. It was thin as a CD and the center was an eight-inch void. Ashur inspected it briefly. "It is what you say it is."

Given confirmation, Eden clutched her hands to her chest. She'd always known, but somehow it was more real when someone in the know confirmed it. All the years she had lived inside her head, fighting to keep her secrets. She was not crazy.

And who else would know such a thing but an— She wouldn't say it out loud after he'd chastised her. Maybe he wasn't allowed to reveal his origins to humans.

"And the others?" he asked.

"I have four," she said proudly. "But I should be getting another in the mail any day now. I found one on a trip to Egypt with my father, and another in Spain. The one on its way, I won on eBay. Some sellers actually know what they are selling. The most I've ever paid is a couple hundred thousand for one."

Ashur whistled. "You certainly are rich, because I discerned last night the average household income is less than half that."

"Trust-fund baby. But don't judge me."

"I have no need to judge you." He handed the halo to her, reverently, then admired the rack of halos. "But you've not hung or displayed them as something of value. Isn't that what mortals do? Display their symbols of wealth?"

"No, mostly it's the new guys come to earth." She

looked over his leather jacket. Designer, for sure. "Sorry, couldn't help that one. As for displaying the halos, I tried once. Had this first one mounted, framed and displayed under halogen lights. The thing fell off the wall two hours later. Glass cracked, and the halo rolled under the couch. I tried once more with another. Same thing happened. I figure they don't want to be fussed over. This coat hook works great. And it's cool working in this room and knowing they are so close. They inspire me."

"I am without words."

She grinned. "Maybe you need to hold it longer. It gives hope to hold one. I've actually got one packaged up to send to a woman I met online a few months ago. She needs hope, so I'm lending the halo to her."

He shook his head, refusing the offer. "Hope is not an emotion I require."

His dismissal made her sad. Everyone could use hope. Truly he was different than her, and she probably would never understand him. But she wanted to. Heck, if he intended to stick around and protect her, then they had time for getting to know each other.

"So maybe this is some kind of weird serendipity?" she said. "Me knowing about angels and collecting their halos. And then one day I've got a Fallen angel chasing after me for some sexin'."

"Do not casually dismiss what the Fallen one intends."

"Sorry. Right. This is serious." She slapped a palm over the angelkiss. She'd tied a blue silk scarf around it this morning after dousing it with more aloe vera, but the soothing effects were wearing off.

"Please." Ashur took her hand and clasped it in his. "It is imperative you wait until I've decided it best to call the angel to us."

She nodded. "So I'm bait."

"That is the correct word."

She did not pull her hand away from his. He was overwhelming in all ways. His height. His size. His deep voice echoed in her head. She liked his voice.

The sheer intensity of his presence had her thinking what it would be like to press her bare flesh against his, just to take all of him in. To know the feeling of a man's skin against hers again, intimately. To close her eyes and sink into trust. And to trust whatever happened between them would not flip her life upside down as intimacy once had.

Eden tugged her hand from Ashur's and pressed it to his chest. The action made him flinch, but he didn't push her away.

"I need to touch you like you did me earlier," she said. "It's overwhelming standing next to you, knowing you've come to me like some kind of supernatural warrior. I want to feel grounded next to you. Not so small."

"I…" He lifted a hand, and when Eden thought he would place it over hers, he dropped it to his side. "Had forgotten about touch. You are bringing it back to me."

"What does that mean? You were not on the earth for almost a thousand years, so you forgot everything?"

"Yes. As I sat upon my throne, the memories of this world slowly receded. And other means stole memory from me. I'm sure it happened over centuries. I released all knowledge of the world as I could not grasp it tight enough to keep. Touch was one of the last things to leave my knowledge. Although…"

"Yes?"

"I never lost one emotion. In fact, I clung to it as a sort of life preserver in the vast black sea which surrounds my throne."

"What emotion is that? Love?"

Why she offered that one surprised Eden. Love was one of those easy yet complicated emotions. Eden had touched love a few times, but it never lasted. Or else it devastated. No matter the result, it always left her feeling slightly tarnished.

Ashur shook his head. "No. Joy."

"You don't say?" A refreshing replacement for love. Truly joy was untainted, and the most inspiring emotion to cling to. "Tell me about the joy that stayed with you for so many years. I want to get to know you, Ashur."

Now his hand did spread across hers. His skin was not warm, but also not cold. His hand was simply there, enfolding her. Perhaps, learning her.

Nice. She liked his slow approach.

"If you must know…"

"I must. I'm curious. Blame it on the artist in me."

"I once witnessed a woman giving birth," he explained. "The actual birthing process is not joyful. It was wretched. She was in pain and agony, mixed with moments of determination and fortitude. But the moment the babe was born and placed in the weary mother's arms, joy suffused her. I felt it in my being. And I knew the babe experienced the same as it was swaddled and placed against the warm, tender breast. Joy. It was exquisite."

Eden tugged her hand from Ashur's chest and stepped away, stumbling as her thighs hit the desk behind her. Memories flooded her brain. She could not push them away. The room wavered. She stumbled toward the door and ran down the hallway, aware Ashur followed silently.

When she reached her bedroom and collapsed onto the plush comforter, she buried her face in the pillow and cried.

Ashur pressed his hand to Six's bedroom door, but didn't push it open. Her sobs were soft. He didn't know how to approach her, and felt odd standing this close to her even with a door separating them.

Women confused him. He'd learned that much overnight. And he felt sure, though the memories were dim, the women he'd previously encountered had been as baffling.

Six's touch had conjured up memories and soft dreams of past encounters. Such power she had, for it had brought his memory of joy instantly to the fore.

Could Six give him joy? Did he want it again?

What was it about mortal women he still could not remember? And the woman he'd watched giving birth… who was she? They must have been close to have witnessed so intimate an event.

He searched his memory but though he'd gained much knowledge last night, his actual life experiences were still difficult to recall. And for reasons he knew well.

Ah! This charge to protect the muse was not for him. When Six decided to come out from her bedroom, he would tear away the scarf and scratch the angelkiss himself. Then he'd wield Dethnyht in preparation for Zaqiel.

Striding down the hallway into the kitchen, he met the maid, who was packing up her cleaning supplies in a rubber-handled tub.

"What did you do to her?" she demanded hotly in Spanish. "I hear her crying!"

"I didn't touch her." She'd touched him first. "I told her about a memory I had, and then…" He splayed his arms and shook his head.

The maid slammed a hand to her hip. "Men."

A terrible crash sounded at the end of the hallway. Glass clattered.

Ashur dashed down the hallway, aware the maid followed. "Stay back!" he shouted.

Six's scream erased the tenderness that had teased at his burgeoning emotions. Her scream had come *after* the crash. That could only mean his hopes to slay the angel would soon be fulfilled.

He quickened his steps toward the closed bedroom door. Another scream sped him to a run.

Reaching for Dethnyht, he unsheathed it.

Thrusting out his other hand, Ashur aimed his will at the door. It broke from its hinges and slammed outward with such force the wall cracked.

Inside the bedroom, upon the bed, stood Zaqiel.

Chapter 7

Zaqiel held Six pinned to the wall behind the bed by her throat. Her legs kicked and arms beat at the laughing angel.

Ashur lowered Dethnyht, knowing the weapon would be futile. The blade could only be utilized against the angel in half-blood form—half his angelic shape, the other half human. It was the form it required to impregnate the muse, for angels were without sex organs.

So what was wrong with this picture? Was the Fallen here merely to tease? Or was he simply slow on the draw? Transformation could occur in the sweep of a humming-bird's wing.

The punkish Zaqiel cocked his head and sneered at Ashur. A sigil circling his left eye flared bright as the mysterious blue flames spotting the Carpathian hillsides. His sigil was *not* a match to Six's mark—the greedy bastard.

Ashur charged, leaping for the bed. With Six clutched against his chest, the angel soared backward toward the shattered floor-to-ceiling window. He stopped, his back to the gaping space. Wind whistled like a banshee through the thirty-second-story window.

"Ashur!" she cried.

"Release her!" Ashur demanded.

He jumped from the bed and slowly advanced on Zaqiel. Holding Dethnyht out in surrender, he loosened his grip, yet did not drop the weapon. He was not foolish.

"Since when does your job entail protecting mortals?" Zaqiel shouted over the wind.

Yes, since when?

"Stop struggling." Zaqiel squeezed Six's gut and slapped a hand across her throat, clenching. "You're late, slayer."

"I'd say I'm early. What's the delay? Take a while to get it up, Zaq?"

Flipping Dethnyht dangerously through his fingers, Ashur stilled the need to plunge it into the angel's skull. That would not serve as a kill shot. Only shattering the angel's glass heart would do. But Ashur needed to be in demon form to wield enough strength to do so. He could shift shapes as quickly as the angel could.

"She is mine," the angel declared. "I have claimed her."

"Ash—"

"She belongs to no man," Ashur protested. If the Fallen held his hand too tightly over Six's mouth he would crush bones. Merely touching her too long would burn her skin.

"And yet here you stand, in her home. Claiming the right to protect her. Interesting."

Zaqiel stepped closer to the window. The wind swayed him so he had to plant his feet. Six's long, dark hair whipped across his face. He would not risk jumping with her, Ashur guessed, for the mortal would not survive the fall no matter how tightly the angel held her. How then would he transfer his diabolical seed to her womb?

"Tell me." Zaqiel slapped Six's face so she looked at him. "Who do you prefer to fornicate with? An angel from Above—" he twisted her jaw to look at Ashur "—or a demon from Beneath?"

"D-demon?" Eden sputtered.

"That is enough!" Ashur charged.

Zaqiel thrust Six out of the window, his grip only about her neck.

Ashur stepped double-time to avoid colliding with the arrogant angel. Six clung to Zaqiel's arm, both sets of fingers clawing, desperate to maintain hold.

"Don't kick, love," the angel chastised. "You'll loosen my hold."

"You would sacrifice your only chance to procreate?" Ashur asked.

"She's not my only chance, and you are well aware of that fact." Zaqiel shook her. Six screamed. "I find this one pretty, is all."

Ashur knew if the Fallen found his muse dead or after he'd mated with her, he could then go on to another. If Zaqiel dropped Six, it would serve little to vanquish his quest to procreate.

Six's life should mean little to Ashur. But he could not stand to witness the senseless loss. Humans were so fragile. She collected halos. She painted angels. There was something special about her, and it wasn't because she dreamed about angels. And though mortals appealed to him on no level, he would not allow her death today.

"Set her inside, Zaqiel," Ashur demanded.

The Fallen one contemplated the idea. The steel ring piercing his chin wobbled as he did so. "I am fascinated you show concern for the woman. Sinistari have no concern for protecting mortals. I suspect you defy orders by doing so. And my own fascination intrigues me. I do like this one. She's a fine specimen, and she knows things, yes? Her hips are wide enough. She would produce an excellent nephilim."

Zaqiel pulled Six inside and drew his tongue along her neck in a wicked, slow trail. Another angelkiss. "I look forward to the challenge, slayer."

The angel threw Six toward Ashur. He caught her flailing body against his chest and stumbled backward to land on the bed. Zaqiel jumped out the window.

Ashur rolled over and pressed Six into the mattress. "Stay here. And don't scratch your neck!"

He ran for the window, serrated with broken glass, and hit the air, his arms spread and his head angling downward to quicken his free-fall descent.

Eden clung to the iron bedpost. Wind whipped about the room, stirring the silk sheers to angry flags and pushing the finer shards of glass across the floor in tinkling slides.

Ashur had jumped out the window. Both of them had jumped!

However, that wasn't the freakiest thing. When the angel had plunged through her window, she had expected it. Sitting up on the bed, she had known exactly what he'd come for. To have sex with her. To create a monster baby.

How did she fight a creature as powerful as an angel?

But what Zaqiel had revealed about Ashur shocked her the most. He was a demon. She'd thought him an angel, on her side.

"A demon has been in my home? And I let him touch me." She stroked the flesh between her breasts where Ashur's touch had stirred her desire. "He convinced me he wanted to help me. Oh, God." She bent over on the bed and clutched her roiling gut.

The maid came screaming down the hallway. "I called 911! What happened?"

"Don't come in, Rosalie!" Eden called in Spanish. "You'll step on glass. Will you get me my boots from the hall closet so I can walk out of here?"

The maid ran off to retrieve the boots.

"911," Eden muttered, forming a plan even as her brain operated on panic mode. "I have to get out of here." How could she explain a broken window on the thirty-second floor? The police wouldn't buy that an angel came crashing through. Hell, she never imagined something like this could happen. She didn't like this strange war between angels and demons that she was in the middle of.

None of her dreams had gone beyond the image of an angel. No wars. No evil angels stalking her.

The maid tossed her a pair of Ugg boots and Eden slipped them on and scrambled across the broken glass to her closet where she pulled down a Dolce & Gabbana suitcase and stuffed it with clothes.

"What happened?" Rosalie asked.

"Not sure," she called. "I need to leave. You'll stay to meet the police?"

The maid could only shrug and watch as Eden opened the closet safe and drew out her passport, credit cards and some cash. She grabbed her blade, something she'd had Todd purchase for her because she wasn't brave enough to go into the knife shop. Then she thought better of it. It would never make it through airport security.

"Are you all right, Miss Campbell?" Rosalie asked when Eden met her at the door. She brushed the shoulder of Eden's shirt. It was torn. "Maybe you should call your father?"

It had been weeks since she'd talked to Peter Campbell.

She'd actually had to make an appointment because he was busy with a new project in Greece. He didn't need to worry about this. What could he do that Ashur—a demon—hadn't already attempted?

"You were crying," Rosalie said through her own burgeoning tears. She had worked for Eden eight years. At times Rosalie acted like a mother to Eden. "And then… this."

"I didn't do this," Eden said, "but I can't explain it, either. You have to trust me." She unbuttoned her shirt and scrambled for another in the closet. The red silk with the ruffled short sleeves would do. "When the police arrive, tell them it was a bird. A big one. And I wasn't here. You were cleaning, as usual."

"But—"

"That's all I can say right now."

She hugged the maid. At that moment the doorbell rang. The police couldn't have possibly gotten here so quickly.

"I'm so sorry to do this to you, Rosalie. I need to get away. Maybe a few weeks."

"Maybe you need to just sit down a bit. Relax." Rosalie got that worried look that signaled she was thinking about calling Eden's father. He had warned her that Eden might get out of touch with reality on occasion.

"Rosalie, I've never been more rational in my life. Trust me. I just don't want to be in New York right now. Lock the door when you leave, and make sure a repairman gets access to the bedroom. The building will no doubt send someone to fix it immediately." She handed Rosalie a small stack of hundreds she'd taken from the safe. "For your trouble."

Rosalie nodded and tucked the money away in her hip pocket. All her children were in grade school; she could use it. Eden trusted her completely.

The doorbell rang again.

Suitcase and purse in hand, Eden ran down the hallway and opened the front door. She slammed into the mailman and he handed her a brown padded envelope. "Sorry, Miss Campbell, didn't think you were going to answer."

She knew what it was, and stuffed it in her bag. "Thanks, Henry, I'm in a rush. Can you hold my mail for a few weeks?"

"Will do, Miss Campbell. Have a good trip!"

The difficult thing about chasing an angel was the Fallen could flash great distances quickly, much like a Sinistari could do, and Ashur had done the previous night to learn the world. But once the angel flashed, his telltale vibrations dissipated.

Ashur followed Zaqiel on foot through Central Park. The angel had dodged the mounted policeman, chuckling and looking over a shoulder to ensure Ashur was still in his wake. He toyed with the slow chase, though mortals barely registered the passing blur as angel and demon sped by them.

When he reached a large pond, Zaqiel leaped into the air and flashed. Ashur, following, had stopped midair because he'd lost the vibration, and landed in the pond. He flashed to shore and kicked the turf. An elderly couple seated nearby on a bench gawked at him, so he restrained himself from vigorously swearing out loud.

No sense in attempting to guess where the Fallen had flashed. He'd lost him.

A glance to Six's building revealed the broken window thirty-two stories up. He wondered if any glass had fallen to the ground, and hoped no mortals had been injured.

Ashur stood straight and shook the water from his hair. What was he doing, wondering after the safety of mortals? He did not care! He should not care.

But he did.

Treading across the dew-moist grass, he slapped the water from his jeans. "I am failing with each breath I take."

For with each breath it was as though he drew in compassion and concern for those surrounding him.

Either the angel would be the end of him, or Six would be.

Todd was waiting tables at Cloud Nine so Eden stopped in briefly to tell him she was leaving and to tell him about the show selling out. The gallery had canceled tonight's showing because she hadn't any pieces to replace the sold ones.

"That's amazing, Eden. All of them?"

"Cool, huh?"

"So you're leaving to…celebrate? This is sudden."

"Um…I'm heading to Italy to meet a friend."

"I'm your friend. Who's your friend in Italy?"

"A girlfriend from college. You don't know her. I barely know her. We agreed to meet for lunch overseas sometime."

"And you need to meet her so desperately you're willing to forego a champagne celebration with friends tonight?" He wasn't angry so much as confused.

"Todd, you're making that up."

"I didn't know you had anything to celebrate until now. Of course I just made it up."

Eden squeezed his arm but couldn't look him in the eye. "My friend…she's in trouble."

"Oh." He bought it, but then he was busy setting up table settings and folding napkins so his attention was divided.

"Is anything wrong, Eden? You don't look right. Your

hair is spilling all over, and you always like to keep it contained—"

"So I'm going with loose and flirty curls for once. You always said the style would look good on me."

"Yes, but the boots are puzzling me."

She looked down at the Uggs that did not go with her pencil-thin skirt and red silk blouse. "I want to be comfortable on the flight."

"Uggs are so five years ago."

"The day I taught you to shop Barneys changed you forever, geek boy."

"Hey, I proudly wear my Ralph Lauren pencil protector."

"So I'll see you in a week or so. Not sure how long I'll be there." She hugged him and squeezed his hand. "I'll let you get back to work."

Todd waved at Eden as she exited the restaurant. Scratching his neck where Eden's neck had touched his as she'd hugged him, he wished her well. The celebration could wait. She needed to get laid. The woman needed real love. She'd been searching for it all her life.

Maybe she'd find a handsome Italian to fulfill those needs.

Chapter 8

Ashur charged into Kennedy Airport, but checked his demeanor. He was aware of the stringent security measures of modern airports so he was careful not to push anyone or draw attention to himself in any way.

He sighted Six leaving the ticket counter. She saw him, turned and walked the other way—quickly. Why was she avoiding him? Didn't she want his protection?

A fine job you've done of it thus far. The Fallen almost dropped her thirty-two stories. And now she knows your ugly truth.

"Six!"

She kept walking. He sped up, using his natural pace and gained her side, slipping an arm through hers. "Don't scream. Don't make a scene."

"Let me go." She struggled but he contained her with a squeeze of her wrist. An older couple passed by, the woman's gaze slicing through Ashur's nonchalant brutality. He nodded to her and smiled. She frowned and turned away.

"What are you doing?" he said in a loud whisper. "I thought you understood the seriousness of having Zaqiel tracking you."

"I do. That's why I'm leaving the country. And getting away from you."

"Me? But I'm here to—"

"To what? Protect me? I thought I was your bait."

He had, too. "It appears Zaqiel wants to play, which is entirely unexpected. Normally the Fallen sights its muse and zooms in for the—" Six's gaping mouth kept him from finishing that thought. "I'm not sure bait will be as effective as I'd hoped."

"Ugh. You have no idea what it feels like to be called bait. So not romantic."

"Where does romance fit into all this?"

"Exactly. I was stupid to consider—" She tugged her wrist from his grip. What she'd been about to say didn't make any sense at all to Ashur. "What he said about you. That you're…a demon," she gasped out. "Is it true?"

Ashur lifted his chin and closed his eyes. No matter the truths of him, the media had designed angels to equal one thing—goodness—and demons the complete opposite. They'd got one side right. Public opinion had not changed since the biblical times when he'd first walked the earth. He was evil to the core of his black heart.

But some evils were necessary to counteract other evils.

Six struggled. "Let me go, or I'm calling security."

"Go ahead," Ashur said low and forcefully. No matter her beliefs, he could no longer risk losing sight of her, especially when Zaqiel was changing the rules of the game. "Tell security a demon is after you. Who do you think they'll lock up?"

He allowed her to wrench her arm from his grasp, but she remained standing before him, huffing and unable to meet his eyes. Six's hair tumbled in soft waves, spilling down to her waist. It was so long and sensual. She'd spilled free of the contained world he suspected was her norm. Since he'd taken her under his care she'd been put through the wringer.

Care? Hell, she was bait. *Had* been bait. Now that Zaqiel had changed the game he wasn't sure what he could actually do with Six. She may not prove an effective lure. But he wasn't prepared to leave her to her own devices.

She clasped a hand at her breast. He'd touched her there. That sweet spot between her breasts was again visible, and the soft skin called to him.

A person should feel some compassion toward Six for what she'd been through, but Ashur was not a person. He was a demon. And he was jonesing for some sin.

"Is it true?" she asked.

He knew what she wanted to hear. Not the truth.

"I thought you were an angel."

"I never said I was."

"Damn you!"

"Do not subscribe to the prefabricated judgments formed by literature and media, Six. What do *you* think I am?"

She lifted a hand to her neck, where she'd tied a blue scarf. The new angelkiss must drive her mad. The one on her forearm would cease to itch now that another had been placed on her skin.

Soft skin. She had touched him. Could she know what that did to him? It conjured up memory. It promised pleasure. It spoke to his easy need for debauchery. Now he wanted more. And want manifested into a desire to protect, to keep what he wished to indulge in safe.

"I think…" she started. "I don't know. I mean, I know angels can be bad, but all I know about demons is they are evil. But there's a possibility you could be good. You rescued me and…"

"I am not good, and do not try to make me so. I am here on earth to do my job, which is to slay the angel intent on making you his breeding bitch."

She sucked in her lower lip. Tears glistened in her eyes. "You're not good?"

"I am demon. Sinistari."

"What's that?"

A cursory glance ensured no passersby were close enough to hear their unorthodox conversation. "My breed. We were forged specifically—and only—to slay angels. I was summoned from Beneath to perform my job. I bear no intent to harm mortals, but must do what is necessary to complete my destined task. And in doing so…"

Should he tell her the next part? Her breath was shallow and erratic as it was.

"What happens when you slay an angel?" she asked. "Do you go back to where you came from?"

"Not unless commanded. And in payment for my task, I take the souls as reward."

Because he was Ashuriel, Stealer of Souls. No other Sinistari had dared do the same. His fellow Sinistari sought the easy way out, a painless escape to a new existence—the possession of a human soul. And yes, he was proud of stealing souls.

An overhead speaker announced the various boarding flights.

Six said hers didn't board for another half an hour. She stepped aside to allow a family of five to pass by, then shuffled up to stand right before him.

Ashur noticed her eyes held color—a soft, pale green. And her lips were tinted with rose. The juxtaposition of such unexpected color against her pale skin startled him.

He wanted to touch her mouth, to see for himself that the color would not rub away.

"What does that mean?" she whispered, while taking in their periphery. "You take the soul."

Ashur exhaled and tugged her over to the wall so they were out of the way of pedestrians. Six touched her neck as her eyes silently pleaded him to speak.

"Don't scratch your neck," he said. "Not in such a public venue."

"I won't. I'm trying not to. Explain. If you want me to trust you."

An explanation wasn't going to forge her trust. But he couldn't justify hiding his truths if it would calm her. Besides, lying was so boring, a mere venial sin.

"Very well, then listen. When angels fell to earth so many millennia ago, they fell with the intent to fornicate with human females and seek their muse. But they also taught man the arts, which was forbidden at the time."

How that had changed over the millennia. The arts were an accepted part of society now, and better for it.

"Forging metal, woodworking and creating cosmetics for the skin—even painting—and other creative endeavors were considered a sin. As a result of consorting with the angels, the mortal man's soul was sacrificed and taken by that teaching angel. The man wasn't aware of it, of course. And when he died, his stolen soul was already trapped within the fallen angel."

Six bit the corner of her lip. Wide green eyes entreated him for clarification.

"When I slay an angel, those souls are released. And before they can go either Above or Beneath, I steal them."

He wanted to touch her mouth, to stroke the softness and offer tender words of reassurance. But it would be a lie. And he didn't do tender.

"I take those souls into my black heart because it gives me agonizing pain."

Her lashes dusted the air. Her mouth fell open in wonder. The expression was far too sensual to keep his thoughts from imagining the texture of his mouth against hers.

"It is what I am, Six. It is the punishment I claim for my task."

"Why do you seek punishment? You're a demon. Isn't murder normal for you?"

He didn't have an answer for that one.

"And the souls… If you didn't steal them," Six said, thinking it through, "those souls would go on to heaven?"

"Presumably. Unless they were destined elsewhere."

"Above and Beneath," she muttered, working over what he'd explained. "The arts? Seriously? If the angels hadn't taught us the arts we would be a boring society."

"The world has changed remarkably since the time when the arts were once considered vile and sinful."

"And what about me? I would not be a painter without what the fallen angels taught my ancestors. Those souls were innocent, not sinful," Six said. "They deserve freedom, the right to go where they must. Does all your kind do that?"

"Only me. If the souls are allowed freedom upon the Fallen's death, the Sinistari wins a mortal soul in reward."

"Then why don't you stop? You could have freedom from—"

"Because it is my just punishment. I have no need for a human soul." *Leave it at that, nosy woman.*

"That's a stupid excuse. You have free will, yes? You can choose to steal the souls or set them free if you wish."

"I wish to steal them."

"I see." She turned away and looked out the window. Cars rushed past, their passengers unaware of the incredible conversation going on mere yards away inside the building. "That's your truth?"

"It is."

"Then why protect me? Why not slay me and take away the angel's opportunity?"

"I do not harm mortals."

"Right. You just steal their souls." She flashed her pale green gaze at him. Tears wobbled at the corner of one eye. Mortals were too tender, especially women. "Are you my protector or my destroyer?"

"I will never be your destroyer."

"What about the other?"

"I offer you protection. I vow it."

She released a heavy sigh. "Until you deem it necessary to sink a hook into me and dangle me before Zaqiel."

He did not answer. She may be tender, but she was also a smart woman.

"So when you've completed the task you'll abandon me?"

"I will leave."

"Typical."

"Of what?"

"My life. Just when I get attached to someone they— It doesn't matter. You think it'll help to put distance between me and the angel?"

"The angelkiss on your neck will still call to Zaqiel the moment you scratch it. But distance makes the beacon weaker. Where are you headed?"

"Italy. My father owns a villa east of Rome. I go there in the summer, but haven't been for a few years."

"Then we'll go."

"Whoa, buddy, I didn't invite you along."

"You prefer to travel by yourself and risk facing Zaqiel alone when the urge to scratch drives you mad?"

She slapped a palm over her neck. "It's already driving me mad. And he can't follow me in an airplane, can he? Can angels fly?"

"Not the ones whose feet have touched earth. Doesn't keep him from flashing, though. He has the ability to track you to the ends of the earth."

"Did you follow him after he jumped from my bedroom?"

"Not far. The angel has the ability to leap great distances, through time and space. Makes tracking them difficult, because I can't grasp onto his vibration after he's flashed."

"Flashing and angelkisses and demons." Eden worried her lower lip. The tear glittering in her eye wobbled and spilled down her cheek. "I can't do this, Ashur."

He put a hand over hers, on her neck. If the tears touched him they might burn. "You will not give up. Do you hear me? You are a strong woman."

"You don't know me. You can't make a statement like that."

"I can see it in your eyes. In the determination you've shown me thus far. And I vow I will do everything I can to protect you."

"You talk a good game."

"Have I given you any reason to distrust me?"

She sighed. "That knife you had. Does it kill angels?"

"Dethnyht," he said lowly, aware they stood in a public place. "It is the only metal that can permeate the angel's true flesh, which is forged of a metal not found on your earth. Soaked in qeres, a poisonous perfume, it is deadly, but only if plunged through the angel's glass heart when it is in half form."

"Half form?"

"The form it must assume to impregnate you. Half-angel, half-human man."

"You mean with wings and everything?"

"Exactly, but not like the wings most mortals imagine they wear."

"Not of feathers, that's for sure. I usually give them steel wings and gears, but that's a steampunk fantasy."

"Your depictions of the angel form are…close."

"What about demons? What do you look like when you're not…like this?"

"You will never know. It would shame me greatly if I were to expose my true form to you. Yet I must assume it to kill the Fallen." But he would then walk away from her and it would matter little if his appearance horrified her. "Now, what flight are you on so I can go purchase a ticket?"

She told him. "But, Ashur." She grabbed the lapel of his jacket. "Would you do me a favor first?"

"Anything."

"You licked the angelkiss on my arm and it relieved the itch. Would you…" She tugged down the scarf from her neck.

Though he knew it a simple plea for relief from the itch, Six's voice entered Ashur's brain on a wave of sensory wonder. Smells and sounds were growing more vibrant to him by the second as he became a part of this world. He should resist, but he had never been one to walk away from temptation.

He fitted her up against the wall and bent close. She smelled salty and powdery sweet at the same time, perfume and adrenaline brewed to a luscious scent.

"What are you doing?" she whispered.

"You smell good."

A nervous snicker softened her defensive stance. "So do you. But just do it, please? I can't do the romance thing right now."

"I'm not trying to romance you, Six."

"You may not be, but your closeness is certainly stirring something in me. Concentrate, Ashur. The angelkiss."

That was one command he was willing to take from a woman.

He drew his tongue along the soft, silken skin of her neck, lingering, prolonging the glide. The contact blasted open his memory vaults and flashed exquisite replays from pleasures once stolen.

Ashur gripped the back of her head, her soft hair coiling between his fingers. The taste of her would be his undoing….

Until the icy lash stung his shoulder. He jerked upright, a reaction to the brief pain. It hadn't been real, only memory.

He stepped away, and Six wobbled, but caught her palms against the wall.

"You okay?" he asked.

"Seriously?" She touched her mouth and bent her head to hide a burgeoning smile. "That was freakin' awesome."

Disturbed by her reaction, Ashur excused himself to purchase a ticket. He was too quickly slipping into the indulgence of the flesh. And the willpower to make it stop did not exist.

Chapter 9

When they reached an altitude safe for electronics, Eden took out her laptop. It wasn't as if she wanted to avoid a conversation with the gorgeous stud of a man sitting next to her in first class. It was because she didn't know where to start.

The stud was a demon. The only thing she knew about demons was that they were evil. The opposite of good. Ashur had even admitted he wasn't good.

So why did her heart feel he was more good than he imagined?

She had always been the trusting sort. After her mother had died, she had literally been raised by the maid while her father worked insane hours. At a young age, she'd grown accustomed to chatting with the grocery delivery-man, the window cleaner, the TV repairman, and knew all the managers at the local restaurants who delivered takeout.

Independence was her middle name. But her trust had

altered a year ago after the nasty breakup with her fiancé, Chris. That had been a horrid time in her life. Ashur's mention of joy this morning had sparked memories of it. That's why she'd left the room crying. It was silly that it still affected her. By now she should be able to handle listening to some guy's story of joy.

In her heart, Eden knew carrying around the pain was detrimental to her mental health. She was over it, and moving ahead, but that didn't mean shrapnel of the experience could ever be completely removed.

So here she sat next to a demon who intrigued her more than frightened her, and she was okay with it. Because if she wasn't, madness waited a step to the left. Seriously, how many women woke up to discover they'd been targeted to give birth to an angel's nephilim child?

"The nephilim," she asked softly, catching Ashur's attention. "Aren't they supposed to be giants?"

"Not like your fairy tales report."

"The Bible is not a fairy tale."

"If you wish. The nephilim are a good foot or two taller than most of your tall mortal men, and stronger than ten men combined. Their appetites are voracious, and they feed upon any living creature they can get their hands on—including humans. They drink blood, Six. The nephilim are wicked incarnate."

"Peachy."

Sorry she'd asked, she scanned through the e-mail files she'd downloaded yesterday and hadn't a chance to look through. Anything for a distraction from the thought of giants sucking people dry of their blood.

"I do not understand the purpose of the seat cushion as a safety device," Ashur whispered to her. "If the plane falls from the sky, what will one small piece of foam do to break the fall?"

"That's assuming we land in the ocean," she said. "They're flotation devices."

"The impact would still kill a man. So strange how modern people are always offering unnatural reassurance for disasters that cannot be prevented. Why not accept the world is a dangerous place and risks are a common occurrence? Mortals accept false reassurance with disturbing ease."

"No sense in worrying about something you can't prevent. But, dude, if you're ever in need of a job after this slayer gig is up, don't try for a counselor or health care services position."

"Why not?"

"Compassion and tact are required."

"I see." He grinned. It was a moment of self-awareness that captivated Eden.

Ashur had come to her, a demon intent on one goal. Yet he was softening as he relaxed into the world and took it all in. Could the world be influencing him? Would that be a good or bad thing when finally it came to slaying the angel?

She took in his face as he studied the overhead controls for air and light, the rough stubble, the hard lines, the scruff of dark hair that looked more pissed than actually styled. Her awareness made him uncomfortable, she knew. He couldn't meet her gaze.

"You don't like it when I look at you." A blast of air beamed onto her forehead.

"Sorry," Ashur offered and switched the air off. "Doesn't bother me when you look at me." The light showered their laps, and Ashur left it on.

"You're not very good at lying," Eden said. "Interesting."

She stroked her neck just above the pearl necklace and Ashur reached to gently clasp her wrist. "Sorry. It's bugging me again. Should have brought along some aloe. I have never been licked by men so much in my life. A girl should really enjoy it, but— Could you, please? It does help."

"The mortal wants a demon to drag his tongue along her flesh, defiling as a means to comfort?" he asked.

"You make it sound very dirty."

The demon's eyes grew deeper in color, capturing Eden with his silent regard. The edges thickened with a bright blue that almost glowed. The effect wasn't so much creepy as enticing.

"Yes," she said on a gasp. "Please."

Bowing to her neck, he took a moment to smell the perfume imbued in her pores. His proximity, nose almost touching her ear, hair skimming her cheek, awakened her senses, made her blood rush. Who'd a thought a cure for an itch could be so sensual?

Across the aisle an older woman with her nose in a book glanced suspiciously at them. Ashur dragged his tongue along Eden's neck. She sighed softly. The old lady dropped her jaw open. Eden couldn't help but smile.

"Mmm," Eden intoned. "That feels much better."

Head bowed over her, he smiled. The smile didn't move his lips into a curve but she saw the satisfaction in his kaleidoscope eyes. Never had she looked into eyes so beautiful, and ever changing. Moments ago they'd seduced, now they appeared…innocent. Learning the world, indeed.

And learning her? Bring it on.

If he was a demon, she couldn't see it. On the surface Ashur was all man. Handsome, powerful, determined to protect her. The combination was so sexy it took away her breath. She could never dream up a man like him, yet now it was as if she were walking through a tempting reverie.

Eden tilted her head and brushed her lips across his. He didn't flinch, allowing her the slow exploration. If he wanted to learn, she was willing to offer. Warm and firm, his mouth felt like a place she'd never been to before, a place she wanted to learn.

This dream she would claim, keep close to her heart as all the others she secretly hoarded.

Her fingers moved across his chest, pressing his rigid muscles. His body felt like steel, solid, and not as warm as most human bodies were, but it was not cold. Not dead. He was alive.

His breath whispered into her mouth as she parted her lips against his. "Six," he muttered. "What are you doing?"

"You don't know what a kiss is?"

"It's been so long. Too long." An achy longing roughened his voice.

"Since you've been kissed? I suppose so."

"It distracts me from the task."

"What can you possibly do regarding that task while in this airplane soaring over the ocean? Just let this happen. Let me get comfortable with you."

"Is this how you find your comfort with all men?"

A weirdly jealous question. The rescuing knight was asserting his claim to her. She liked that. "No. I'm following my heart right now."

And even if he insisted this had nothing to do with romance, Eden couldn't flee the desire to rush forward and dive in.

She opened her eyes to find his were closed. And he did not move away so she kissed him again, firmer, at the corner of his mouth. The tickle of his mustache made her smile and dash out her tongue to trace his lip. She glided her fingers along the line of goatee framing his jaw and mouth.

For a moment of undiluted bliss she forgot she sat in an airplane, fleeing from a mad angel, and in the presence of a disapproving old lady who observed from across the aisle.

"Your kisses are good for a man who hasn't done so in a thousand years," she said. "Thanks for letting me kiss you."

Eden sat back and looked out the window. She had kissed a demon…

…and I liked it.

Whatever happened from here on, she had to trust Ashur. He was the only one she could trust.

But could she trust her own heart not to leap into uncharted waters?

Five hours into the flight, the old woman across the aisle drowsed. Six observed her, and Ashur settled back in the seat to give her a better view. The laptop still sat open on her lap, but she hadn't tapped at the keyboard for a while. She'd dozed for a few hours, as well.

He was fascinated by the technology, and really wanted to crack the laptop open to see how it worked, but would not do it in front of Six. She seemed very possessive of the computer.

He glanced at the screen and saw another of her paintings that made him hiss. What in the black sea Beneath? That one was not an angel.

Fashioned of black steel, angled row bar, metallic mesh, gears and menace, the creature had horns centered down its skull and small wings that stretched beyond the elbows and flared out in silver flames. There was no sigil on that creature. And why should there be?

Ashur clenched the armrest until it cracked.

Six switched her gaze to him. "What's up? I think I dozed off a bit there. We almost there?"

She was not aware of his anxiety as she pulled down the cover of the laptop and closed it.

Never had he been so blatantly revealed. It shamed him. He did not like the feeling.

The creature Six had painted was him.

Her tender expression prompted Ashur to look away so she would not see the tight anger on his face. "Ashur?"

"A few hours yet," he replied. "You are not going to work on your paintings?"

"Oh, this piece I was dabbling on always gives me trouble."

"Why is that?"

"It's just…not right yet. It's the first piece I've ever created without having a dream to refer to."

"Then why create it?"

"I don't know." She tapped the top of the laptop. "He appeals to me. But he's not a dream angel. Just something I felt compelled to try."

Ashur huffed out his breath. Foolish mortal muse.

"I'll look at it again in the morning when my head is clear. So, do you like the airplane ride?"

"It is monotonous."

"Sorry. I've been in my own world. Let's talk and make things less boring."

She reached for her purse and pulled out a lipstick and smoothed it over her lips. She pressed her lips together, rubbing the gloss around. He liked her mouth. It was too soft for one as rough as him. Perhaps that was why it attracted him so much.

Upon noticing a couple sitting ahead of them, their heads bowed together in sleep, he wondered if Six had left a man—boyfriend, lover—behind. Would she have simply up and left New York without notifying him? Perhaps she'd contacted her lover using the laptop. He wasn't sure how it worked, but he knew people used a plethora of electronic devices to speak instantly with their loved ones nowadays.

"Do you have family?" he suddenly asked. He nodded toward the sleeping couple.

"It's me and my father." She sat back and rummaged in her purse for something else. "What about you?"

"I told you I was forged, not born."

"That's…weird."

"It is what I know. That means no family, no relatives of any sort. Just me and the ranks of Sinistari." None of whom he knew well. They were dispatched on separate missions when needed. Only once had he assisted a Sinistari who had encountered two Fallen at once. "So only you and your father?"

"Yep."

Good. There were no other men in her life. And why was that important?

"Last time I spoke to him was a month ago, I think."

She pulled out a bottle and spritzed her face with what he could only guess was water.

"That seems an inordinate amount of time not to speak to someone so close. He must live far away."

"No, he lives down the street from me in the Wilson penthouse. He's very busy. We're not close like some families who do lunch or go on vacations together."

"I find that startling. The two of you live so close and yet…?"

"Really? You, who do not have family, can be surprised at another person's choices?"

"You have me there. I don't think I would normally be concerned, but with you it seems I am. Is that water?"

"Yep, keeps my skin moist during the dry flight." She offered it to him, but he shook his head, and she tossed it back in her purse. "Don't worry about me. My father loves me, I'm sure. Although, he never actually says 'I love you.' I don't think it occurs to him."

"But you need to hear it." He searched Six's expression, and was disturbed by what he saw. A tear glimmered at the corner of her eye.

"I don't— No, I'm cool not hearing it. I don't need love." She winced.

She denied her own desires. Interesting.

"You do want to hear it—and you do need it—otherwise you wouldn't have mentioned it."

"Don't go all psychiatrist on me, demon. I've had enough of them."

He flinched at her use of the word. It hadn't been accusing, but he preferred she use the name he had given her. Ashur. It sounded human. Not evil.

"My father gives me gifts all the time," she said. "After the, er, a recent hospitalization, he gave me a diamond tennis bracelet."

"I've learned women like diamonds. They are a girl's best friend."

"Oh dear, you did soak it all up, didn't you? Diamonds are not my best friend. I gave the bracelet to a girlfriend. I don't need all the bling. If I need to dress up for a charity event, I actually prefer paste jewels from the turn of the century."

"What about those pearls at your neck?"

She touched the necklace. "I took these from my mother's things the night before a crew my Dad hired arrived to pack away her stuff. She used to always say I love you. I think Dad did, too, but he changed after Mom's death. He works all the time now. Has ever since her death. I was ten. I had to grow up fast after that."

"Had you no one to talk to about your dreams of angels?"

"No. And when I finally did… Well, I've learned to keep that knowledge close to my heart now."

"Yet you just put all your paintings out for the world to see."

"Yes." She smiled a wondrous, wide smile. "It was my way of speaking about it, without really doing it, you know?"

"I'm sure your father must be proud."

She shrugged.

"What if I suggested the gifts are your father's means to express what he cannot verbally? Everyone has his own way of expressing feelings. You must know that."

"I suppose." She sighed. "You're right. I know I'm too hard on him."

"You want something everyone else wants."

"Really? Do you want love, Ashur?"

Just then the flight attendant leaned in and asked if they wanted drinks. Ashur asked her what she had to offer, thankful for the escape from Six's question.

"What would you recommend…?" Zaqiel handed the waiter the embossed menu and leaned forward to read his name badge. "Todd. And don't let my slim physique fool you. I'm all for hearty fare. What's the house specialty?"

"The lobster was caught fresh this morning."

The waiter rambled on about the catch of the day, but Zaqiel concentrated on picking up signals from this mortal regarding the muse. He was marked by his own kiss so she must have rubbed against him—there, where he scratched his neck.

"Allergies?" Zaqiel commented. He fingered a steel ring dangling from his nose.

"Huh? Oh, sorry. I think they switched to different soap in the kitchen, or something." Todd eased a palm over his neck. He flashed a gaze across the room toward the hostess station where Zaqiel assumed his manager must be the one glaring a hole into the waiter's forehead. "So the lobster, then?"

"Excellent. And can you suggest a good club in the area? I've some friends coming to town for a visit and I'm not sure where to take the young and adventurous. Where do you and your friends go, Todd?"

"We usually check out Pearls on weekends. Their DJ is sick, in a good way, you know."

"You going there with friends this weekend, Todd?"

The waiter adjusted the silverware before Zaqiel. "Probably not. My best friend just left for Italy. We usually hook up on Friday nights."

"Ah, so it's a female best friend."

He shrugged. "Eden is a female, that's for sure. Did you want white wine with that, sir?"

"Where in Italy?" Zaqiel nodded toward the wine list and Todd handed it to him. "Rome?"

"Probably. She likes to visit the Vatican whenever she's in the country. She's an artist and paints angels."

"Fascinating. I think I saw that show yesterday."

"It sold out."

"You don't say. I'll have the merlot. That soap must be some nasty stuff, Todd."

"Sorry." Todd dropped his hand to his side. "Anything else?"

"I understand a rash is going around."

"What? Really?"

"Yes, it's called angelkiss. It burns and itches like a mother for days."

"Oh, man, that must be what I have. Angelkiss? Sounds too good to be so bad."

"Well, it's a hell of a lot better than an angel bite."

"Angel bite? Dude, what's that?"

"It's an angelkiss ten times over. The bite introduces contagions to the infected mortal's system. It scurries through the victim's veins and brings about a slow and painful death. The victim's veins literally harden and turn solid. Sort of how it is for angels, don't you know."

"Shit, I'm glad I caught the kiss and not the bite."

"I can remedy that."

Zaqiel grabbed Todd's wrist and latched onto his arm, all his front teeth growing into vicious fangs and sinking into flesh and ripping through muscle.

The waiter screamed. Patrons seated nearby scattered. The manager rushed the table.

Releasing the waiter in a stumbling flail of limbs, Zaqiel stood and strode down the aisle between the tables spread with white linen.

"Somebody call the police!" a diner yelled. "Stop him!"

With a wave of his hand, Zaqiel parted those patrons brave enough to stand before him. They were flung left and right.

"Just like parting the Red Sea," Zaqiel muttered. It was a nifty trick he'd utilized for the actual Red Sea. "Damned Moses took all the credit. Ingrate."

Chapter 10

They landed in Rome at sunset. The Fiumicino Airport bustled, yet Eden hadn't checked her bags so they didn't have to wait around after landing.

Eden was content to hold Ashur's hand and allow him to lead her through the airport. At stressful times she appreciated someone taking control while she got her head together. She handled stress well; it just took a bit to order her senses and inhale some cleansing breaths.

Walking hand in hand with Ashur felt incredible. She wanted to shout, "Hey everyone, look who I'm with. Sexy, isn't he? Dude's a demon, but that's cool. I like him."

Well, she couldn't claim complete rationale at this moment. By morning she'd probably regret inviting him along.

How he'd gotten through customs without a passport had made her wonder. He merely handed the customs official the stub of his ticket. He must possess some sort of mind control.

Would he use it on her? Perhaps he already had. She was allowing a demon to escort her to her villa. And she didn't mind at all.

Shuffling through the rush of people headed toward the cab pickup outside, Eden was tugged off course by a toddler who reached out and grabbed her pearls. She stopped and clasped the delicate little hand. "Careful," she told the boy in his mother's arms.

The mother shook his fingers loose of the necklace and apologized profusely to Eden.

"No worries," she said in Italian. "He's sweet."

The little boy, who looked about a year old, cried. His prize had been taken from him. He shoved his fingers in his mouth and chewed on them around the wailing.

"Shh," Ashur cooed.

The babe stopped crying and blinked teary eyes at the imposing man with the gentle voice. The demon stroked the child's forehead, further rendering him silent and sleepy eyed.

The mother stepped away from them, obviously uneasy about anyone touching her son.

"We'll catch a rental car," Ashur said as he tugged Eden along. "How far away is your villa?"

"Couple hours to the east. We should be there by sunset. What did you do to that baby?"

"Just touched him. Was that okay?"

"Not sure. You didn't use some kind of mind control on him to make him stop crying?"

"No. Just averted his anger from the loss of your pearls. Children are so innocent."

"You surprise me with every word that comes out of your mouth and every one of your actions."

"The child required comforting, that is all."

"I would expect you to be the last person to provide it."

He shrugged and offered a weak smile.

Eden squeezed his hand, and he squeezed back.

With one last glance at the now fussy baby, she turned to focus on what lay ahead: Avoiding an angel intent on having sex with her.

"After we get a rental car, let's stop and pick up some food. I'll never survive without the energy, and the villa will need to be stocked."

"Sounds good. Can we get tacos?"

"Tacos?"

"I had a few of them when I walked the world. I like Chipotle."

"Tacos in Italy? We can do our best."

Michael Donovan paused outside a door carved in the Art Nouveau style. It was open slightly. The hallway was filled with assorted construction ephemera. He'd seen from street level before entering the building that a window was boarded up, probably thirty or more stories high.

He wasn't too surprised his destination was the same one that had the damage.

Nodding to a worker in white overalls, Michael decided on a plan of action. He'd walk in and belong. From what he knew of construction crews they were contracted from various firms. Many workers from different places all worked in unison to get an assortment of jobs completed. No one would know whether he actually belonged on site.

Pushing the front door open with confidence, he followed the tracks of dry-wall dust and dirt down the hallway toward what he suspected would be a bedroom. Eden Campbell's bedroom.

"Señor!"

He turned to the maid. Her dark hair was secured in a ponytail and a wondering look brightened her sallow complexion. "I'm with management," he said. "Just taking a look at what's going on."

She shook her head. "Not good English."

He gestured to the workers and pointed at his chest. "I'm with them."

"Ah. You want lemonade?"

He smiled at her and nodded. "On my way out, thank you."

He'd passed the test. He felt sure none of the workers would question him. They were busy replacing the window and fixing the framework.

Wonder what had happened to knock out the window? It wasn't as if a bird could actually damage the tempered safety glass used in these high-rise complexes.

Avoiding the room from which he heard a skill-saw buzzing away, Michael veered right and touched a closed door. He pressed an ear to the wood. Must be closed to keep out the workers. He walked inside and shut the door behind him.

Afternoon sun lighted the all-white room brilliantly. He guessed it was an office. Its style was completely different from the rest of the house, which was odd.

Michael booted up the computer, and with one eye to the door, he quickly opened the e-mail program.

He'd gotten the lead after tripping over a casual mention of halos in a chat room on angels. Cassandra Stevens had posted that Eden Campbell collected real angel halos. The idea had given her solace in a world she felt was going insane.

Overly dramatic, but Michael had been hunting halos for a decade. He never passed up a lead. Miss Campbell had ignored his e-mails asking if she was in the market to sell. He'd decided she was a buyer and not a seller. Not good, because that took some off the market and Michael wanted to know the location of every halo on earth—if not own them all.

But where was Campbell finding her contacts to buy? And why hadn't he gotten to them first?

Sliding onto the chair and scanning the room, Michael's focus on the various file folders in the program was averted by the iron coatrack standing in the corner of the room.

All alone. Not even decorative. Almost as if shoved aside and forgotten about for the lack of coats it should hold. And yet it instead displayed remarkable objects.

Rushing to the door, Michael peeked out. The hallway was clear. Construction noises buzzed, hummed and clattered. Closing the door, he dashed across the room to the coatrack.

"Three of them. Just hanging here." Too incredible.

He spread his fingers to touch, or grab, or— He slapped his palms to his chest. He couldn't touch them. It was sacrilege.

Yet he'd done far more sacrilegious things in obtaining the eighteen halos he currently owned. Yes, he had stolen a couple from unknowing owners. And don't get him started on the vampires.

Could Miss Campbell know about the vampires?

Eden Campbell was far from unknowing. She knew what these simple circles of metal were. She must have also realized to frame or display them wasn't possible. Michael wasn't sure why—he'd tried it himself—and had decided the answer to that question was ineffable.

But she couldn't know their power. What they would mean in the wrong hands. Or could she?

If the halos fell into certain vampiric hands the world could be in dire trouble.

He wouldn't take them. They would be safe here. He'd

make certain they were. He shoved his hands in his pockets and turned his back to the coatrack. A colored printout had fallen to the floor below the printer.

He picked it up. It was some kind of computer artwork. Very detailed, and masterful. "An angel?"

He followed the fluid lines of steel that represented the angel's wings. It was in man form, but of metal. His abdomen was marked with an— "Angel sigil."

Looked like two sevens butted head-to-head. Maybe Campbell knew more than he could imagine?

He turned to the halos. "Changed my mind. I'm going to have to take these with me."

Six insisted on driving the rental car, though Ashur had protested. He had driven the Ferrari, so it wasn't as if he didn't have the skill. Though this little puddle jumper had no power. It was a woman's vehicle, for sure.

He was glad he'd conceded because now he could watch the countryside zoom by. New York City had not been green at all, save the park below Six's window. Italy was green and lush and the fields blossomed with flowers and butterflies.

Appreciation of beauty was not beyond him. It just didn't produce an emotional response. He could take it or leave it. Mostly. He found he did enjoy it. That was certainly some kind of response.

One beauty he did not want to disregard sat across the stick shift from him. Intent on her path, she focused straight ahead, unaware of his observation. Her neck was slender and long, graceful. She'd tied the blue scarf about it in lieu of asking him to lick the angelkiss once more after they'd secured a rental.

She enjoyed their contact. It was she who had kissed him in the airplane, not the other way around. And he'd responded as any man would. Resistance was not in his repertoire. Of course, she could be regretting that move now. Regret was a great mortal burden. So was ego.

Ashur had no ego that he was aware of. Though certainly any time spent here on earth would bolster that lacking bit of inner angst. He tipped down his sunglasses and studied the tiny dark mole at the base of her earlobe.

"See something you like?" she asked.

"Uh…you?"

"Not very sure of that answer. You said you'd never had to protect a muse before. So what happened this time? Why'd you change your mind about me being bait?"

"As you've seen, the Fallen will not approach you if he knows I am near. Quite opposite of you, he cannot sense me, only see me, so that is why he attempted you at your home. How did he find you originally?"

"How should I know? I was standing on the sidewalk, hailing a cab… Wait. He must have seen the mark on my arm when he was in the gallery. That's when my arm started tingling. When I was standing by him."

"He got very lucky."

"Why is that? He found me! And yet he was standing right next to me after the accident, but it was as if he didn't see me."

"The Fallen one's senses are enhanced and scrambled. He sees voices as color and shape."

"Yes! He said my voice was green. I thought he had synesthesia."

"If he heard your voice again, that is how he would recognize you. Their senses are so enhanced they have difficulty retaining faces."

"Really? I think I've heard of something like that. I thought it was something a person got from brain damage. I can't remember the name for it…"

"Prosopagnosia. It is a mortal condition, contributed to a damaged brain, as you suspect."

She flashed him a look.

"I know all, or most. I just have to access the information."

"Lucky you."

"There are many things better left unknown in this world," he said solemnly.

"I didn't mean to imply you were more fortunate for having so much knowledge."

"I understand. The world has changed. Anyway, the Fallen's inability to remember your face is similar to prosopagnosia. The only other way he can recognize you is by the sigil you wear. When he's in half form, though, he is compelled to mate with his muse, and if you're within breathing distance, he will find you."

"Peachy."

"Will we be there soon?" He pulled down the sun visor and a broken mirror dropped onto his lap.

"You're worse than a little kid." Six smirked and clicked on the blinker. "Yes, we're almost there. Just a few more miles."

Chapter 11

Zaqiel startled upright from the bench outside the Rome airport. The sound of a wailing child alerted him. Mortal younglings were obnoxious.

He glanced to the overhead clock. It was five minutes after the estimated arrival time he'd verified earlier. He'd not missed her, though he'd fallen asleep, which was weird. He never slept. Didn't have to.

Standing and tugging the ragged jean jacket closed over his bare chest, he sneered at the old woman who cringed upon sight of him. Mortals were so judgmental. Everyone had a judgment.

Even his master.

"Former master," he muttered, and spat on the ground. "Time to get this show on the road."

He kicked open the glass airport door, which shattered. Safety glass skittered across the tiled floor. As he entered the building, glass shards rained off his body without cutting his hard mortal flesh. A few people yelled in surprise, but no screams were more audible than the insufferable wails of the child held in a woman's arms outside a restroom.

Zaqiel focused beyond the noise. The beacon was strong. He scanned the crowd's faces, seeing eyes and mouths open in dismay. Everyone had a discernible expression. None was unremarkable as had been the muse.

If she spoke he would see her voice. But right now the calamity of cries would mask the clear green color he sought. It felt like she was near, within arm's reach. Unless his kiss had transferred to another by touch, as it had with the restaurant waiter.

Zaqiel eyed the crying infant. Damnation! The beacon was coming from the babe.

Strutting up to the loathsome lump of noise and snot, Zaqiel gripped the babe's wrist and saw that the angelkiss had reddened his stubby fingers and meaty palm.

"Let go of my baby!"

He shushed the mother harshly in Italian. "I'm not going to hurt the bitty thing. See here, he has a rash. Poor ugly lump of mortal skin."

"It's been bothering him a while," she said frantically. "I don't know what it is."

"It's a contact rash," Zaqiel said over the wailing. "Where is the woman this babbler touched? Hmm? The child touched someone. I know it."

"I…" The mother, confused, tugged at her baby, who only screamed louder because Zaqiel had no intention of letting go of its arm until he got answers. "Are you a doctor?"

"Do you want me to be?" he asked, and influenced her mind to calm and cooperate. It was easy to enter a mortal's mind, especially when it was not focused.

She nodded. "A while ago a woman walked by and my boy grabbed her pearl necklace."

"Ah, yes, the neck. That would be her." He snaked out his tongue, remembering the salty taste of his muse. "Where did she go? Who was she with?"

"A man. Tall. Handsome. In a hurry. But he was so kind to my baby. Is it dangerous? Will the rash go away?"

"How the hell should I know? I'm no doctor."

"Help!"

Grabbed from behind, Zaqiel struggled against the security guards who had the nerve to touch him. He released the baby's arm, because to wrench it loose would serve him no boon. The security detail literally dragged him down the slick, tiled floor, away from the woman and child.

"Don't you know it's illegal to assault babies?" one of the pair said in Italian as he kicked Zaqiel in the spine to force him off his feet and to his knees.

Enough. He would not endure humiliation from mere mortals.

Zaqiel stood, spreading his arms and flinging the officers away from his body. Thrusting back his shoulders and opening his chest, he let out a cry to Above that pierced the higher ranges of human hearing. Overhead the windows shattered and glass rained down. Before him, the crowd parted with a sweep of his hand, bodies flying through the air and landing in the cutting glass.

How he relished chaos.

Reining in his cry, Zaqiel stomped toward the woman who still held the blubbering child tucked to her breast. The glass had avoided her completely, as he'd commanded.

He placed his palm onto the babe's forehead and sought its vision. A flash of dark hair curling about its fingers.

Glossy pearls. The gentle coo of a dark-haired man as he tugged the faceless woman away from the child. The Sinistari had attempted to quiet the child?

What in Beneath was wrong with that demon? He wasn't playing this game right. By all means Zaqiel should fear the Sinistari's approach. And yet the demon was holding back, lurking in the shadows. It set Zaqiel off. He wasn't sure how to play the return hand.

But he would. He'd find the muse. But he couldn't kill her until after she'd given birth to his child. Yet the demon wouldn't allow her to conceive, let alone give birth. What to do?

"They cannot have gone far," he decided, shoving the woman aside and tromping over the fallen glass.

Eden parked the car under the canopy of ancient chestnut trees before the villa. She hadn't been here for years. The place looked the same, thanks to monthly visits from the groundsman and a housekeeper. Ivy snaked across the stone front of the three-story house, spreading pink blooms across it like a fairy tale. Each story was painted a different shade of yellow, for the painters were never too concerned about matching. The wood shutters were various shades of gray with some slats missing on the lower floor.

The fieldstones tiling the front courtyard were in need of sweeping. The tree boughs hung low and a double-wide hammock swung in the breeze opposite the courtyard where she stood.

Eden remembered the summer her father had tied the hammock between the cypress trees. She'd been upset about missing her best friend's sweet-sixteen party back in the States. Why had her father insisted she come along with him to Italy? She'd spent half of July pouting in the hammock. By August she'd resolved that a vacation away from the city wasn't so life-crippling as she thought it to be. And she did have a cell phone with unlimited long distance. She and Cammie's friendship had survived despite her exile to a beautiful, sunny foreign country.

Now she got out of the car, stretched her legs and twisted at the waist. Jet lag was imminent but the evening air, tainted with lavender, worked wonders on her drowsy state. She leaned on the car hood, breathing in the freshness.

The Italian air was so different from New York City's. More expansive. Old, yet subtle, steeped with centuries of strife, endurance and joy.

Since that dreadful summer turned wonderful, Eden always felt as though she could stretch out her imagined wings here and float.

Ashur peeled his large frame out of the car. She hid a laugh at the sight. Like a giant contorting to get out of a clown car, he twisted his head and shrugged his wide shoulders to pop free. He set her suitcase on the ground by the front tire and stood beside her, silent.

She was too tired to figure out his mood, and perhaps he didn't have moods because he'd said he'd lost all the emotional stuff.

Though the way he'd calmed the baby in the airport still impressed her. She suspected he wasn't aware he had expressed compassion.

"I'm tired," she admitted. "Of running."

"You can get a good night's rest here."

"Sure. And then what? Another day of running away from the maniacal angel?"

It was apparent Ashur couldn't kill the angel unless it was already attacking her. She did not like being bait. Surrendering her control was not tops on the menu. It made her feel small, humiliated. A feeling she was all too accustomed to whenever she brought up her dreams.

"I don't think I can do this, Ashur. I'm not as strong as I like to believe. Why don't we…let the angel do his thing?"

"I am surprised at your easy defeat. You would allow Zaqiel to rape you?"

She didn't like hearing it put that way. No, she would have nothing of the sort. But what could she do?

Eden walked to the stone wall edging the courtyard that spread before the house. From here she could look down over the vineyard. Beyond that, a few kilometers, lived a family who tended the vines year-round. The wine was put out under the villa's name, though Eden's father oversaw all the profits and marketing.

"I'm good with a blade," she said, "but as you saw, the angel is too quick for me. Besides, I left it at home."

"That little stick is worthless against an angel. The best defense against Zaqiel is to allow me to handle the situation."

"Right. I'm the bait. Got it. Don't like it. But I don't have much choice. Though, really…"

"What?"

Something about the air here always loosened her defenses, made her want to be open and true. And perhaps the truth would stop it all.

"Ashur, there's something you should know. It doesn't matter what the angel does to me. If he tries to get me pregnant it won't work."

"He will not try. He will succeed."

"He may, but it won't matter." She sighed and hugged her arms to her chest. She hadn't spoken of this since it happened, not even to Cammie, who, thankfully, had given her space.

It was late and she was tired. But she had to get this off her chest before she went to bed. It was something Ashur needed to know.

"I can't carry a baby to term."

He rested his elbows on the stones beside her. She could feel his intensity permeate her pores like the warm sun. But he did not speak. She was grateful for that.

"A year ago," she said, "I was engaged. And pregnant."

She didn't look to him for confirmation or any of those awkward nods or smiles of understanding she'd gotten so sick of seeing after it had happened. Probably he didn't know such things were expected, though completely unnecessary.

"I'd been dating my boyfriend for six months when I found out I was pregnant. It wasn't something we'd planned. The condom broke. And honestly, I wasn't sure I wanted a baby. Well, I knew I did not. But he proposed, saying he wanted to do the right thing."

The right thing. Catching her chin in hand, Eden closed her eyes. Those were the three most unromantic words she had ever heard. Though at the time, she'd thought she was a princess and her knight in shining armor had rode up to rescue her.

Funny how a few months, and the ability to look over one's past, changed their perspective. She was grateful for that now.

"I was excited about the prospect of being married— and you know, a ten-carat engagement ring always clouds a woman's heart to reality. And I was relieved I wouldn't have to do the single-mother thing, so I accepted the proposal. Afterward, though, I felt my fiancé draw away from me every day.

"After about a month, I didn't care that he was growing distant. I changed. My heart altered. I could feel my body changing, my stomach expanding. I was going to have a baby. And I could love it and it would love me and never judge me like so many others have. It was amazing. I felt so blessed. I wanted that baby so much.

"I miscarried at four months." She bowed her head, but the tears didn't come. She was all cried out for the baby. Or so she had thought. A tight ball clenched in her chest, a smudge of blackness that yet remained. "When you mentioned how you remembered joy by witnessing a birth, that stirred up things for me again. Sorry to have freaked on you."

"Do not apologize for something that is not your fault. The loss must have devastated you and your lover."

"Yes, well, my fiancé broke up with me before I was discharged from the hospital. But the weird thing is, I wasn't upset about losing him. I felt I'd lost him the day I told him I was pregnant. But the baby…" She reached down now, stroking her flat belly, remembering the sweet mound that had begun to develop. "The doctors told me I have a T-shaped uterus. I can get pregnant, but I'm not able to carry a baby to term. So."

She turned her back to the wall of stone and propped her elbows on it. A glance to Ashur found him standing stiffly, arms crossed over his chest in a defensive pose. It disturbed her. Men were not keen on emotion and girl talk. And demons were obviously less keen on it all.

"Your angel can do his best," she said, "but I'll never carry the little monster to term."

"Why would you be a muse if you cannot carry the child?"

The look he gave her burned through Eden's heart.

"Way to make me feel afflicted," she managed. But she was shaking. Her confession had been difficult, and then Ashur's castigation… Well, she hadn't been prepared for that.

She charged past him toward the front door and slipped her key into the lock. She didn't want to talk about evil angels and guardian demons tonight. Nor did accusations help. She'd gone beyond reason. She'd laid out her greatest heartbreak. She just—

Ashur stood in the doorway, his features darkened by the shadows coaxing night closer. Eden hadn't flipped on the light. She knew the house by heart. This house held only good memories. She did not want to taint it with her sorrow.

But it was too late. Tears pearled down her cheeks. Her vision blurred, and the grief returned as if it were new.

"Ashur, I…need someone to hold me and tell me everything is going to be okay."

Chapter 12

Ashur clamped his arms across his chest. It was automatic to resist connection. But it felt wrong.

Six stood there helplessly. She simply asked for what she needed. It wasn't a few words, but emotional contact that would reassure her. He knew it worked like that for humans.

But a hug?

Hell, where was that damned Fallen?

On the other hand, he never backed down from a challenge.

Opening his arms felt awkward, but when Six saw his movement she slid close to him, fitting her body to his. Her arms slipped around behind his back and she nestled her head on his shoulder.

Nice.

What was necessary was to close her in a hug with his arms. He'd never done the sort before, not even a millennium earlier when he'd dallied with mortal women. Tease 'em, please 'em and leave 'em had been his MO.

He wrapped one arm across her back. The move had her snuggling her warmth against his chest. The heavy sweetness of her breasts and the taut line of her stomach melded to his body. Women shouldn't feel so good. Such a delicious sin.

His other arm he hugged gently along her back, lifting his hand to caress her soft hair. It smelled like some kind of fruit, as did her flesh. She was a treasure to hold. He had been denied softness for so long. He didn't deserve it.

Didn't need it.

His life had been spent Beneath, tapping, tapping, ever tapping away the moments that moved like the sludge sea behind his throne. Trying to hang on to the goodness he'd experienced on earth, yet unable—save for joy. And though he'd kept it, he had never pulled it out to experience for fear of losing it like a wisp of a forgotten past.

Until now.

Six was good; she was warm. She was ripe for him. He was hardening for her. She must feel his erection growing, but she made no indication.

He should indulge when opportunity presented itself. But could he expect carnal relations after her tragic tale of lost love and hope? She'd relayed the information so clinically, as if it meant little to her.

Women were more complicated than that. That much he did know.

Nuzzling his face into her hair, Ashur stifled a groan of pleasure. It was weak to show such reaction. He couldn't allow her to expect less from him because he'd touched her.

Yet he didn't want to release her. He wanted to be closer to her. Inside her. Surrounded by her. He didn't have to commit the one sin of the Sinistari.

"You can do that second part now," she whispered.

"What part is that?"

"The part where you tell me everything is going to be okay."

Something inside Ashur pulsed. It was not a heartbeat, but a rap upon the hard walls of his heart. The stolen souls wanted release.

He was called Ashuriel the Black for a reason. A demon didn't collect myriads of mortal souls, hold them within forever and not suffer the consequences. He'd come to accept it as his bane, a bane he required to balance the evil he performed upon earth. A bane too wicked to force upon one as good as Six.

"Ashur?"

"I can't tell you that," he said, stepping away and pulling her arms from around his neck, "because I don't know what tomorrow will bring. Even what the next hour will bring."

She nodded. "Sleep." A sigh lifted her shoulders and breasts. She was still so close to him, he could breathe in her scent. It dizzied him. "Thanks for listening to my silly rambling. The bedrooms are made up. They're both upstairs."

"I want to see if I can track Zaqiel."

"You said you couldn't kill him unless he was in angel form. And that would only happen when he tried to have sex with me. So, shouldn't you stick close to me?"

"In theory, but if I can find him and keep an eye on him, I'll be able to control the situation. An angel loosed on earth is a vile torment. He will leave chaos in his wake."

"He won't harm others, will he?"

"He is capable of anything."

She looked down and rubbed her bare arm. "Would you stay if I asked?"

"Ask and see."

"Stay, please. I don't want to be alone, knowing some

creepy dude who wants to rape me is out there. And what if I itch?"

Close to the muse or tracking the Fallen—either place would put him in a position of strength. He had simply thought distance would quell the ache he suddenly felt for Six.

So be it. "Stay I shall. I'll watch you through the night."

"You mean like stand over my bed? That would creep me out, too."

"If you were to scratch in your sleep it would alert Zaqiel."

She nodded and sighed. "You can watch me, but don't be obvious about it. I think I'm tired enough to fall asleep with a guard standing over me."

"I'll carry up your suitcase," he offered.

"Thanks." She took her purse up the stairs with her, and Ashur left her alone in the bedroom, thinking she'd like some time to settle into sleep.

An hour later he crept into her room. She slept on her side, still wearing the red blouse and skirt. The brown boots sat on the floor before the bed.

Moonlight spilled through the window she'd opened and the night's perfume tempted him to sit on the wide sill, his legs up and his head against the stone casement. The vines climbing to the house were in bloom, but he didn't access his knowledge for their name. Didn't matter. The sweetest perfume emanated from Six.

She didn't stir until the night grew long and morning teased the horizon. When he suspected she would reach up to scratch her neck, Ashur dashed to the bed and caught her wrist gently.

"Sleep," he purred. "I'll hold you, Six."

She made a noise, sweet and sleep-drenched, as he carefully lay on the bed and clasped her wrists against his chest. She smiled and nuzzled her head against his shoulder.

Eden woke in the arms of a demon. Sunlight softened the hard angles on his face. His skin was not so pale but hardly tan, and stubble marked his jaw where he would normally shave. He was exactly as a man should be.

Tiny laugh lines curved out from the corner of each eye. She was intrigued that he would show signs of age when he had existed so long already. Surely they were not laugh lines. Ashur did not laugh often, she suspected.

She wondered what he looked like when he was in demon form. He said he would never show her that side of him. Probably she didn't want to see it. While appearance mattered little to her, if he brandished horns, a tail and hooves she knew it would be difficult to maintain indifference.

On the other hand, it was she who tried to get the world to view angels in a different light. Perhaps standing before a demon incarnate would be the thing to challenge her sense of right and wrong.

No. As brave as she was, she suspected facing the demon would have her crying for mercy.

Wiggling her hand within his clasped fingers, she tried not to wake him. He held her wrists loosely to keep her from scratching the burning fire strafing along her neck. He'd said the beacon would grow weaker with distance, but obviously distance had nothing to do with itch intensity.

When all but her fingers were free, he grabbed her roughly.

"Please," she whispered. "It's driving me nuts."

"Don't bring the angel to us right now," he said, his eyes still closed. "I want to spend this time with you."

He wanted to spend time with her? She could get behind that suggestion. The more she prolonged the inevitable, the longer she prevented her own anxiety over being abandoned. He was here now. She didn't want this to end, either.

Ashur moved in to nuzzle against her cheek. Something a lover would do.

Did he realize what he was doing, or was he still half asleep?

It was a weirdly sexual thing when he drew his tongue over her skin. She knew it was merely a means of protection. But separating the two—protection and desire—was not so easy. The heat of his tongue against her flesh stirred delicious sensations at her neck and throughout her body. Her nipples hardened. She arched her back, pressing her breasts against his sleeve.

Digging her fingers into Ashur's shirt, Eden tugged him closer. She moved her hips forward, meeting his thighs. He still wore the jeans and heavy leather jacket. It was difficult to feel his muscles beneath the clothing, but she wanted to know if he was experiencing the same desire as she. It wouldn't be fair if this was a one-sided seduction.

He whispered aside her ear, "What are you doing?"

Seduction. When had *she* changed the game? Well, she was a woman. It was her prerogative.

"I want to feel you." Pressing her breasts against his chest, she hoped he could feel her desire manifested. "Give me more than protection, Ashur. Kiss me."

"You ask very much."

"Is it so difficult for you to kiss me?"

"It is too easy."

"I'm distracting you from the greater cause?"

"Something like that."

"I have a feeling the angel can wait a few minutes. But if you'd rather not—"

He buried his face into her hair, drawing his nose along her ear. Shimmers of champagne bubbles effervesced through Eden's veins. His breath burnished a blush at her cheek, which melted down her neck and across her breasts.

She hadn't simply lain beside a man like this for a year. She'd begun dating last month, but hadn't allowed herself to enjoy anything as intimate as this. Two bodies crushed against each other. Breaths mingling. Skin flushing and aching for touch.

Desire clasped hold of her senses with a determination she'd not touched for…forever.

When Ashur's mouth found hers, a whimper escaped her throat. It was a surrender to something she wasn't sure about, but knelt before, willing to succumb if asked.

Eden slid her hand down Ashur's abs, surfing the solid ridges as she snuck up under his shirt. Her fingers explored as determinedly as he did at her mouth. He felt like sun-warmed steel, curved and powerful, yet pliant against her skin. Beneath her touch the sudden rise of goose bumps tickled the whorls on her skin. The normality of it pleased her. She stroked her palm over the bumpy skin, warming it smooth.

The rough scruff of his beard softly skated along her chin. Moving her kiss higher, she tasted the fine trim of his moustache. She drew her tongue along it then dashed it inside his mouth to tangle with his.

Somehow she got tangled in the need, the utter desire for touch. For connection. Could she draw him into her without actually pushing it to sex? They had known each other but a day. She just needed this kiss.

Wrapping her leg over his thigh, she pressed her groin against his. Ashur moaned into her mouth. She felt him harden against her mons. He moved against her, putting himself in a commanding position. He thrust his tongue inside her and dashed it over her teeth, her tongue and behind her upper lip. More demanding now. Discretion abandoned, he sought the intimate edges of her. She wanted him to trace her, to learn her, to keep her.

"You make me remember," he said into her mouth.

"Remember what? Touch?"

"Passion."

Yes, the ferocious desire to become a part of another person through skin, mouth and scent.

"It's been too long for you." She licked a trail down his chin and kissed the fine beard dashing a thin line along his jaw. "I want this, Ashur. This touch."

"Yes, touch."

His body clenched against hers as if he'd been seized by pain. He gripped her hair and pressed her face against his neck.

"What is it?" she murmured.

"Just a twitch. Don't stop. Brand me, Six. Use your tongue to mark me."

The throaty hoarseness in his voice further enticed her wicked intent. Eden touched the tip of her tongue to Ashur's clavicle. She could not get over how hard his body was. The flesh was warm and malleable, yet his muscles were solid. She'd never been with a man who worked out. Wall Street suits were more her style, and they preferred manscaping over muscle. The difference was so delicious. She did not want to cease exploration.

Pushing up his shirt, she shoved it high and he tugged it off, along with the leather jacket. He rolled to his back and she straddled him, tending his fiery skin with her tongue. At his nipple she teased it and laved the tiny hard jewel.

Again he flinched, or maybe all his muscles tensed. His body tightened. It could be a sexual reaction, but she felt it was not. Pausing and seeking his eyes in the morning light, she silently wondered if she should continue.

"Just a muscle twitch," he reassured. "From…an old injury. More," he said and let his head fall onto the pillow.

Whoever had designed this man had made him tall and lean, offering Eden a vast stretch of tightened abs to tease with her mouth. Licking, kissing, gently biting, she worked along his side. Ashur's fingers twisted in her hair, gripping and loosely possessing. When she pressed her breasts to his stomach and her hard nipples poked through her silk shirt and skimmed his skin, he moaned long and racked with desire.

The sound of his pleasure reassured her. She liked control, liked to be the one on top. Rarely did that happen, so when it did, she refused to shrink in dismay or play the innocent. She may be the astute society girl on the outside, but underneath the pearls and silk a darker rebel sought release. Eden knew what she wanted from this man, and she intended to have it.

He tugged at her shirt. "You want me to take it off?" she asked.

This time when his muscles clenched, Ashur sat up and gripped her by the shoulders. Eyes closed in a wince, he held her as he rode out some inner pain she could not fathom. It was awful, for what could make this big, strong man shudder?

"Something's wrong," Eden said. "Is it a demon thing?"

Coming up from the pain, he opened his eyes—they were brilliant blue, not the mixture of colors she had seen previously. Glancing aside, he stroked her shoulder absently with his thumb.

"Ashur? Your eyes… Is something wrong?"

"*This* is wrong." He pushed her off him and rose, grabbing his shirt from the floor as he did. He pulled it over his head. "I shouldn't take advantage of you."

"I think it was quite the opposite. I was taking advantage of you!"

He smirked, but didn't meet her eyes. "And you did it well."

"Tell me it wasn't wrong." She smoothed her palms up her arms, feeling small sitting alone amidst the rumpled sheets. "Touching another person, showing them you care about them is never wrong."

"Care? Six, you don't know me. I am…not like you."

"I know. You're a demon. Your body is like steel and your eyes— They've changed color. They were bright blue, but now they've returned to all colors."

"And does that not disturb you?"

"It should, but, nope, not feeling it right now. Remember, I'm a little touched in the head to begin with, dreaming angels and all. Ashur, you can't deny you liked kissing me."

"I won't." He looked out the window where the sun blurred the edges of the walls with a brilliant white glow, again granting him an aura as she'd first seen in the warehouse. Her white knight. "I could kiss you all day. But touching you brings back memories."

"From when you used to walk the earth?"

"No, of after that time. When I was consigned to Beneath for my sin."

"Your sin? But if you're killing angels, that's beyond sin—"

"When angels hate, they commit the only sin recognizable by their kind. Demon sin is the opposite."

"You mean…?"

"The only sin a demon can commit is love," he said sharply. With that, he marched out of the bedroom.

Kneeling on the center of the bed, Eden clutched the pillow to her chest.

"Wow. He's capable of love."

Chapter 13

Ashur stalked out from the cool morning shadows before the house and paced the stone-tiled courtyard under the shade of the chestnut boughs. He couldn't leave Six's bedroom fast enough. Pain had rended through his body.

By the time he reached the courtyard, he was bent over, clutching his head to stop the grotesque shouting and moans of macabre delight the torturer had emitted.

He stumbled down the steps and into the shadows at the base of the stone wall and fell to his knees. Beating the grass with a fist and clamping his jaw, he maintained control on the yowl seeking voice.

He must not allow her to see him like this, weakened by something as insubstantial as memory.

But the memory was so real. And Six's intimate touches had conjured it.

The world had once been simpler. Yet in those years of

walking the earth, he'd indulged in all mortal sins. It had been recreation for him. And his kind approved.

It was only when he'd stepped over the line from those mortal excesses and began to embrace emotion and consequence—and morality—that his fellow Sinistari took offense.

He'd fallen in love. And if ever a demon could sin, love was the ultimate.

Sent Beneath without trial or recourse, his punishment had been a thousand years of torture. At first they'd tortured his mortal costume, and when that was shredded and oozing he had been allowed to heal and resume his natural form. It is difficult to whip the steel-like flesh of a Sinistari demon, to open it wide and bleed out the black blood. But it had been done, over and over.

Eventually, after sixty or seventy decades, Ashuriel began to scream and yowl. No longer could he clasp the pride he had learned from the mortals.

And when he was left to heal, the scars formed, bulging and glossy in his metallic flesh. All emotion had fled. Any speck of morality. Memory of fine moments. He had been reduced to a shell.

After a thousand years of torture, though, he had still retained his crown. The Sinistari—all demon breeds—regarded him as the master slayer, for following each slaying he never chose the cowardly consolation of a mortal soul. And the Sinistari held him in higher regard for having stolen the sweet mortal pleasure of love and taken his just punishment in return.

Love had been beaten out of him. With the lash of the bladed whip, Ariel, the Master of Punishment, had beaten away emotion, the exquisite ring of kindness, the subtle flavor of whimsy. Compassion had bled out, humility raped from his veins and solace shattered. It had all been taken, even the lust, greed and the desire for excess all Sinistari embraced.

But as he'd told Six, no one could take away joy. He'd hoarded the emotion in his darkest recesses, crammed deep within the horde of souls that had writhed in ecstasy during his torture. The souls he'd stolen had sensed their prison master's punishment and had rejoiced.

Ashur sat against the stone wall. The pain had begun to recede. What he'd done all those years ago, he would never regret, even after the torture. He had known love. He had received a just punishment.

Now but days upon the earth, Ashuriel the Black had succumbed to mortal sin again. It wasn't the sin that bothered him or his fellow breed. Sin he could indulge in and receive an approving nod from the Sinistari and master.

It was the forbidden love. It could prove his undoing.

He didn't love Six. But he did desire her.

Desire and love were different beasts. There was nothing wrong with indulging lust. It was his right to partake all pleasures the mortal realm offered while he inhabited earth.

So why did the vicious memories stab at him when Six touched him intimately? Almost as if a warning against the great sin he may yet commit.

Though the Sinistari and others looked up to him, it was the psychopomps who truly despised Ashuriel. He had stolen their booty. He held no fear for the soul bringers. Come at him with their worst; he would defeat them all.

He clutched his chest. On occasion he could feel the souls within his black heart flutter, as if seeking escape. They had been consumed by the Fallen who had taught them the arts and other crafts once deemed a sin by man—until Ashur had stolen them.

How the world had changed to embrace those masterful arts. No longer were those forbidden crafts considered vile, sinful or obscene.

But he would never release the souls. They were his. Prizes won for the kill. Yes, it was agonizing as he received them into his black heart. As it should be. Yet once there, it comforted him to know he carried them within, his rightful trophies.

Six had been horrified to learn about his hoarding proclivities. But she was mortal and could never understand the ways of the Sinistari.

Though she did accept him amazingly well. She'd kissed him. And continued kissing and touching him, even with the knowledge he was a monster.

He'd never revealed his demonic nature during his previous earth walk. None of his female conquests had a clue to his origins. It had been better that way. Yet would they have been as accepting as Six had they full knowledge of him?

Likely not. Times were different now.

Six saw him only as human. She could not begin to comprehend standing before his true demon form. Or perhaps she had some idea. Her painted images astounded him. She was so close to capturing the angel in her works. Combine bits and pieces from each of them and she'd be right on.

But the image he had seen on the laptop while they'd flown over the Atlantic Ocean disturbed him most. Could she know she had painted him? It was not an exact portrayal, but many parts and features were right on the mark. She had not anticipated that his demonic form bore scars.

Perhaps all muses had instinctive connections to the Fallen. Did they all dream of angels and attempt to recreate their dreams artistically? Six knew the angel sigils. That knowledge was forbidden to mortals.

He had not remarked such connections before because he'd never gotten to know a muse personally.

He recalled Six's confession that she could not carry a baby to term. He did not understand that. Obviously she had lost a mortal child. So why then had she been chosen to carry a Fallen one's child?

Random women were not selected as muses. They must have ancient ties to the Merovingian line of kings, and further back, to the very Christ.

Could Six carry a Fallen's child?

He didn't have those answers, and it baffled him. What a waste, should the Fallen actually attempt her.

What would Zaqiel think to learn that truth? Perhaps he'd leave Six alone and be on to the next muse. That would solve one problem Ashur had.

No, it was best he killed the angel before he could move on to another innocent muse.

The fiancé Six had told him about had been a bastard, leaving her in the hospital to fare on her own. Had she loved him? Had she loved the unborn child?

Yes, she'd said she had loved the child but not the father.

Children were exquisite. Pure and innocent, they compelled Ashur when he saw one. So vastly opposite of what he was.

It shouldn't matter to Ashur what happened to Six— but it did.

Mortal emotion was so confusing. It wasn't black and white, but so many shades of gray, as his sight had been upon first arriving on earth. He would have strangled the bastard for what he'd done to Six.

Did that mean Ashur cared for the mortal muse? Perhaps.

"But it's not love," he muttered, and stood. "It is merely lust." Of which, he was free to dive in headfirst.

Six stood in the kitchen slicing a pear on a cutting board

placed on the table. "Sorry if I offended you," she offered without turning to him.

"You did not. I needed some air."

"Get some thinking done? Strategizing?"

She expected him to defend her, which he would. So why did he seek means to extend their time together before the angel arrived? "Six, did you love the man who fathered your unborn child?"

She swung around to look at him. The cut pear wobbled on the table behind her. Running a palm down the simple flowered dress she wore, she finally managed a shrug. "No. Yes. Maybe for a while. I'm not sure what love is. Well, there are so many forms of love."

"You mortals tend to make everything more complicated than it needs to be."

"Is that so? And you are a master of love?"

He hung his head, sighing through his nose.

"Sorry. I didn't mean— I meant, well, take young love. When you're a teenager and you share that first kiss and the boy tells you he loves you, you believe him and you want to marry him and have his children."

Ashur lifted a brow.

"That's love," she countered. "You can't tell me it's not. And there is the adult, passionate love that totally blows teen love out of the water. It is sexy and sometimes dirty and so wonderful. And that's real love, too. And there's parental love for their children. It's complicated, as you say. I think I've known different kinds of love at different points in my life, but never a true love."

"True love is yet another kind?"

"It's the kind of love I desire."

"So many means to ultimate punishment, then."

"What do you mean?"

He shook his head. "Nothing."

"I think you've known it," she said.

He had not told her he loved a mortal woman. And love had been tortured from him. There was no way she could read conflicting emotions from him now.

"When you described joy to me," she said. "I don't think it was joy, but rather love."

"It was joy."

"Maybe at first, but seriously? What you witnessed was love the mother had for her child. And a new and perfect love a child has for its mother. My God, that would be so wonderful." She smoothed a palm over her stomach. Her eyes did not smile as did her mouth. "And I think you loved them both."

"No." He reared back, flinging a hand through the air, not sure if he wanted to punch something. Instead he shrugged his fingers through his hair. "Love was tortured from me."

"What?" She set down the paring knife. "You've… been tortured?"

He'd said too much. Ashur stalked to the doorway, but slammed his palms to the frame.

No. This was not the way to remain strong. He would not leave again. No mere woman would defeat him twice in so little time.

"Torture is a way of life for the Sinistari," he said. And leave it at that.

Turning, he crossed his arms over his chest and defied her to question him further. He'd silenced her with his force. She nodded and turned toward the table, toying with the pear halves.

"We are not alike in any way," he added. He must push her away though he wanted to pull her closer and nuzzle his face in the luscious waves of her hair.

She again nodded and brushed her neck with her fingers. She'd tied her hair in a loose ponytail with a bright blue scarf.

"Don't scratch, Six."

"I won't. I have to. It's… Oh." She slammed the knife on the table and turned to him. "Please, will you…?"

Ashur inhaled shallowly. If he crossed the room and put his tongue to her flesh right now, he wasn't sure he could stop there. His fingers curled into his palms. The woman would be his undoing. He should allow her to scratch, to call Zaqiel to them and complete the task.

But he wasn't prepared for Zaqiel yet. He'd learned the world; however, now he wanted to learn this woman. Because if he didn't do it now, the opportunity would not exist after he'd slain his prey.

Six clasped her hands before her and twisted them in an attempt to keep from scratching. The fix was simple—but too easy.

Ashur crossed to her and swept her into his arms. So lithe and weightless, she felt like a captured bird in his grasp. If he held her too tight she would break.

Perhaps you should break her so Zaqiel will have no use for her.

That angry thought had come from his darkest depths. His black heart burst with caged and angry souls. It didn't shock Ashur. Yet if he killed Six that would take care of nothing at all.

As well, she was already broken, wasn't she? Unable to carry a child to term. Once Zaqiel learned the truth—or if the muse was damaged by Ashur—the Fallen would be on to the next muse. The angel would not stop until he had procreated.

Six's fingers dug into his shirt. Her whimper stabbed through his skin and prickled beneath. It was a good feeling. One he must indulge.

Bending to her neck, he licked the flesh. Salty and sweet, he tasted the tang of pear juice from when her fingers had stroked her flesh. "That is the scent," he muttered.

"Pears?"

"Yes, I had no name for it the first time I smelled you. It is your scent."

"It's a fruity perfume I always wear. Why does demon saliva counteract an angelkiss?" she wondered aloud.

"Not sure. I just know it works." He licked a trail up her jaw. Her hair feathered across his face, tempting him to dive into the lush darkness and lose himself in a softness he had not touched for literal ages.

"Can a demon give me a demonkiss? And would an angel's saliva counteract that?"

"Stop talking, Six."

"Sure. Mmm… Yes, right there."

"Does it itch here?" He stroked his tongue down the opposite side of her neck.

"No. Just…"

The subtle sweetness of her threatened to push his ramparts wide-open, to release the demon's needs. *Don't deny yourself.*

"I want more of you," she murmured.

"You should not." He kissed her jaw. Her mouth found his and their tongues kissed. "But I do. I must have you."

"Yes. More of you, my demon lover."

"Stop talking, Sex."

She abruptly pulled away from their kiss. Her green eyes sparkled mischievously. "You just called me Sex."

"No."

"Oh, yes you did. Got a certain topic on your mind, big boy?"

"I did not."

"Did, too." Now her eyes smiled as wide as her mouth. "Doesn't matter. Just kiss me and no pulling away this time."

"I am finished arguing with morals. Those are your mortal devices. We Sinistari heartily partake in lust. I want to touch you, and I will."

He lifted her and set her on the table. The plate clattered and half a pear rolled to the edge to balance precariously. She wrapped her legs about his hips and he stroked his palms over her smooth legs.

Gliding his way along her body, he pressed her hips to secure her tightly against his groin. The position moved them close, a tight hug that allowed her to know exactly how hard he'd become.

Moving his hands up her torso, he thumbed her breasts, stroking the nipples. She reacted by arching her back, giving him free rein over her intimate zones.

In between kisses, she managed to breathe, and asked, "Where will you go when you are done here? When the angel is slain? Will you… Can we…?"

He suspected she was looking for him to say they could be together. And that sounded like an interesting future, but it wasn't his reality. "I will go where I am commanded."

"Oh." She kissed his ear, and used her teeth to tug the lobe. "So who is your commander? Some great demon from Beneath?"

"I am the great demon from Beneath," he said with a growl. "Ashuriel the Black, Stealer of Souls, Master of Dethnyht."

"Cool. You have a crown or something?"

"I do. It is fashioned from the feathers which remain after I've slain an angel."

"Oh."

And she was starting to think too much. Never good in a situation better left to lusty abandon and surrender.

"You would not believe me if I told you who directed my actions."

"Try me." She leaned back, pressing her palms to the table. Her nipples peaked beneath the silk blouse, tempting him deliciously. She hugged his hips with her knees. "I believe in angels and demons walking the earth. I bet there's not much you could tell me that would shock me."

That was a bet he would win. Unfortunately.

The makeout session had officially ended. Ashur stretched back his shoulders. A goddess posed before him, displaying herself for his admiration. Her cheeks were flushed brightly and her lips were bruised red.

Damn, if he didn't want to strip her bare and kiss her everywhere.

It could wait. Everything could wait.

She wanted truths?

"My commander," he said, "is Raphael. An archangel."

Chapter 14

Obviously he could shock her.

"An angel?" Eden slid off the table and accidentally stepped on the pear slice.

Ashur stood with hands at his hips. His lips were still burnished from their kisses. She wanted to lick his bare chest, to fuse herself against him as if she were the filings to his magnetic field.

But first she needed to get things sorted out.

"I thought the angels were the bad guys?"

"The Fallen are. The upper echelons are most definitely not. The archangels are His right hand. Raphael is the one who forged me, sent me on my task, had his lackey punish me for my sin and then summoned me again."

"Seriously? Raphael. I've read about that angel."

"Whatever the mortals have recorded about the angel is likely inaccurate. It is Raphael's concern no Fallen should accomplish its task. Though some have. That was an oversight made while I was Beneath."

"You mean fallen angels have actually had sex with women? Gotten them pregnant with…?"

"Nephilim have been born to walk the earth. They've been quickly dispatched, yet not always by slayers. David took out Goliath, the giant of Gath."

"No way. Really?" The whole bible lesson was fascinating, and frightening. "But Goliath was a grown man."

"When the nephilim is born it matures to adulthood within seventy-two hours."

"Oh, my God. That poor mother."

"The mother may not be aware if she is dead. I have not heard of a muse who has survived the birth."

Eden's legs wobbled. She clutched the edge of the table and tried to keep her mouth from gaping. She wouldn't survive the birth? Not that it mattered. She couldn't carry a child to term.

But what if she could? What if, after some supernatural entity had been placed in her womb, it was able to grow and be born? What kind of freak of nature was she? Seeing angels in her dreams and wearing an angel sigil…

"You're calling Raphael a *he* and saying Fallen angels can have sex with women," she blurted out nervously. "I thought angels were without sexual assignment. Or is that another mortal falsehood?"

"It's easier to speak of them using the male pronoun, and Raphael often manifests in male form. Fallen can have sexual congress with mortal women only when they are in full or even half human form, thus rendering them with the correct anatomy to complete the task. In fact, they can shift no further than half angel form, and can never achieve complete angelic form again. Their feet have touched the earth so they lack divinity. It is why they cannot fly or look to the heavens."

She clutched Ashur's arm for support. "You won't let Zaqiel get to me, will you?"

"Six, you know what I have told you."

"Yes, I will have to draw him to me so you can slay him. But you'll do it before he has sex with me?"

"Yes, I promise you."

"I'll hold you to that promise."

"It is all I can give you."

Meeting his eyes, Eden wondered at that statement. Was a promise all he could give, or all he wanted to give? Had she been luring him from the task by kissing him and encouraging his exploration of her body? He was a warrior with one sole purpose, and had been sent to accomplish it by a freakin' angel.

"So this Raphael dude—"

"Do not speak his name unless you wish his audience."

"Seriously? You mean I could call an angel to me by speaking its name?"

"Not any mortal can do it, but I suspect a muse probably could."

"Cool."

"Do not abuse the power, Six."

"I won't. I just wondered if you and he were tight."

"I have been in his presence three times. Each time I did not speak, only accepted his command. We are not tight."

"I suppose not. Demons and angels would not be friends."

It was too much for her to think about right now. A change of subject was necessary. "So, are you hungry?" She toed the crushed pear.

"Not at the moment. Have you a cross or holy objects in the house?"

"I…don't think so. What do you need them for?"

"If I can ward the house, that should keep you safe and leave me to track Zaqiel. I remember seeing a church in that village we passed through."

"Villa Columbina. Are you going to raid it for holy water?"

Ashur lifted a brow, and she nodded in acceptance.

"I won't be long."

Antonio Del Gado ran his palm over the painting that had just been delivered by FedEx. All together, eight paintings sat unpackaged and lined along the wall of his studio beneath the streets of Paris.

He had never seen an angel like the ones Eden Campbell depicted. Well, he'd never seen an angel, save for the fluffy things on the pages of books he'd gathered for his research. Some, though, had been depicted wearing armor and wielding medieval weaponry.

"Are they truly fashioned from metal as she has painted?"

He wasn't sure what to decide about that, but one thing was certain: she possessed some knowledge. On each angel, in each painting, a sigil had been placed. Different parts of the body displayed a symbol that was unique to each angel.

Antonio knew about the sigils. The Book of Common Angels had touched briefly on them. Four had been illustrated. He'd been lucky two sigils had been associated with a name—Zaqiel and Xymyr. The summons required the sigil and the name. He'd collected quite a few sigils, but hadn't names to match beyond those initial two. And until he had more names, no more Fallen.

But more importantly the exact match of Fallen to muse must be made. The blood grimoire he used to conjure the fallen to earth was most specific.

"Has she any idea?" he murmured to himself. "I think I need to talk to Eden Campbell. But where to find her if she is not in residence?"

He'd instructed Bruce to give his name to the artist at the gallery. He could sit back and wait until she called him, thanking him for such a large purchase, or he could be proactive and send out hunters now.

The demon wasn't so stupid he thought he could tell her about the power she wielded, and then expect she wouldn't try it out. Besides, she needed to know things, right now, that would affect the outcome of this nasty chase.

Thinking the angel's name over and over, Eden walked the sunlit path along the vineyard.

"Raphael," she called softly. "Raphael?"

What had she read about angels? They were almighty and powerful. Humans could not look upon them in all their glory. They could smite or impart feelings of well-being. They could change a human's emotion through vibrations. And they were ruthless warriors.

Yet were the kind and benevolent guardian angels even real?

Zaqiel didn't appear so almighty, and she could certainly look at him, much as she wished not to. Must be because he was not in his glory. Ashur had said a fallen angel could not resume the appearance he'd once possessed while in heaven. Make that Above.

And the only way a Fallen could have sex with a muse was in half form. Half man, half angel. Eden had painted a few like that. Their bottom halves male and human, while from the torso up steel and glass made up their bones and flesh.

Much as she admired the angel on canvas, she did not want to see one in half form standing before her with lust in his eyes.

She glanced to the clouds floating through the pristine blue sky.

"Maybe I shouldn't do this. I don't know what I'm calling to me."

A flash of lightning through sunshine flooded Eden's peripheral vision. Shivers racked her shoulders. She gasped on her own breath. Foreboding tightened her neck muscles and clenched in her gut.

It was too late to change her mind.

A tall, thin man with golden hair that shimmered in the sunlight walked the stone path bordering the vineyard. The brown plaid suit was not fitted well, tighter at the shoulders and hanging at his hips. Hands clasped behind his back, he reminded Eden of a schoolteacher, perhaps a nice one, but one could never be sure when he might show his true colors and pop a quiz on the classroom.

"Eden Campbell," he said. His tone admonished and accepted at the same time. "What's up, love?"

A British accent? That was weirder than the suit.

"Yes, well, bespoke certainly isn't what it once was." He tugged at the hem of a short sleeve.

Where were his wings? The blinding light? A plaid suit?

What had he asked her? What was up? She couldn't say she was just checking to see if her summons had worked. That would anger him. If Eden knew anything, one mustn't anger an angel.

"Indeed not."

"Can you read my mind?"

"I know all about you, Eden Campbell. Reading your mind would be banal and, frankly, beyond me. So get on with it. My time is not your time."

She bolstered her bravery with a deep inhale and asked what she wanted to know. "If I cannot carry my own child, how can I carry an angel's child?"

"Your womb was designed exclusively for the Fallen's progeny. As are the wombs of all muses. I would offer an apology for the personal pain you've been forced to take on, but everyone has their own burden to bear, eh?"

Gasping out her breath, Eden struggled not to fall to her knees. The realization she'd been born into this world for such a task was too large and shocking to wrap her brain around.

And yet it made bizarre sense. All her life she'd been drawn to angels…

"So you've become attached to my Sinistari, have you?"

"Ashur? I wouldn't say attached." She couldn't look at the angel. Was she a pawn set down on the board decades ago? A piece in a game played by greater forces? "He's a friend."

"Of course. And love would be ridiculous. Forbidden, actually. But is the muse interested? Desirous? Does she want to do the nasty with the angel slayer?"

She would not dignify those accusations with a reply. Besides, he likely knew the answer already.

"I do," he replied to her unspoken thoughts. "You seek safety, Eden Campbell. Safety in the arms of a lover who will be true. But you mustn't dally in love with the Sinistari."

"Why is love off-limits to the demons? Ashur said it was their only sin. Love should be the greatest gift."

"Without evil there can be no good. You know how that whole balancing of the scales works. Angels are innately good and cannot hate. Demons are innately evil and cannot love. If demons were allowed to embrace love then we'd have a real problem with lacking evil, wouldn't you say?"

"That's…just wrong. Especially when the angel I've met seems to have mastered evil. Ashur told me love was why he was banished Beneath," she said.

"Indeed. I was the one who banished him. What more is there to know? And why is that particular tidbit so important to you?"

"I'm…" *I care about him. Too much, already.* "…curious."

And she was angry at the injustice Ashur suffered simply because he had succumbed to an emotion everyone deserved to know. Did she seek some human part of the demon? Some means to justify her attraction to him? Because she was attracted and Raphael was more right about her wanting safety than she cared to admit.

"Why torture him?" she asked. "Why not allow him to keep his memories? Wouldn't that have ultimately been more cruel?"

The angel clucked his tongue admonishingly. "You are offended by the use of torture?"

"Yes."

"It's not punishment unless it hurts." Raphael smiled, but the curve of his lips smoothed away as if it had only been an illusion. "I observed Ashuriel following the slaying of thirteen Fallen. Released of his task, he tracked the world, experiencing all it had to offer. Thievery, adultery, bearing false witness, murder."

"Murder?" Eden gasped.

"But of course. Ask him about it some time. He hasn't only murdered angels. Ashuriel revels in all sin, as Sinistari are wont to do. It is their nature. And yet, love is not permitted a demon. Well, we had no idea the Sinistari were capable of it, you understand. It was offensive one of his breed should embrace love. Utterly abhorrent."

"Some might say an angel stalking innocent mortal women was abhorrent."

"Exactly. Which is why the Sinistari were forged."

"Maybe you should have warned them before you sent them out into the world that love wasn't allowed?"

"Look at you, all about the rules and nicey-nicey. It was a learn-as-you-go situation. It's not like we'd had angels fall previously and had written up a rule book on how to manage them. Please."

She'd offended him, yet Eden lifted her chin. One point for the mere mortal. But he quickly snuffed out her pride.

"I knew the moment Ashuriel felt love for the Macedonian woman. When it was seen the Sinistari master could love, it was decided love must not be allowed their breed. As I've said, one must maintain the balance. But I did not banish him then. I waited."

The angel made a skipping step, hands still behind his back, as he marked the grass bordering the limestone path.

"I was there when he committed himself to the woman with his body and heart. He could not marry her. He was not allowed, for she was huge and ripe with another man's child. Score one point for adultery." He notched the air with a long finger as if marking the scoreboard. "Yet still, I waited."

Eden clasped a hand over her mouth. Ashur had loved a woman who was pregnant? Could she have been…?

"When the child was born, I witnessed Ashuriel's joy. It was the first time he felt that emotion. Still, I waited."

Not joy, Eden thought, but true love. She knew it now.

"You are correct. Love embodies joy. You basically cannot have one without the other. So, where was I? Ah, yes, only when the woman was days away from death— she had a cancer in her body—and I knew the child was yet too young to fend for itself, only then did I step in and banish Ashuriel to Beneath. I left him to my assistant, Ariel, who is a master at punishment. Or if you prefer, torture."

Malicious glee curved the angel's smile. He skipped again and danced down the path.

Eden lunged before him, halting his giddy jig. "You bastard! You are crueler than Ashur will ever be. You're… you're worse than a demon!"

"Demon. Angel." Raphael bent over her and Eden felt the heat of his presence burn in her throat. "Those are names. Titles. Words bandied about by humans to label a thing they can never truly know. You humans put wings on our backs, shining halos over our heads and paint us on greeting cards. We are a symbol of hope and grace to you all. Yet is that the truth?"

"Apparently not. Are you saying demons are the good guys?"

"I cannot say. It is all in the perception."

"Then the balance shouldn't be entirely weighed upon Ashur's head. You can have some good demons if you also have bad angels."

Raphael offered a dismissive gesture. "Now I will leave you. I feel this conversation was unnecessary."

"It was necessary. I needed to sort out some things."

"I did not help that."

"No, but you did bring other things to light. And much as you don't want to discuss what you've done to Ashur, I know you feel regret. It was wrong to torture him."

"Is that so? And was it so right he be allowed to steal souls? He would not accept a human soul for his actions. He was the one who chose the darkness. He chose it!"

"I don't understand all of that."

"You never will, and should not concern yourself with it. Eden Campbell, listen to me. If you care one iota for the Stealer of Souls, Ashuriel must not fall in love with you."

"Don't worry about that. Love is stupid." She winced. She thought she'd stopped lying to herself.

"Ah? Who tore your heart to pieces, mortal?"

"Doesn't matter."

"The ex-fiancé." He nodded knowingly. "Shall I smite him for you?"

She whipped her head around to gape at him.

Raphael shrugged. "Angel humor. But you know that wasn't real love the two of you had. You're not a stupid woman. A child does not ensure matrimonial bliss."

She clasped her arms across her chest. Indeed. She wasn't stupid. And she would not be stupid about what she expected from Ashur. If he did fall in love he would be banished again—and tortured. She would not be the instigator of such pain.

When she turned to Raphael he was gone.

Chapter 15

The gold-plated cross on the altar was cracked and had been fixed with Krazy Glue. Ashur grabbed it and tucked it under an arm. Now for some holy water. He found the font at the back of the church and dipped the cross in it. The water splashed onto his skin and sizzled into steam. It didn't hurt, but he got a kick out of the reaction.

He stepped out of the church, but a scream alerted him. It was not heard by any but him for it echoed in his brain much like the vibrations the Fallen put out scurried through his marrow. Instinctually he knew a Fallen one had found its muse.

He could flash to the scream, dispatch the angel and return to Six's side in no time. He risked Zaqiel finding her while he was gone, but if that should happen, he should hear her cry for help, as he heard this one. Besides, he couldn't resist the call to real danger.

Flashing to a neat hillside neighborhood in Andalusia,

he landed on the courtyard of a red-tile-roofed home. The screen door hung loosely on its hinges. Spike-leaved agave plants clawed for space along the wall.

Another scream tingled across his brain. And now the Fallen's distinctive vibrations shuddered through his steel marrow.

Ashur raced through the house toward the screams, drawing Dethnyht and raising it above his head.

The scrape of metallic wings growing out a bedroom door focused his determination. The wings, designed of twisted black and copper wire twenty to thirty feet long, would obliterate anything in their path as they grew.

He shifted, shrugging away the mortal coil. His true form emerged, hard, metallic and black. He charged the door and butted it with his head. His horns tore the wood frame to shreds and twisted in the Fallen's wings.

A woman scrambled across the pillow-strewn bed, groping for the iron head rail. The Fallen easily shoved her down to position beneath his parted legs. He tore away the mortal garments yet clothing his lower body.

Ashur leaped, landing on the creature's back. Metal collided with metal. He slipped, but maintained hold by gripping the angel's hollow rib cage that resembled no human form. The angel bucked at him, but his intent remained on the screaming woman, who, with a slap from the angel's palm, was knocked unconscious.

The angel roared in myriad tongues Ashur had not heard since biblical times. The noise clattered with the growls and vocalizations of all the earth's wild beasts and languages long forgotten.

Leaping high, Ashur flipped over the top of the angel, and landed on the bed, planting his hooves to either side of the unconscious woman's head. He saw the sigil on her forearm, shaped like a square with spikes.

With one hand he crossed himself from shoulder to shoulder, head to chest. With the other hand, he thrust Dethnyht up and into the angel's glass heart. Shards of red glass dispersed; a few caught in Ashur's eye. He closed that eye, growling against the cutting pain, and jammed the blade deeper.

The angel struggled and vocalized like a stuck elephant trumpeting the battle cry. Under his jaw Ashur saw a sigil to match the muse's—it glowed blue.

The Fallen managed to knock Ashur aside the head, but his face merely dented inward. He threw off the angel, pushing it away and to the wall. Plaster flaked and cracked about the angel, fit into the wall, its wings crushed to the right and twisted metal bent over his shoulder.

Dethnyht dripped red glass droplets over Ashur's thigh. They *tinged* and slid to the bed where they became liquid and melted into the torn sheets. The blade was tipped with qeres, an Egyptian poison which was the first sweet breath of the afterlife.

And the angel dropped, landing on its face with arms outspread. Wings scraped the walls and ceiling, cutting deep gouges through the plaster. Some of the wing wires made contact with the electrical wires run through the mortal home and orange sparks snapped. It was like a bad car wreck.

The entire being dissipated. The angel shimmered into a pile of crystal dust.

As he stepped off the bed, Ashur's hoof crushed the angel dust. In the middle of the glamorous destruction lay a single copper feather. He snatched it with his muscled black fingers. The feather marked the angel's death, each one unique and different from all others, much like the sigils.

A satisfied growl purred in Ashur's chest. His prize.

The angel dust rose in a fog before him, swirling and emitting a beautiful chirr of release. It was not the angel's remains, but rather the souls it had carried within for endless centuries.

Ashur breathed in, taking the souls through his mouth and swallowing them as if a thirsty man two weeks in the desert. As each soul hit his heart, the solid black muscle sucked them in. Red-hot pain pierced through his nervous system with each glutinous gulp of his heart.

Crying out and thrusting out his arms, Ashur received the agony of his success. Souls trapped once again, but not without a torturous twist at his heart. Over and over, the electric bite of anger and rejection and terror shot through his system. He fell to his knees amid the angel dust and slapped his palms into the glassy mess. Wrenched forward and seized about the middle, Ashur took it all.

And when it was done, and the room was still and dark, he heard the woman on the bed stir.

"Sleep," he murmured, and reached up to stroke his fingers across her forehead. Hypnos captured the woman in gentle arms and lulled her away from the sight of a Sinistari demon kneeling on her bedroom floor.

Standing, Ashur strode from the room, the feather in hand. He grabbed the knife sheath from the floor. As he walked, he shook out his shoulders and thighs, shrugging off the demon to resume mortal form. He eyed the laundry room and found a pair of men's black jeans. They fit snuggly. No shirts, but the pants would serve until he could find something better.

Stepping out back, the setting sun made him blink. Exhaling, Ashur sucked in the fresh air. He tucked the feather in the sheath next to Dethnyht. As he did, a question formed. Raphael had not sent a Sinistari to slay this Fallen? Someone was slacking.

"Sinistari!"

Squinting, Ashur made out the shape of a man standing before the whitewashed garage, which was fronted by a cobblestone walkway. Shoulder tilted against the wall, one leg angled before the other, the man spun a black cane lazily before him. Long black hair hung straight over his shoulders. Dressed in pin-striped black trousers and a matching coat that revealed wide white shirt cuffs and black leather gloves, he glowered at Ashur.

"You have something that belongs to me," he announced.

The man did not smell entirely human, yet a strange, deathly miasma coated his preternatural odor. In fact, he smelled of so many souls, he should be sick from the overload.

"Psychopomp," Ashur addressed him.

The man bowed. "Blackthorn Regis, Soul Bringer."

Ashur could guess what was coming and cared little.

"How many did you steal with that kill?" Blackthorn asked. "A couple thousand? Tens of thousands? Those are mine."

"You want them?" Ashur spread his arms out in challenge. "Come and get them."

The cane stopped spinning. Before he could figure what would next happen, Ashur dodged to avoid the deadly pointed cane soaring at him with ultrasonic speed. It landed in the wall but inches from his ear, cutting through the red-clay tiles with diamond-edged precision.

"Is that all you got?" he challenged, knowing it wasn't wise. Following a shift he was always less strong than usual.

The psychopomp tugged off his coat to reveal a gold-shot damask vest beneath. Threading his gloved fingers together and cracking them dramatically, he then charged Ashur.

Ashur had only to step aside to avoid a collision with the man who was equal to him in height and likely strength. Not a wise move, however, because Blackthorn claimed the cane, and twisted around, swinging.

A cut to Ashur's cheek drew black blood. It went in so deep he felt the tip of the cane cut his gums.

Spitting blood to the side, he grinned and swung up a foot to pummel the psychopomp aside the head. Blackthorn wobbled, but managed to stab the cane into Ashur's bare foot.

Ashur swiped Dethnyht through the air, but pulled back before it could decapitate the man. He had no reason to kill the bastard. He simply needed to show him he couldn't ask for what Ashur wasn't willing to give.

"You damned Sinistari!" The psychopomp dodged a punch and slammed Ashur against the wall. He beat him in the chest with rapid fists. "Why steal them? You're the only one who does it. Take the freakin' mortal soul and have a damned life, why don't you?"

"Not going to happen."

"Because you are afraid!"

Ashur kicked the man off him, but maintained hold on the cane. He whipped Blackthorn around and slammed him against the wall. Winning the cane, he tried to break it across his knee but it had a steel core, so it only bent into a U. He thrust it aside.

Afraid? Preposterous. He simply had no need for a mortal soul. Because if he did not annihilate the Fallen walking this earth, who would? Apparently Raphael was sleeping on the job.

"You've more than enough souls to keep you satisfied," Ashur countered. "These are mine. My reward for the ugly task I perform."

"Oh, boo hoo. You need a reward every time you do

something good? Get over it, demon. Next time I'm not coming alone."

"You bringing the entire brigade? All with canes? You can do a little song and dance for me."

Blackthorn smashed a fist into Ashur's nose. The broken bone—actually, a metal shard—pierced his sinuses, and he swallowed thick blood. Spitting, he shot the black spray across the psychopomp's face.

They offered an equal match. The psychopomp was an earthbound angel assigned here by an archangel—not Raphael—but Ashur cared little beyond his own master. They could beat on each other through the night and never get any further than broken bones that rapidly healed.

"You stop taking souls," the psychopomp said as he leaned against the wall to catch his breath, "and I promise you I'll make sure the muse's soul goes the right direction when her time comes. Which, I'm guessing is gonna be soon."

"You—"

The psychopomp's only job was to ferry souls to either Above or Beneath, wherever they belonged. Ashur believed this one would take Six Beneath even if she was intended for Above.

"I can't do that. I'll take my chances with you next time. And she will not die. I'll be sure of that."

"Uh-huh." Blackthorn spat. His blood was bluish red. "We'll see about that when the time comes. Ta."

The wall was bare, save the crushed stone where their bodies had hit. The psychopomp had vanished.

"I won't let her die," Ashur growled. "I would die to protect her."

Chapter 16

After a shower, Eden descended the stairs wearing a pink tank top and yoga pants. The afternoon sunlight hit the opposite side of the villa, rendering the kitchen cool and shadowed. It reminded her of quiet days she'd had to herself as her father would walk the vineyards with the field workers. They'd only vacationed here a couple times together, but she cherished those memories.

She figured Ashur was around somewhere but she was too hungry to bother looking for him.

She pulled a new pear out of the fridge since she hadn't gotten to eat the one she'd cut earlier, and some hard white cheese. The wine cellar sported some old vintages, but she wasn't inclined to go sort about in the cellar that gave her nightmares. Attribute that to her sixteenth summer here and spiders. Instead she'd have the bottled water or fruit juice she'd picked up at the grocery store on the way here.

As she sat at the table and ate, she thought back on her

hasty exit from the penthouse, and remembered colliding with the mailman. The package. She tugged it from her purse.

"Another halo," she said, recognizing the return address. "I wonder if Raphael knows about my collection?"

She glanced upward, thinking she wouldn't be at all surprised to hear a British voice agreeing he knew about her quest for halos. And how interesting it was that while she'd been searching—and dreaming—she'd been destined to collide with angels and demons all her life.

Did other muses paint or draw angels obsessively? Search for halos? She'd like to meet another muse, ask her if she'd went a little crazy when she was younger, too.

Tearing open the package, she shook the metal circle out onto the table. It flashed blue briefly, as if a flickering LED light.

Eden dropped the pear slice. "I've never seen one do that before."

Tentatively she touched the cool metal. It felt like the others. Thin and a bit rinky-dink. "Like a 1950's Hasbro toy," her father had once commented. It looked like it could be easily bent, but Eden knew otherwise.

It didn't glow again, so she rapped it against the edge of the table.

"Weird. I must have imagined it."

But now that she thought on it, it reminded her of the freaky blue circle around Zaqiel's eye. He was the weirdest looking angel she had ever seen. Not that she had seen a lot in person…

True, she painted them more bizarre than Zaqiel's appearance. But seriously, Zaqiel had been covered in tattoos that had appeared more burned into his flesh than inked. Numerous piercings dangled from all parts of his body, and his shocking hair had been whiter than snow. He'd fit right in with the punk crowd or a Goth crew, but not heaven.

"I see you have another for your collection."

Eden looked up as Ashur walked into the room. His entrance didn't surprise her. She was just relieved he was here now. She pushed the plate of cut fruit and cheese toward him as he seated himself across the table. "Hungry?"

"A little." He sampled the fare. "When is taco night?"

"We can do it tonight if you like. I bought avocados for guacamole, too."

"I love guacamole."

The utterly normal comment struck Eden. He smiled at her with a little-boy grin. He loved guacamole and touching things, and—well, not her, which was exactly how she had to keep it. She had taken Raphael's warning to heart.

Or was she fooling herself? When was the last time she'd admired a man's sexy smile after he'd confessed a passion for guacamole?

Oh, Eden, watch it. You want something that scares you.

He pointed at the halo. "Where did that one come from?"

She turned over the envelope to display the address. "Turkey. Cost me fifty thousand because the woman knew what she had. This one glows."

He lifted a brow, midbite. "Glows?"

"Just like the blue sigil around Zaqiel's eye. You think maybe it was his halo?"

Ashur sat back in the chair, as if to distance himself from the halo, yet he eyed it keenly. "I don't know much about angels and their halos, beyond that it holds their earthbound soul, and not a Fallen walking the earth would want it back."

"Why not? I would think a soul would be the greatest prize."

"Not going to happen."

"What makes you think Zaqiel doesn't want a human

soul? Just because you won't take one after you slay an angel doesn't mean the Fallen might not kill for his own human soul."

"When the rewards of walking the earth with divine powers are so much greater? Think about it, Six. No angel is going to sacrifice such omniscient immortality."

"What about when all the muses have been found and have given birth to the nephilim?"

"I don't know. I only—"

"—know what you've been sent to do," she finished for him. "It's a good excuse not to become involved, I guess."

"You accuse me of undertaking the task I was forged to do."

Eden sighed. "And it's a heroic task. I just wish…" No, she didn't wish. Well, she did, but it was wrong to do so, so she'd keep that one close to her heart. Which was where it resided anyway.

He nodded at the halo. "They can be used as weapons, but only by the original owner. If it should fall into the angel's hands who once wore it, then look out. He could do deadly things with that innocuous-looking circle of metal."

"Cool." Eden never imagined it could be utilized as a weapon. Somehow the halo should be a perfect conductor of all that was good and right. Made of gold and emanating pure love, or some such. Of course in her dreams it appeared in rainbows of color, different to each angel. "Would it harm you?"

"If wielded by the owner? It could kill me, I'm sure."

"Is that the only thing that can kill you? You said only your knife and some poison could take out an angel. Is it the same with demons?"

"A halo could strike my head from this body, and yes, I'd be finished." He narrowed a look at her. "You're not getting any ideas, are you?"

"To kill you? Heck no, you're my protector."

She hoped. When Ashur had left on his errand she'd felt so desperately alone and yes, a little frightened. She wanted him to stay by her side always. And how needy was that?

Get over it and grow a pair, she inwardly admonished. *You don't need a man in your life.*

Yes, but a need was different from a want. And she wanted…so many things.

"This doesn't belong to me," she added, "so it probably wouldn't serve me— Whoa! Did you see that? It glowed again."

"I did." Ashur grabbed another pear slice, but didn't make a move to touch the halo. "You've never before had one that glows? Perhaps it senses you are a muse."

"No, never one that glows. But do you think if this halo belongs to the angel that's after me…?"

"You're not Zaqiel's match. The blue circle around his eye is his sigil."

"So that means he's already raped one muse, and now he's after me."

She grabbed the halo and held it against her chest, feeling the subtle calming effect. If this had belonged to an angel who wanted to rape her, she couldn't make the connection with the hopeful feeling it gave her.

"Can we talk about what happened in bed this morning and then here in the kitchen?" Ashur asked.

"Seriously? You want to talk? Like discuss feelings and all that? Wow, you are not the average man."

"No, I am not. In fact, I have no human moral code. In the demon realm, to master the seven deadly mortal sins is a matter of pride. And I have mastered them all."

"Even murder? Raphael told me—"

"Raphael?" He lifted a brow, but didn't admonish as

Eden expected. "Killing an angel would be considered murder, yes."

"He said you'd killed more than angels."

"Hmm…possible. You need to know I'd forgotten all that after I was sent Beneath. But you are stirring up memories. Especially of lust."

"Lust is not as sinful as it sounds." She leaned forward, eyeing him through her lashes. "Is that why you were flinching when we were making out? You were remembering?"

"Yes, the pain of torture."

"Was it bad? Can you tell me about it?"

Propping his elbows on the table, he shrugged his fingers through his hair, bowing his head and shaking it. When he looked up, his eyes were dull. "All things worldly and mortal were tortured out of me—including lust. I bore the sting of a bladed whip for hundreds of years."

"That's horrible to imagine. And you remember that torture now? I'm so sorry."

"There's nothing to be sorry about. The torture was just. I can survive anything. Except…."

"Except?"

He stood and shrugged a hand through his hair. "Right. This talking stuff is a little overboard. So what did Raphael have to say?"

She didn't want to look up, but she did, and he'd mastered the admonishing expression well.

"I expected you would contact him," he tossed out.

"You didn't trust me?"

"Trust isn't necessary to complete my task. I don't need to know what you and the angel talked about."

"Then I won't tell you."

"Fine. Obviously he mentioned my penchant for sin. You already know about that."

She got up and cleared the dishes into the sink. He'd

murdered others. That was troubling. But surely he'd had a good reason, like self-defense.

"I need to focus on tracking Zaqiel or you'll be running forever."

"Well, I'm sure he'll give up when I'm dead. I thought you were out tracking him earlier?"

"I was sidetracked. I sensed a muse was being attempted by a Fallen one. I arrived just in time."

"You slayed an angel while you were gone?"

He nodded. "It is what I do."

"I know, but you mention it as if it was an errand your boss sent you to run."

"It was."

"Right. So…the woman is safe?"

"Traumatized, but sleeping it off."

"And the angel?"

"Dust. I claimed the feather and stole the souls."

"The feather?"

He produced a copper feather from the dagger sheath behind his hip. "All that remains of the angel following death. I put them in my crown as a warning to the Fallen. And it is a prideful show, as well."

"Can I see?"

He handed it to her. It wasn't what she had expected. It was as if carved from fine copper wire, yet soft and pliant as a downy feather when she ran her fingers over it. "This is beautiful." She handed it to him. "Your battle prize. I've never dreamed feathers on angels."

"They don't have feathers. Save when they perish. I assume it is sort of like their divinity, abandoned amidst the fallen angel dust."

"That's very poetic. You said you steal souls from the angel?" Head bowed, she tapped the table. "To be truthful, that disgusts me."

"What? Me doing what my nature demands?"

"Raphael said you don't have to take the souls. You could set them free. Let them go to heaven."

"Or Beneath."

"Yes. He also said you could claim your own mortal soul if you simply asked for it."

"I thought you didn't intend to tell me what you two had discussed. You had quite the chat, it sounds."

Eden sighed and walked up beside him. She wanted to touch him, place her fingers on his shoulder, but he was too distant right now. Too much the myth and not enough a mere man. Like the figures she painted, he seemed untouchable and alien.

"Does it make you happy? Stealing souls?"

"Happiness is not something I strive for. It is my right to take a prize for a task completed, no matter how painful that reward might be."

"It's painful? You get off on torture?"

"I…" He looked aside. He'd obviously never thought about such a thing.

She obviously didn't understand the whole demon thing, and was asking all the wrong questions. They were different, as much as she wished they were the same.

Yeah, no problem avoiding the love thing with this guy.

"How come I'm the chosen one? A muse?" she asked. "If the Fallen have been away or imprisoned for centuries, then how is it I was born with this mark at this particular time? How could the universe know someone would conjure the angels now?"

"You are of Merovingian descent."

"How do you know that? I don't even— Weren't they French kings?"

"It is what is known. All the women in your family, for

ages, have worn the sigil. It only becomes evident, actually seeable, when the prophecy will become real."

"So two hundred women are walking around the world today with weird birthmarks? And they're all targeted by angels intent on getting them pregnant?"

"Close. Two hundred angels fell in biblical times. I, along with my Sinistari brethren, were able to slay forty-seven."

"That leaves…" She did the math in her head. "One hundred fifty-three angels remaining."

"Something like that. I believe the numbers are not accurate. There are fewer angels than you count, but I don't know why."

"With fewer angels than women, some of those women will luck out?"

"No. As I've said, once the angel has completed his task with his muse, he can go on to another muse. It can cause chaos within the Fallen ranks."

"I don't think I like those rules. So, what's the plan? You going to lock me up and leave me alone as angel bait while you go out searching?"

"I want to ward your home. There are sigils I can put up that will keep most angels out."

"Most?"

"The most determined can defeat anything." He tugged a small gold cross from the inside of his leather jacket and laid it on the table.

"You stole that."

"If you already know, then why state it?" She saw no guilt in his expression.

Eden looked away. "I hate this."

"Have some faith."

"Seriously? You're going to play the faith card on me? You? A demon? What about your faith?"

"I am beyond the reach of faith. But that doesn't mean

I cannot utilize it to affect the actions of others." He tapped the cross. "I'll need this to draw the wards. But Zaqiel displayed some unusual munificence in that he didn't immediately attempt you in your home yesterday. He actually gave me a choice."

"He's taunting you. Playing."

"Yes, and I've never encountered one who has before."

"He sensed you cared what happened to me."

He pierced her with a glare, but Eden knew he understood what she meant. "Dude, you like me, admit it."

He evaded the question. "Zaqiel is dangerous."

"Aren't they all?"

Eden touched her neck. It was beginning to burn, but she cautioned herself from asking for the easy fix, because she didn't want to push Ashur toward something that would cause him pain again. And after Raphael's warning, she seriously didn't want him falling in love with her.

As if.

Eden, you think you're so special? He was merely lusting after you. He's a male. It's what they do.

"I can ease your discomfort," he offered.

"No." She gripped the halo. "There's an old bottle of calamine lotion in the bathroom. I'll try that."

"I noticed limestone spread around the base of the vines earlier. I can use it for the warding. Go get me some before you run upstairs."

"Just like that? You snap your fingers, and I react?"

He leveled the malevolent glare on her again, and Eden felt the prickle of his anger at the back of her neck. Do not make the demon mad. "Will do."

Eden headed out to the vines with a basket and collected some limestone, as directed.

Back in the house, Ashur was preparing to ward it.

Whatever that meant. He'd said he wanted her out of the house while he smudged it clean.

She swatted at a fly and tugged up the spaghetti strap of her tank top. Sitting on a mound of grass near the edge of the vineyard, her legs splayed, she'd forgotten how good it felt to get away from the busy rush of the city and breathe in the clean, country air.

She closed her eyes and inhaled the rich scents of leaves, earth and the dusty limestone.

She felt glad she hadn't let her past bring her down, particularly the episode with Chris, her ex-fiancé. A man who had controlled her, and when he could no longer, had dumped her like yesterday's trash.

Losing the baby still hurt. So much. But Chris's exit from her life had actually made her see things more clearly.

She did not need a man to feel complete or loved. When the right man came along he would be her friend and lover, but neither would require the other for happiness.

If a woman couldn't walk through the world by herself, take care of herself, stand without the assistance of a man to back her up, then she hadn't reached the point in her life where she was truly ready for a relationship.

Eden was ready now. Or at least, she was ready to enjoy herself with a man. She didn't need love. She simply required acknowledgment, and some hot sex.

For years she'd applied the means that love meant money. Her father, never home, had given her material things to appease her aching need for his presence. So she'd grown up believing men showed their love with gifts.

"So not true," she said and chuckled. "You're learning, Eden. Slowly but surely."

She tossed a few more limestone pebbles into the basket and stood with it looped over her arm.

Ashur had been tortured? And kissing and touching her brought those memories back to him. How messed up was that?

He'd been punished for falling in love.

Well, it didn't have to happen that way with her. Sex did not mean love. It was a means to share more of yourself with someone you trusted and cared about. And, strangely, she'd quickly come to trust Ashur. She cared about what happened to him. She wanted to take it to the next level.

"Six!"

She smirked at his name for her. "Coming!"

Chapter 17

Eden could not recall the last time she had seen a pair of jeans hug a man's hips and legs so sensually. The fabric greedily clung to every part of him, wanting the touch as badly as she.

He wore no shirt or shoes. His coal-black hair looked bed-tousled. His arms arced out from his body, displaying his fine form. Impossible abs and chiseled muscles angled down beyond his jeans and tempted her to trace them. In the hazy afternoon light his body glimmered as if a sheen upon forged metal.

Was it right a demon could look so nummy? Shouldn't he be ugly and smell like brimstone and make a person want to run in the opposite direction?

Perhaps that was the plan. Lure the hapless female closer and then…

Then what? She'd already learned kissing a demon was beyond incredible.

With images of naked bodies hugging each other under the moonlight zipping through her brain, Eden almost dropped the basket of limestone, but caught it before it slipped from her fingers.

"You wanted me?" *Please say yes.*

"I need the limestone to draw protection sigils on the floors. And…"

She handed him the basket. Her fingers almost touched his skin, but not quite. "And?"

"I'll need some of your blood."

"Seriously? I gave to Red Cross last week. I'm all tapped out."

His eyebrow arched. "Just a few drops to mix with the limestone. It's necessary for the ward to protect you in particular."

"All righty, then. I suppose I can manage another drop or two." She pointed her index finger up. "You got a pin?"

He reached behind his hip and drew up the wicked-looking knife Eden had seen him wield against the angel. It was like one of those fantasy weapons with a fancy serrated blade that sported three deadly points curving dangerously on each side.

"I thought you said that had poison on it?"

"It won't affect you…it's an angel poison. You won't feel the cut, either."

Clasping her arms across her chest, she took a big step backward. "I don't think so. That thing looks like it could sever a limb."

"Six." His tone chastised.

Eden did not like being told what to do. "I have a knife in the drawer."

He gripped her arm as she turned to the cupboard. A fine pain streaked across her forearm. The slice was minute, yet throbbed like a paper cut. And before Eden could protest, glossy crimson dribbled down her arm.

Ashur resheathed the blade and tugged her toward the table. He held her arm above the basket of limestone. Crimson droplets splattered over the dusty white pebbles.

"You're not much for arguments," she said.

"This is for your benefit."

"Right, keeping the angel at bay. Or is this the bait?"

"That should be good." He dropped her arm, apparently having heard her question, but not about to answer it.

"I don't think I have bandages." She inspected the cut. It was long and, though not deep and not at all painful, she would need something to staunch the bleeding.

Again he grabbed her arm and this time he bent to lick the cut. Eden reflexively pulled away, but he held her securely. Licking away her blood from his lips, Ashur freaked her only as long as it took to notice the cut on her arm was no longer there.

"That's…" Though her heart beat faster, she couldn't quite get frantic. She was in awe. "That was cool. I forgot you could do that."

"A trick of the trade."

"But you just drank my blood. Are you a vampire demon?"

"I did not drink it. I merely licked it clean from your flesh."

"Yeah, but do you like the taste of it?"

He crushed the limestone with a marble mortar and pestle he'd found in the cupboard. "Everything about you tastes delicious, Six. But I'm not going to start feeding on your blood if that is what worries you. It is not necessary to my survival as it is a vampire."

She inspected her arm but could not find even a red line

where the cut had been. "You're very commanding, you know."

"You like it."

"I do. Why *am* I so attracted to you?"

He continued to crush the mixture, without looking to her. "You don't know?"

"I think it's your honesty. You have a pureness about you. An innocence."

Ashur scoffed. "As I've said, you do not know me."

Eden wagered that she knew some things about him that he wasn't willing to admit to. He was a complicated demon, intent on his goal, yet willing to take the time to learn the world—and her.

"Now, you'll need to change," he ordered.

"Into what?"

"Less is more," he said, busy with the crushing. "You must come to the warding unfettered and open to receive the blessing of protection."

A blessing? Engineered by a demon? She kept her mouth shut.

"Skyclad is preferred." He studied her, no guile in his expression, though his intense gaze reeked of desire. "I'd ask you to go bare, but I don't think it necessary. Have you a simple sheath dress or something less confining?"

"Is this your way of trying to get me naked?"

He smiled. "I would remove your clothes with my teeth, and slowly, if that were my intent."

Pleased, Eden bristled gleefully. When she didn't move, Ashur nodded for her to run along.

Right. She had to remove articles of clothing for the sexy man. Easily done.

She skipped up the stairs. She hadn't a nightgown because she usually slept in the buff. If he thought the yoga outfit was too much, she wasn't sure jeans or even the long skirt she'd brought along would be much different.

Eden stripped to her bra and panties. The red lace matched set had been imported from Paris, made especially to her measurements.

She curved her palms beside her breasts and eyed her figure in the dusty mirror on the vanity. Slender yet curvaceous, she was proud of her curves and her taut stomach. Did she dare? "He did say less is more."

She hadn't anything more revealing without stripping naked. This would have to do. It was like wearing a bikini. In fact, Eden was sure she had some bikinis that showed more skin.

"Hello, Angel Slayer, my name is Eden. Want to touch?"

She winked at her reflection. The guy didn't even know her name. She'd best stop fantasizing—or else start initiating her fantasies—before he was gone without a trace.

When she reentered the kitchen, she almost stepped on a chalk marking dashed upon the floor.

"Avoid the—" Ashur, kneeling near the front door, his torso twisted to look at her, simply stared.

"The marks," she finished for him. "What's wrong?"

The man's jaw dropped. The chalk he held slipped from his fingers. He noticeably swallowed.

Eden posed with hand to hip. *Hello, Angel Slayer.* "I didn't have any slip dresses. This is as bare as I could get without going nude. Just think of it as a bikini."

"Fine," he croaked, and turned away.

Eden smiled. Someone was getting a hard-on. If all went well with the warding process, she seriously wanted to see how much he liked this ensemble. And why waste those perfect abs that had tightened at the sight of her? They deserved some licking.

"Shouldn't you get naked?" she asked.

"I am half clad," he mumbled.

Eden pouted. Should she be more serious about this whole affair? Definitely. Though, it would be very difficult. Eden couldn't recall when she'd been so attracted to a man.

Did she regularly tease men in her underthings? Only after she'd been dating them awhile.

It had to be the allure of the bad boy. She'd never had a dangerous lover before, and she was seriously buying into the appeal of all things dark, dangerous and oh, so sexy.

"What do all these marks mean?" She tiptoed across the kitchen floor. There was one below the stairs, one at the back of the kitchen that lead out to the garden, and he was finishing one that spanned three feet in diameter before the front door. "Are they some kind of angel repellent?"

"Exactly. I'm going up to draw them by the windows and bedroom doors. Stay here, because if you follow me in that attire I, well…" A lift of his chest preceded a lusty exhale. "Just stay here."

Again she smiled, and sat at the table to toy with the halo. When Ashur returned she jumped up to follow him to the center of the kitchen. "What next? It doesn't seem like I'm helping all that much."

"You need to stay in the room. Your energy is important to the ward." He turned to perhaps grip her shoulders, but instead slapped his palms to his chest, awkwardly uncomfortable. His eyes darted from her breasts to her belly, and lower, appealing to Eden all the more. "Stay back, near the wall. There will be an outburst of…stuff."

"Stuff?"

"I don't know how to put it into words you would understand. It is remnants of the universe answering my incantation. I'm going to work here by the door, and I'll be chanting the ward. I'll be speaking in tongues."

"Impressive."

"Six, it may frighten you. I may, in fact, sound… demonic." He winced. "To use a term I gathered while learning this world."

"I'll be cool." After all, the demon was protecting her, and she was grateful for that. And who knew? The reward for enduring this whole warding ritual may be some snuggling afterward.

"Good. Go stand by the wall."

She waited for him to lean down and give her a reassuring kiss, a rub of his palm over her arm, but he instead turned and knelt to his task.

Sighing, Eden wandered over to the wall. Rubbing a palm up her arm, she chased the goose bumps she knew were there—because of the man filling the room and not because of anxiety over the unknown. Could he sense her desire? Hell, what couldn't he sense about her when clad in a few bits of red lace?

She had better tone it down. He didn't need the distraction.

Ashur knelt on one knee and bowed over a limestone circle drawn on the stone floor. His back to her, his bared muscles rippled with movement as he stretched his arms out and lowered his head. It was a worshipful pose.

Eden traced her lower lip with her tongue.

Every move he made softened her insistence to keep him at a distance. She could not look away from him, and found the sensual in everything he did.

He was unlike any man she had ever known, and more dangerous. Hell, she had never known a dangerous man. Ashur drew her out of her perfect, ordered, upper-class lifestyle and forced her to comprehend things she could never have imagined. Like the bad boy's allure. And the precarious call of surrendering to the unknown.

And facing that which scared her.

She had thought she'd faced something pretty horrific when she'd lost the baby. And all those who had shaken their heads pitifully when she'd tried to explain her dreams hadn't bolstered her confidence level. Yet now a stranger banished from heaven wanted to get her pregnant. How twisted was that?

What she feared most clambered against her personal walls, clawing for her submission.

"Let this work," she whispered. "Please, let him know what he is doing."

And then the whispers began. Ashur spoke lowly, head bowed over his work. His voice echoed off the walls, and doubled, then tripled itself. Suddenly his words took weight and presence. Myriad colors formed before Eden, dancing darker and lighter as his voice rose and fell.

His voice continued to multiply until the room was filled with many voices of all colors, slipping over her flesh with untranslatable noise. The sound was eerie and reminded her of strange horror movie effects utilized to creep her out so well. Yet the color was gorgeous and sparkled like a ten-carat diamond beneath the sun.

Now his voice moved through the air as menacing clouds. Eden pressed her spine to the wall.

Ashur rocked forward. Arms still extended, he commanded some otherworldly presence she felt creep along her neck and tickle the hairs upon her scalp.

Something moved over her. Not across her flesh, but rather, through her pores and into her veins. Like molten lava cooled by ice. Its journey was slow, yet she dared not move to shake it off, because it wasn't real.

It couldn't be real.

It is real.

He was only trying to protect her.

Ashur thrust back his head and shouted something that sounded like Latin. The house shuddered. His arms were spread, his fingers flexed, and from his palms flashed beams of blue light that danced over the walls in symbols similar to those drawn on the floor. When the blue light lined up with the drawn symbols it was sucked in and the symbol flashed. Limestone dust burst out from the drawn line, fogging the room.

A spinning metal object soared toward Eden. What the— It was the halo! It careened sharply. It buzzed like a storm of insects. Bright blue flashed in her vision.

She dodged and screamed.

The room clouded, and as her muscles gave way, her body hit the floor.

Zaqiel didn't need to be knocked over the head to sense the repellent wards that rumbled across the countryside. He dropped the puppy he'd been dangling from the leash its owner used to tie it outside the pastry shop.

He strode to the middle of the cobbled street in the Villa Rialto outside Rome. Spreading out his arms and tilting back his head, he read the air upon his closed eyelids and mouth.

The Sinistari was attempting to protect the muse.

The only thing wrong with that plan was Zaqiel now had a lead on their hiding spot.

Dropping his arms and striding forward, Zaqiel decided against flashing there. He'd take his time. All good things came to those who danced when others least expected to find anything on the head of a pin.

Whenever the Sinistari put out energy into the world the psychopomp felt it. They were connected by the shared means of handling souls. Ashuriel was in Italy. He'd put up wards against a Fallen one.

Odd. Blackthorn thought the Sinistari's only purpose was to slay Fallen. So why the wards? Shouldn't he be welcoming the angel with open arms and a poisoned blade?

"This demon will not have his way." Whatever he was up to.

Unceremoniously dropping at the pearly gates the handful of souls he'd been delivering Above, Blackthorn flashed to earth.

Something odd disturbed the air.

Sitting on the hood of his rental car, Michael Donovan looked up from the wind-rumpled map of the Italian countryside and scanned the sky. Didn't look like rain. The sky was bright and white. He should have picked up some water at the store before venturing away from Rome.

The address on the package he'd found in Eden Campbell's penthouse had led him across the ocean. After vacillating on stealing the one halo, he'd taken all three she'd had hanging on the coatrack.

All was fair in the game of collectors. At least, that's the way he saw it. And Miss Campbell could have no idea the greater evil building behind the scenes.

He needed to know where all the halos were, and keep them from the hands of the unsuspecting, from those who could easily be tricked by the evil that would use the halos against them all.

Chapter 18

Eden startled awake to find herself cradled in Ashur's arms. Worry glistened in the multicolored coronas of his irises.

"I'm okay," she whispered. "I just…" She saw flashes of what had happened. The halo careening toward her. The spray of wall plaster hitting her cheek. She grabbed her neck. "Oh, my God, my head…"

"It's still there. And a very pretty head, I must say."

"I was almost decapitated."

"Shh," he murmured. "It's all over. You fainted. I will lay you on your bed."

"No, I…" Oh, hell, she was wearing nothing but a bra and panties and he was carrying her! "Set me down. I'm fine now. Still alive. Those halos are deadly! Oh, look at me. I'm covered in white dust!"

He set her down at the open bathroom door. "I told you there would be fallout."

She hadn't expected anything like that. The halo had come so close to decapitating her. She stroked her neck again, avoiding the angelkiss.

So much had happened over the last couple of days. She'd discovered that angels were real. And she had thought to seduce a demon. She was out of sorts. She needed time alone to think about this, about where things had gone oh, so wrong.

Brushing the dust from her stomach, she said, "I think I'll take a bath."

"I'll go down and put things in order. I should check the halo didn't damage the ward."

"Did it work?"

He called as he descended the stairs, "Won't know until we need it!"

Great. So her bloodshed and near decapitation could have been in vain.

Eden rubbed her throat, and cautioned herself against scratching the angelkiss. It didn't itch, actually. Maybe the ward had something to do with that. No matter, she was glad her head was still attached to her body.

She wondered what made the halo take flight like that.

Could Ashur have— No. He'd said the halos were only viable weapons if returned to the original owner.

He'd also said something about the halos containing the angel's earthbound soul. So if an angel wanted to become human it simply had to find its halo?

Could it belong to Zaqiel? Could any of her halos belong to him?

She thought of her collection at home, hanging so modestly alone in her office. What if they had the ability to attract their original owner? It could explain how, in the entire world, Zaqiel had managed to run into her in Manhattan.

What if the halo downstairs was drawing Zaqiel here now?

It was what Ashur wanted—most of the time. The demon vacillated between drawing the angel to them, and not. It was as if he didn't want the end to come.

Was it because it would bring an end to their relationship? Once Zaqiel had been dispatched, Ashur would leave and seek out the next angel.

Unless he asked for a mortal soul and stayed here with her.

It was a nice thought, but Eden suspected she was only daydreaming a better ending to this story. Really, she was too frazzled to think straight.

She bent to turn on the water, then selected some bubble bath from the closet shelf and poured that in. The room blossomed with lavender, and Eden stripped off her bra and panties. She left the door open about a foot. Being able to hear Ashur shuffle about below gave her a sense of comfort.

And if he wanted to clean up after his heroic efforts, who was she to stop him?

Ashur inspected the halo stuck into the wall. He blew off the pulverized plaster dust from the blade. The curved halo had easily cut through the solid plaster and embedded itself two inches deep.

He reached to touch it, but when it flashed blue, he retracted.

It was the strangest thing he'd ever witnessed. He'd not known of a halo being reunited with its owner. Perhaps it was Zaqiel's? And if so, could it sense when a slayer was near? Is that why it glowed?

It confounded him, but he would worry about it later. He was thankful it had not harmed Six.

Hell, if it had, this mission would be over.

And what if it did belong to Zaqiel and he could control the halo without being present?

No. Ashur dismissed that idea. The Fallen would never purposely destroy a muse. Of course, it could have been off course and intended for *his* neck.

"Nah." He gave the Fallen one little rein in the forethought and planning department. It had been a fluke the halo was now stuck in the wall.

Straightening the toppled kitchen chairs, and noting the debris of paint chips and stone dust all over the floor, he decided sweeping was not in his skill set. Besides, he didn't want to disturb the sigils. A walk through the house to ensure nothing else had fallen down or gone untoward was necessary, and to ensure all windows were locked and no glass had cracked.

He took the stairs two at a time to the upper level and checked the first bedroom, which Six had indicated he could use. A single bed with a white woven comforter mastered the room. A housekeeper must have placed the vase of fresh lavender on the windowsill. He'd noticed the purple flower was abundant in the fields as they'd arrived. The paned window was locked. The glass was thin, easily cracked, but it remained intact after the shaking the house had taken.

This villa reminded him of old-style housing from Greece. Made of stone and plaster quarried from the land, it was cool and airy. Nothing like Beneath. It was something he could get used to—but mustn't. He didn't belong here.

He wanted to belong here.

And why was that? Certainly the world appealed more than Beneath did. But a Sinistari without purpose was nothing more than another face lost amongst the billions who inhabited this earth. Slaying was the only purpose Ashur had.

Could anything else satisfy him as much?

Crossing the hallway, he ensured the windows in Six's room were still locked up tight.

At the end of the hallway he heard water splash. The bathroom door was ajar. She'd left it open?

Did she want him to enter, or was she merely teasing him?

If she wished to break him, she was on the right track. The emotions creeping back into his memory delighted in release, good, bad and/or ugly.

He'd not experienced pleasure in so long. It was his right. He had taken no vow to remain chaste while he pursued his prey. He was only restricted from the one emotion.

So why not go in search of a woman to appease that ache?

It didn't feel right. Because it threatened his only means to satisfaction?

"You loitering?" she called.

Her voice rang cloyingly, like forbidden church bells clanging together in his gut. He wondered what color it would be if he could see voices as the Fallen did. Purple and crimson, he decided, lush and sensual.

He stepped into the doorway and leaned against the frame that didn't meet the wall snuggly and which creaked with his weight. The walls were tiled, but here and there a few tiles the color of spring grass shoots were missing. All the old plumbing was visible, running along the ceiling and down to the toilet and tub. The claw-foot tub was mounded with bubbles.

Six sat upright, her wavy hair pulled loosely onto her head in luscious waves. The bubbles covered her as if an iridescent gown with a neckline dancing below her shoulders. That didn't keep him from wondering what the skin below was like.

If the Fallen touched one portion of her flesh…

Ashur's fists tightened. He sucked in a breath. So quickly he assumed jealousy.

"There's a chair," she offered.

Did the fair mortal attempt to seduce him, Ashuriel the Black? That red bra and panties hadn't been warding wear at all, and she had known it.

Ashur sat on the wing-backed wicker chair and stretched out his legs. He still wore no shirt and was dusty after the warding. He twitched his dusted toes. He could use a bath himself.

He caught her eyes as they took in every inch of his abdomen and chest. He wondered at the gears and pulleys working in her brain. Women were never thinking what he thought they were. When he thought "sex," they were probably thinking "balance the check-book." And vice versa.

"Very well, I am sitting in the chair," he said. "Does this please you?"

"Very much. I can't recall when last I had a more delicious companion."

"Do you often bathe before men?"

"Only the ones I like."

That sexy smirk of hers reached right out and tweaked at his desires.

But not so fast.

"I like modern women," he said. "I observed many when I walked the world. You all are so to the point."

"Not all of us. Some are demure and polite. I don't believe in playing coy. Not anymore. If I want something, I ask for it." She blew at the bubbles about her neck and a thick pouf dispersed, exposing the glistening rise of one of her breasts. "Otherwise, what's the purpose of waiting silently and perhaps missing the opportunity?"

"Then you must be even more to the point. Tell me—" he leaned forward "—what is it you want, Six?"

"You."

Much as he had anticipated that answer, it still challenged his sense of what he expected from a woman. The last time he'd dallied with women they'd been mostly subservient and sex was more a means to an end, unless he'd found a whore.

Indeed, the modern women were independent and strong. He liked that. Yet he couldn't deny the sense of unease that kept him firmly planted on the chair. He was not ready to approach her yet, though parts of him had already crossed the room and stood over her, ogling her exposed, wet skin.

This modern woman could prove his undoing.

"I haven't forgotten what you told me about when you were previously here on earth," she said. "You were tortured because you fell in love."

"Yes."

She blew a thick froth of bubbles before her, which revealed her knees, bent before her chest. "Then don't fall in love with me."

"I don't intend to."

Her poker face momentarily stalled. Ashur caught the flicker of disappointment in her eyes. She hadn't wanted to hear that answer.

"Fine. I don't intend to fall in love with you, either." She spread her arms along the tub rim and lifted one leg out to point in the air. Water glistened on the gorgeous limb. "Were you…scarred? From the torture?"

"Yes. In my true form I bear the scars of my sin. The rage of angels is more wicked than the worst evils you can imagine."

"I still can't believe it is an angel who commands you, and was responsible for your torture."

"Torture is my past."

"Yet it seems present with you now," she said.

"It has made me the demon I am today."

"Everyone can change."

"You can't change me."

"You and I change every moment we're alive. It's unavoidable. You might think you can't change, but it's already happening, buddy."

He hung his head. He did not want to discuss the impossible when she had so cleverly set the bait for a more seductive liaison. "Back to what you want."

One of her eyebrows arched in a delicate curve. Ashur envisioned drawing his tongue along it, tracing her interest. The corner of her mouth curled up, begging for a kiss right in the crease.

"Indeed," she purred. "What I want. Very well. Can we have sex?"

Mercy. The direct approach was certainly unique, and amazingly effective. "You wish to have sex with me, knowing exactly what I am?"

"Why is it so hard for you to believe a woman could fall—er, would desire you? You've had nothing but my best interest in mind since you tugged me away from the scene of the accident. You quickly decided against using me as bait."

"I refuse to learn your name. Does that not offend you?"

"Nope."

Well. That was all the argument he had. No sense in conjuring false reasons to display a morality he did not possess.

Ashur stood and approached the tub. Anticipation sweetened his disposition. She wanted it? He had plenty to give her. And since no angels were knocking down her door right now…

"Get in the tub with me," she said.

By the great void Beneath, this woman worked fast. "I'm not sure I do bubbles."

She parted the thick froth and pushed some over the tub sides. Raising her hands above her chest, she dribbled water from her fingers. It slid down the insides of her arms and melted away more glistening bubbles at her shoulders and chest.

The sight of her gorgeous wet breasts, half-concealed at water level, quickened Ashur's fingers to his zipper. He had to ease the tight jeans down or risk scraping his erection with the metal zipper. In biblical times the clothing had been much less confining. He looked forward to letting everything hang loose.

Six's tongue teased at her plump lower lip. Her dancing, bright eyes fixed on his crotch, her delight growing as much as his hardness. He stepped from the pants and straightened, naked, stretching back his shoulders and displaying himself for her approval.

Pride, thy mortal sin is mine to own.

"That," she whispered, "is amazing."

Of course it was. But he didn't say so. He could feign humbleness with the best.

He stepped into the warm water and sat at the end opposite Six. Water splashed over the sides, sluicing away the remaining bubbles. The room smelled like lavender fields, and it felt great to settle into the hot water. His muscles softened. Ashur let out a satisfied murmur.

The luxury of self-indulgence generally manifested in physical activity, not this languorous melting of tension. He liked it.

Six swished forward and moved up to kneel over him, knees to either side of his thighs. Water glistened on her lean body. Her high breasts teased near his mouth. The wicked water sprite enchanted him with her supernatural beauty.

Ashur slicked his hands up her sides. Bubbles popped and burst in renewed fragrance. She did not sit down on him, which was good, because that would be too much, too fast. Right now he wanted to admire every bit of her.

"Your skin is like wet silk," he said. "I have not felt something so exquisite. Ever."

"Or in a very long time." She dipped her head to kiss his upper lip.

"No. Ever."

He plunged his tongue into her warm mouth, skating along her lips and the porcelain beauty of her teeth. Slow and tender wouldn't serve. He needed to enter her, to claim her and make his mark.

Too long he had been kept from this pleasure.

No longer.

Her moans spurred him to kiss her harder, bruising his want upon her flesh. Her fingernails clawed into his shoulders, trailing dribbles of water down his back.

Yes, torture me sweetly. I need it. It is what I thrive upon.

The hard beads of her nipples slicked across his chest and he broke from the kiss to suckle them. She reacted to the new touch by thrusting back her head and gripping the tub sides.

Her heart pulsed beneath his fingers and he wanted to eat it away, own it. He had no pulse. She could become his heartbeat.

"That's so good," she said on a gasp. "Yes, suck me hard. I want to give myself to you, Ashur."

Tightly he gripped her rib cage, holding her where he needed her. No escape now. This union had begun. Whether right or wrong, it mattered little to him. He simply needed to devour it all.

She swayed back, breaking the connection he eagerly sought. Six slid her groin against his loins. She wanted him to touch her there. Words were not needed. He read the command in her parted lips, her softened gaze.

Drawing his fingers down her mons, he noted she shaved a unique pattern and pushed against her spine to tilt up her torso so he could inspect. "Curves?"

"You like?"

"I do. Do you like this?" He slipped a finger inside her and she clenched him tightly. He moaned. "Mercy, I do."

"I like every way you touch me, Ashur. It burns in the best way."

She moved upon his finger, finding a rhythm that pleased her. Ashur massaged her breast with his other hand. He tickled the finger embedded within her forward against her inner wall. That move ignited a noticeable tremor in her body. She was close to coming.

"Another," she said. "Two fingers. Please."

He obliged. Her demand set his black heart to a curious flutter. The stolen souls were privy to his pleasure. Let them revel in the indulgence. It was but a small reward for their imprisonment.

A muscle twinged in his shoulder. Ashur winced. The memory of torture would not defeat his quest for pleasure. He didn't care what he'd suffered for his betrayal. This was no sin. This was carnal indulgence at its finest.

"Ashur!" She came at his command, calling out and thrusting back her head as her body shuddered upon his. She lunged forward and bracketed his face, kissing him deeply. Tasting him, eating him, devouring him.

"That was so good," she said, breathlessly. "Now it's your turn. I need to feel you inside me. All of your amazing length and width."

"Then put me inside you," he gasped harshly. "Now."

She gripped his cock with a determined possession. Their skin slicked and slid against each other's. Bubbles floated in the air, shimmering as they captured the moonlight. As he entered her, her inner walls squeezed him so tightly Ashur thought he couldn't possibly make it in the entire length. But he did, and she rocked upon him, creating a dance only they knew the steps to.

The ecstasy was immeasurable. Each time she moved down she sheathed him fully, then she drew forward to glide him slowly out until only the tip of him was grasped tightly by her. The buildup of orgasm clutched his core. The stolen souls shuddered to anticipate his success.

He gripped her hips and quickened her pace, pistoning himself inside her until he could not hold back. Calling out, Ashur surrendered to the intense rapture no angel could know. Only he, a dark demon, could indulge in so wicked a treat.

Six's hands bracketed his head, holding him there, riding his tremors. And when she dipped her head to press her forehead to his, she whispered softly, "My name is Eden."

Chapter 19

Ashur gasped and uttered her name after she'd said it. It came out like a prayer one whispers swiftly in dire circumstances.

Eden wasn't sure he'd completely comprehended that she'd just told him her name, because he'd been mid-climax when he'd said it. Well, now it was out there.

Three orgasms and a migration to the bedroom later, and now they lay on the rumpled sheets, heads toward the foot rail and toes pointing into the pillows. Eden glided her hands up his arms, pinning them above his head. He allowed her the easy capture. He'd already had his way with her. Now it was her turn.

Lavender tainted their skin and seeped into her senses, lulling her between orgasms. She laved her tongue down his abs, exploring each ridge as if a sand surfer skimming the dunes. His odd belly button fascinated her. It was a perfect circle, filled with a single coil. She wondered about it. If he had been forged—whatever that meant—he may not have come from maternal beginnings.

That thought bothered her, so Eden quickly averted her attention to the dark hairs trailing down his loins. His cock grew mighty and hard, pulsing against her breasts as she moved lower. She pressed her breasts over it and he groaned. His fingers slid through her hair, as he gently made her understand he was willing to receive what she intended to give.

She licked him and took him into her mouth. Such control she brandished by the stroke of her tongue. She could reduce this man, a powerful demon, to wanting growls and, quickly enough, body-shaking tremors.

At this moment she owned him. He belonged to no other woman but her. And that provoked her wicked grin as she mounted him. He came powerfully, bucking up deeper inside her and clutching the bedsheets as tightly as his jaw.

"You're mine, demon," she purred. Working herself upon his shaft, she found her sweet spot inside and massaged it with the hot tip of him. "All mine."

And when she came, it bound the two of them in a peculiar blending of species and ideals, desires and needs. Ashur gave her something she had never had. Raw, uninhibited sex. A reason to enjoy life again. The truth of her insane dreams. And a desperate desire to keep this gorgeous hunk of lover who had rode into her life as the rescuing hero.

"Promise you'll protect me?" she whispered.

"Always," he said on a sigh.

Zaqiel left the dancer against the wall, sighing as she came and gripping for hold on the nearby iron railing so she wouldn't collapse. He turned and stalked away through the strobe-lit darkness, zipping his fly. Though he'd only been walking the earth a few days, he'd quickly learned sex with any human woman was very doable.

And very dissatisfying.

A Fallen could only achieve pleasure by mating with a muse. That was how it worked.

"Stupid rules." He shouldered past a dancer in black leather and headed toward the club's back door. The atmosphere appealed, dripping with sweat, alcohol and the vein-throbbing beat. "But I got her off, lucky girl," he muttered. "Talk about being kissed by an angel. Ha!"

His own muse had been on her deathbed when he'd located her in a village east of Berlin. One look at him, in all his angelic glory—okay, half—and she'd seized and gone into cardiac arrest. He hadn't attempted her dying body. Wasn't as though a dead woman could carry his child to term.

"Bitch."

But that meant he was entitled to go after whatever muse stepped in his way. If he chose a muse who had a Fallen tracking her, he'd have to battle that one to win her. He wasn't sure the fight was worth the outcome.

On the other hand, he was itching for his own pleasure.

Lucky thing he'd stumbled onto number six. She wasn't matched to a Fallen one. That meant either her match had been slain before the flood, or it hadn't been conjured yet.

Why he had been conjured to walk the earth was a puzzle to Zaqiel, but he didn't ponder it. He was free. He intended to get him some muse.

Maybe he could seduce the poor bit of breasts and legs and convince her he would make a lovely boyfriend. He could get his rocks off while she carried his child. Of course, she wouldn't survive the birth. But by then he'd be on to another muse. Another nephilim unleashed to inflict havoc.

Such a lovely circle.

Only problem was the Sinistari in his wake. Rather, he wasn't tracking Zaqiel, the damned demon had beat him to the muse and waited with poisoned blade poised.

"He's probably bedding her," he muttered. "Tainting the muse. Idiot Sinistari. They live for debauchery."

Not that he couldn't get behind a healthy helping of debauchery.

"All's fair, then. You taint my bitch. I'll snatch her from you and see she gives birth to your most hideous nightmare."

"Inside you is the best place on this earth," Ashur whispered at Eden's ear.

Yes, Eden. She'd given him her name as she'd climaxed earlier. He hadn't immediately known what to do with that information. It wasn't as though he could unhear it. Forget it? No, the name fluttered lushly within his brain, spinning reminders of earlier times and yet invoking sensory dreams of gorgeous gardens where they could romp naked.

They snuggled on the bed, she before him, her back sealed to his chest with perspiration. He was still inside her, pumping slowly, not wanting to leave. Ever.

"Ever Eden," he said. "Mine."

"You mean it?" she said from her drowsy slip into sleep.

"I could be. I want to be."

"You are." For now, he thought. And that was all he could give her.

Yet what if he could claim her? Keep her as a lover while he stalked his prey? It would be doable. Love wasn't necessary to share one's body. And he couldn't imagine seeking any other woman now that he'd lain with Eden.

She gave him things she couldn't be aware of. A soft

place to rest his head when he was not stalking the Fallen. Escape from duty. She easily accepted him and the bizarre events surrounding them. She touched his joy with a smile and laughter that echoed inside his chest so gaily it ached.

Eden was his sweet ache.

He would claim her as his own. Damn the angel who thought to attempt his woman.

Chapter 20

He didn't need a soul to claim Eden as his lover. He definitely didn't require a soul to slay angels. In fact, a soul was out of the question. The moment Ashur decided to claim his earthbound soul his slayer days would be over.

Then he'd be left a common mortal to walk this earth.

With Eden. If she would have him.

Ashur weighed the choices. He had no compunction toward slaying until all the Fallen were extinguished.

And then what? He'd be left to walk the earth as a Sinistari, forever in fear of finding love, of being banished Beneath. It was an option he could live with, because it could take millennia more for that to occur.

Of course, Eden's natural death would arrive too quickly in that time. And he doubted she'd prefer him as a demon lover when there existed an option to make love to her as a human.

And with a human soul he need never fear a return to Beneath or torture.

Was he so weak he would succumb to the lure of the mortal flesh? He could have it and not take a soul.

"But not without Eden."

It all hinged on Eden. Eden, Eden, Eden. Why had she given her name to him? By speaking her name she had fixed herself into his black heart with tenterhooks.

And by the black sea Beneath, he'd no desire to snap those hooks loose.

Sure, if he walked the world for centuries he may find another Eden. Someone who may appeal to his black heart. But he didn't want to. He'd sat Beneath for too long. Waiting. Just…being. Knowing he was without the joy he jealously guarded deep within his heart.

This time on earth he could make things different. Why not? It was his right to take the soul he was owed. Why deny himself again? For once ne had a reason to want to change.

Promise you'll protect me.

He'd vowed to her he would protect her, and he had no intention of breaking that vow. Eden Campbell, his sweet ache, soft on the outside and wild on the inside.

Decided, Ashur flashed to a quiet hill in the Italian countryside. Around him fields of tall grass waved in greens and gold. A cavalcade of honeybees buzzed the flower tops, their legs weighed heavily with fragrant gold booty.

Nothing like this existed Beneath. And should he remain on earth long after slaying all the Fallen, he would not see this world as he saw it now. Unadulterated and pure, untainted by his vicious desire to grab all the sin he could handle and devour it.

Eden could give him this pureness.

"Raphael," he whispered, putting intent into the syllables.

The air shimmied through his hair. Clouds zipped by overhead, much faster than usual. Imminent rain flavored the darkening sky. Ashur could taste it in his inhalations.

The sky brightened as if a nuclear explosion occurred.

Ashur fell to one knee and lowered his head. Though Raphael appeared in form viewable by mortals, the Sinistari were not allowed to look upon such divinity. And if they were allowed, Ashur respected the archangel far too much to taint him with his black regard.

"I am surprised at your change of heart," Raphael said.

Ashur sensed his master would say more and remained submissive.

"Have you grown tired of the hunt? How is that possible when you've only been on earth this short time?"

"It is that I've tired of Beneath," he said, truthfully and with conviction. Yet he winced. Was he doing the right thing?

"It is a rather dismal place."

"I wish to receive an earthbound soul upon my next kill. With Zaqiel's death."

"It is every Sinistari's right…"

That pause meant something else was coming.

"Except for the Stealer of Souls."

Raphael's declaration pushed through Ashur's chest like a wave of sludge. He wanted to choke it up, expel it, but he could only listen—and obey.

"You push the rules to fit your needs, Ashuriel. I do not dispute your desire for reward. You would not be demon, otherwise, if you were not selfish."

So true. He would bring his demonic mien with him when he was human. Yet he would shuck off his demonic hungers. He must show Eden he could be a good man.

"Such determination, Sinistari. Very well. But first, tell me, why do you want a soul?"

Ashur sucked in his breath. If he revealed the truth, even thought it, Raphael would know, so instead he said what was mostly true. "I remember what it was like before, when I wanted a soul. That wanting has not left me."

Yet her name eluded his grasp. The woman who had given birth to a beautiful child. The woman he had loved.

"Even after the torture? Impressive. I will see to granting your earthbound reward when Zaqiel is dispatched. With one stipulation, if you will."

The exception. "Anything, my lord."

"Since you are the master Sinistari you will be greatly missed amongst the dwindled ranks. Situations must be remedied. Loose ends tied up."

Ashur nodded compliance, but he didn't understand.

"You see, I wish to ensure all details of this unholy match between the Fallen and muse are ended. Destroyed. Rendered complete. In other words, after Zaqiel is slain, you must then kill the muse. Eden Campbell's death is the key to you gaining a human soul."

The angel flashed away, leaving a brilliant sheen before Ashur's eyes. He blinked but it didn't matter, he could not immediately see. His black blood grew icy. His muscles twitched as if sensing imminent torture.

Kill Eden?

He clutched his chest and yelled to Above, loosing his voice as he had never done before.

Chapter 21

Peter Campbell took Eden's call after a ten-minute hold. He apologized. "My secretary did not tell me it was you, Eden. I was in a meeting."

"It's all right, Daddy. I'm lying here on the bed looking out at the lavender fields and thought I'd give you a call."

"Lavender fields? You on vacation with friends, sunning yourself?"

"I'm at the villa. By myself, actually. I felt the urgent need to get away from the world." She toed the rumpled sheets that she'd not made up after she and Ashur had made love. "There's something I need to say, and I don't want it to go any longer."

"Is everything okay, Eden? I know it's been a while since we've seen each other—"

"Everything is…" Everything wasn't *near* okay, but it wasn't so bad when Ashur was here. "I love you, Dad. And

I needed to say it, because it's not something that is ever easy or obvious to me."

"I understand." He didn't return the endearment, but Eden found she didn't need it right now. She had taken to heart Ashur's suggestion that she accept her father's means to express love for what it was.

The sun filtered through the tree boughs and twinkled across the wood floor. Eden closed her eyes, loving the warmth of summer upon her face.

"Do you believe in angels, Dad?"

"Eden, we've had this discussion before."

Yes, as she sat in the psychiatrist's office and denied her dreams as a means to simply be free. He'd never understood. Eden felt only her mother would have truly listened to her and given her the benefit of the doubt.

"So, you don't believe in them. Not even the idea of a guardian angel?"

"Eden, are you okay? If you need to talk to someone—"

"Daddy, I've never been more sane in my life than I am at this very moment. Please don't patronize me. I know you will never understand the dreams I have, and I accept that. Perhaps I shouldn't have called."

"No, wait. I'm sorry. I haven't been a very good father. I should have been there for you after your mother's death. Perhaps things could have gone differently for you."

"My life has gone exactly as it was meant to. And as I move forward it continues on a destined path. I guess it was foolish to try to reach out to you."

"No, Eden, please." A heavy sigh sounded like frustration, but Eden wondered if it might be tinged with surrender. "Okay, I'll play, then. I do believe."

Eden actually took the phone away from her ear and looked at it as if she'd just received an alien transmission.

"I've been in the presence of them twice, that I'm aware of," he said as she put the receiver back to her ear.

"Really? Did you see them? Were they physical beings?" Why had he never mentioned this before? Could she have inherited her dreams from her father?

"No, I merely felt their presence, but it was such a remarkable feeling I had no question that is exactly what I was experiencing."

"Tell me about it. I promise I won't call you crazy."

His chuckle lasted only two seconds. "Well, the first is humiliating."

"I won't tell a soul."

His sigh startled her. Usually her father's sighs indicated how long he had worked and meant that the exhaustion would keep him from putting a puzzle together with her or reading her a bedtime story. She had come to know her father by his uttered noises. But why were all her memories of her father from her childhood, so long ago?

Because after her mother had died, they had changed, grown apart and grown away from the innate trust family must share.

"You were younger, about four," he said. "And I was...well, I was spanking you for having broken your mother's vase. I didn't abuse you, Eden, you have to know that."

"I do. And I don't recall ever being fearsome of your punishments."

"Yes, well, I did it rarely, and usually it was just a swat. But I was angry that day. It was a vase your mother bought. I know you didn't mean to break it. I spanked you once, but when I tried to do it a second time, I could not. Something stopped me. It was as if I could feel a force pulling my arm back. I knew at that moment your guardian angel was in the room. I never spanked you again."

"Go, guardian angel."

"It wasn't like the things you once claimed to see, Eden."

She'd give him that false comfort. It didn't matter to Eden now who believed her. She had the truth.

"Thank you for sharing that with me." After all these years her father finally trusted her enough to tell her. Her father... It had been so long since she'd had real family. She felt a stirring for one of her own. But could she ever have her own family?

Ashur will leave you when the angel is dead. Don't be stupid.

Swallowing a tear, Eden said, "What about the other time?"

"I had one of my migraines and went to the emergency room. I'd just received a dose of Imitrex and lay there on the exam table shivering. My eyes were closed, and the room was dark. When I heard a female voice ask, 'Would you like a blanket?' I knew it was a nurse. But when she brought the warm blanket and laid it over me it felt like heaven. My shivers stopped and my muscles relaxed. I think I cried. And again, I knew an angel had been present."

"You're very lucky. I've never felt the presence of an angel." Until Zaqiel had entered her life.

"But I thought..."

"You never listened to me, Dad. I dream of angels, and I know they're real, but I've never seen one."

"I apologize for what I put you through after your mother's death. I think a part of me died with her. I shouldn't have let that affect our relationship. I'm sure my angels look nothing like the ones you paint. Your work is amazing. I don't think I've ever told you that."

No, he had not. He'd never commented on her work. Eden's eyes teared up.

"You have so much talent, Eden. And the way you put

the images from your heart onto the computer screen and canvas…well, I love it. Is that…? I think it's my way of saying…well, you know."

She did know. He loved her. And she had always known it. Even though he didn't exactly put it into the words, she could accept the way he'd expressed the emotion.

"Thanks, Dad. I love you, too."

Ashur lingered by the back door, watching a sparrow collect bits of twig for a nest. Eden sauntered down the hallway, a long skirt flowing around her legs and a floaty shirt billowing about her. A change from her usual tighter, revealing clothing. It wasn't half as delicious as the red underwear, but since it made him wonder what was beneath the fabric, it had the same effect as the lacy bits.

He nodded and winked. It felt natural to simply exist alongside her. As if he belonged here. Alongside his sweet ache.

Eden Campbell's death is the key to you gaining a soul.

That bastard Raphael.

But he could not blame the archangel. There was an order to the world. Ashur had violated that order by stealing souls. Of course order must be restored if he wished an earthbound soul.

He sighed as Eden wrapped her arms around his waist. In turn he hugged her tightly. If he could squeeze her into him, he would. Forever imbue her upon his flesh, imprint the soft pear smell of her in his senses. He wanted to bite her, lick her, enfold her within him and keep her from the rest of the world.

She pressed her head against his shoulder and he smelled the salt in her tears. He tilted her chin up and brushed the wetness from her cheek. "They don't seem like sad tears," he said. "Are you okay?"

"Actually I've never been happier. I told my dad I loved him this afternoon. I feel like the world just flipped on the sunshine."

He hugged her to his chest again.

"Wow," she said against his shirt, "that's a mighty big hug. You miss me?"

"Always," he whispered.

Something burned in his eyes. It wasn't tears. Demons couldn't cry. Yet it was painful and made him swallow hard.

Then something incredible happened. The hard black muscle forged of steel in the center of his chest…pulsed.

"I do need love," Eden said. "We all do. Even you."

Ashur's heart pumped again.

Eden placed a palm over his chest. Her wide, green eyes flashed up at him. She had heard it, too, or may have felt it. The wonder in her eyes asked all the questions rushing to Ashur's tongue.

"You did this to me," he said. And though his words were soft and admiring, his feelings were accusatory.

"What are you saying? What did I do? Your heart, Ashur. It's beating. Does that mean…?"

"No, it's not. It's just the souls." But he couldn't help wondering if he'd just lied to himself.

Chapter 22

"I can't get a read on the Fallen." Ashur exhaled and leaned against the wall.

He was locked inside the house with Eden, waiting. Waiting for the angel to strike. For his reality to crash. Could he kill her for a soul?

Should he?

Any Sinistari would. And he was master of them all. What kind of demon was he if he considered the consequences of his actions?

"You've been concentrating all afternoon."

"Huh?" He realized Eden had been in the kitchen the whole time as he struggled with the conscience he suddenly hated.

"Let me show you my favorite place in the whole world." Eden waved an open bottle of wine, directing Ashur to follow her.

"Wait! You're going outside? I need to open the wards."

She stopped abruptly, her hand on the doorknob. "Sorry. I wasn't thinking. I desperately need a breath of fresh air. Is it okay?"

Ashur nodded as he focused his open palm on the ward marking the door. The ward glowed blue, and he moved it with a gesture of his hand to the side wall.

"Cool." Eden walked through the door. "You have to reset it when we come back in?"

"Yes. Don't let me forget."

Eden walked backward across the stone courtyard. She gestured with her forefinger as if luring him to a secret location. He followed, his eyes never leaving hers. The connection stirred everything that had developed between them. She was feeling frisky, and he was, too.

With a human soul he could have moments like this every day.

If he had a human soul, that would mean Eden was dead.

She sat on the hammock and patted the ropes beside her. "Like it?"

Shoving the dire thoughts out of his brain, Ashur forced a light mood. "Can we both fit on there?"

"This is a double-wide. You sit and we'll slide back at the same time." They managed the maneuver with some chuckles, and Eden held the wine bottle high until they were comfortable on the creaky, but sturdy rope swing. "This has always been my favorite spot. Look at the sun through the leaves overhead. It's beautiful here, isn't it?"

"I suspect the beauty is enhanced by your memories." Ashur clasped her free hand and brought it to his mouth. He kissed the space between her thumb and forefinger, then dashed his tongue along the curve of it.

The taste of her was addictive. He wanted it all the time.

"What of your memories? Do you remember what it was like on earth so long ago?"

"Simpler. Tougher," he said.

"Not so many people?"

"Exactly."

"I know you've only been here a short time," she said, "but I wonder if you ever think about becoming like us?"

"Like you?"

"Just human. Mortal." She drew his hand to her mouth and pressed her lips to the side of his thumb. "Not living with the threat of being banished to some weird hell I can only imagine—and probably don't want to imagine. Not having to kill."

"You will never understand killing is my mien."

"I get that part. You're a demon. Demons kill. Someone has to keep tabs on the nasty angels."

"And you would wish me to sacrifice what I am and leave all those nasty angels, as you call them, to torment innocent women such as yourself?"

She shifted on the hammock, rolling to her side, and ran her palm up under his shirt. That touch he liked. Brazen, demanding, it quickly stirred him to desire.

"I like that you're a hero and all," she said, "but sometimes I think I'd like to keep you all for myself."

He thought the same, impossible as it was.

"Ashur."

His name on her tongue sounded too good to be demon. Her touch did not preach patience. He was no master of virtue, yet he wanted to hold this moment, to cleave to it as he had joy, because it may never again be this sweet.

"I must be selfish," she said, "and tell you I wish you wouldn't leave me after this is done."

"I won't know what the morning following Zaqiel's death will bring to me. Let's not look that far ahead. Actually let's look ahead. Like at what my ass is going to look like when I stand up from this torture device. It's uncomfortable."

"You think? I love this hammock." She rolled and stepped off, reaching back a hand. "Come on, wimp."

Ashur stood and lifted her over his shoulder in one fluid move. He swatted her ass and charged the house. "For that, you will be punished."

Once inside, he turned and with his free hand, directed the ward back over the door. It settled into position and flashed blue once.

Laughing, he ran up the stairs, her body held easily over his broad shoulder. Indeed, he did not know what the morning after Zaqiel's death would bring. But he wasn't about to kill Eden to gain a soul. Because with her gone from this world, what would be the value of his human soul?

What was different about making love to a demon rather than a man? Physically, he was completely human. No horns or…well, Eden didn't know what anomalies to look for. But she didn't find any as she explored Ashur's gorgeous body. Hot and moist with perspiration, he was perfection.

She glided her fingers up his leg, enjoying as his muscles tensed with her touch. A moan from her lover danced in her heart. It was as if he'd awakened to her, and she in turn had found someone so unique, she felt as if only he fit in her life.

And inside her. Eden nestled her mons against his soft penis. He was spent after half a dozen orgasms. As was she. Though she sensed he was ready for another round when he began to harden against her stomach.

The man had stamina. She'd never been so thoroughly sexed in all her life. Must be because he wasn't human.

He was certainly demonic in bed. And she loved it.

Eden moved up as Ashur rolled onto his stomach and dropped an arm over the bed's edge. Pressing her breasts to his smooth hard ass, she kissed his back and traced her tongue along his spine.

Ashur growled lowly, a satisfied sound.

She smiled against his skin. "You like that? You're so hot. It's like you're a furnace. A girl would like to have you around in the wintertime."

"I haven't seen snow for a millennium."

"Then I hope you stick around to see it this year. I want the first sledding date in Central Park to be with you. We'll follow by stripping down to bare skin before the fireplace in my penthouse and sipping hot chocolate."

"If I am on this earth when the snow falls, you will not be able to keep me from you. Eden," he said on a purr. "Beautiful name."

"You're crossing the line of getting personal by using it."

"You've tugged me over many lines, Eden."

"You like it."

"I do."

Fingers gliding along the rumpled sheets, Eden tickled her tongue toward the back of his neck where fine dark hairs flowed into the thick tousle upon his head. He had a few freckles.

Eden glided her fingers up his neck and into his hair. There she saw something dark against his skin. A design? It was as if he'd grown hair over a tattoo.

It struck her as odd. "Ashur?"

He grunted, halfway to sleep.

"Lover, there's something on the back of your skull."

Another grunt, but he was listening.

"It looks like a tattoo, but could be something else, though I don't know what. It's black, like ink."

"Never had time to get a tattoo. Not particularly interested in one, either."

"It's shaped like— Oh, my God."

"What?"

She stretched her arm up by his face, revealing the sigil. "It looks like this. A six!"

The mattress bounced as Ashur rolled over and slid off to stand in one fast motion. Eden was flung off him and sat sprawled across the rumpled white sheets.

"Are you sure?"

She nodded and gestured with a shrug. "You want me to get a mirror and show you in the bathroom?"

A flash of realization thundered her heartbeats. She hadn't made the connection until she'd said the number herself. And Ashur had to think the same thing as she—

Ashur shuffled into his jeans and grabbed his shirt. His abs flexed as he tugged it over his head and stretched back his arms, fisting his fingers. Concern narrowed his brows. His eyes were dark, lacking in color.

Eden gave his eyes a double-take. She'd never seen them like that. "Where are you going?"

"I need to go talk to someone."

"Right now? But what about—"

"You'll be safe. The wards are strong so long as you don't leave the house without my assistance. It won't take me long. I'm sorry, Eden." He leaned in to kiss her on the mouth. The kiss was too quick, but his fingers lingered in her hair for a moment and he drew away to trace her gaze with his. "I cherish you."

She caught her breath as her heartbeat stalled. Cherish her? That was awesome. Was it close to love? Almost. Maybe it was his form of expressing love?

No. Love was forbidden to his kind. What would that mean to them being together? He'd be banished again. Sent Beneath. She did not want his love if it meant he would be tortured for it.

By the time she'd summoned her voice, Ashur had marched out of the bedroom, leaving her alone on a sea of sheets.

"I cherish you, too," she whispered.

She stroked the birthmark on her forearm. It had been there since birth. She'd not associated it with the number six until third grade when they'd learned Roman numerals.

Did it mean what she now thought? Were she and Ashur meant to be together since before they both walked this earth?

Chapter 23

The interspace between earth and Above was colder than the Arctic Circle. The mortal clothing Ashur wore did little to protect him from the elements. The cold couldn't kill him; it would just give him a hell of a brain freeze. He could shrug off his human costume, but his demonic form would offend his master, so he endured.

Ashur shivered and called again for Raphael.

He slapped a palm across the back of his neck. Six?

In all his uncountable centuries he had never known. Never before had any of his lovers noticed the telltale mark. Not even the woman from Macedonia. *What was her name?* She'd probably never seen the mark because their couplings had been more tame, not as exploratory as those with Eden.

Yet as soon as Eden had described the mark to him, he had innately known. What else could it be?

"Now what?" The angel beamed before him, partially

formed with shoulders and a torso, but mostly light. It wasn't a warm light, either. Angels were never warm, despite popular belief. "You're going to freeze your mortal dick off if you spend any amount of time here, Sinistari. Then what fun will you have tromping through sin as if it were an all-you-can-eat buffet?"

Much as he wished to snap at Raphael, Ashur held his tongue. He revered the archangel, for reasons beyond his comprehension.

"Why is Zaqiel still alive?" Raphael prompted. "And for that matter, the muse still breathes."

"Zaqiel will not live another day."

"That had better be a promise and not hope."

"Hope is not in my arsenal."

"If that is what you wish to believe. What of the muse?"

"I am…considering the task."

"Considering?" The archangel scoffed. He knew all truths and lies. But it hadn't been a lie. Ashur was almost sure he would not kill Eden. But almost wasn't completely.

"Was I once…?" Ashur's teeth chattered. He couldn't believe it, but he'd never known exactly how the Sinistari were born—rather, forged. "How were the Sinistari created?"

"They were forged of a metal unknown to mankind before their feet hit the earth and then they were matched with the blade previously crafted from their rib bone."

He'd known the blade was created from his form. But what form had that been?

"*Before* my feet hit the earth?" he asked. It was impossible, but only one explanation made sense. "Was I once an angel?"

He felt Raphael's disappointment in his icy bones. "Yes. But now you are demon."

Incredible. And completely insane. "Was I one of the two hundred?"

"Yes."

Raphael's abruptness afforded Ashur little time to process the truth now, but he needed to understand. "Explain," he insisted. "Please."

"When the two hundred fell," Raphael said, "their ranks were decimated. Those twenty were chosen to become Sinistari."

"Why?"

"It was anticipated there would be a need for them," Raphael said sternly. "You've got willful angels walking the earth in search of human females. It's not all romance and roses. So the demon Sinistari were forged from the hard metals strafing through the earth."

That Eden was so amazed at the hardness of his body had only reminded him of his origins.

"We are tough to exterminate, we angels," Raphael said, "but our own kind can do the job rather nicely. Fact is, only an angel can slay another angel. The Sinistari were a necessity born of the fall."

"But if I was forged from the earth's metals, then how…?"

"The blade. You are a different substance than Dethnyht. Earthly. But that blade is pure divinity, created from your angelic form as you fell."

He ran a palm over the blade sheath at the back of his hip. "And the poison?"

"Softens the hard angel flesh. Makes the blade go in real swell."

The archangel tilted his head wonderingly. That he allowed Ashur to process this now was a boon he did not have to offer.

"I was once an…" Ashur slapped a palm over his still heart. Icy wind permeated his steel flesh. Feeling anything, even pain, was not to be disregarded. For how soon before he was returned Beneath? "That means I had chosen to fall. That I was once Grigori. I was once a part…"

"Of the mutual curse that formed the wicked pact to fall. Yes, yes, get over it, demon. You have always been and always will be divinely created."

This was difficult to digest. "I was once divine?"

Raphael nodded. "Divinity alters little with the form. It is still within you."

"Impossible. I am Sinistari. I am evil."

"Your perspective, which, I gather, is based on the perspectives of others. I was startled you so easily accepted the label all those millennia ago. There are billions of perspectives, depending on who is doing the looking. One must never subscribe to any other than his own."

"But the Fallen—they are not divine. His divinity was swept from them as the halos left their heads and their feet touched the earth."

"That is true. A halo was swept from your head, but your feet did not, indeed, touch the earth. You were forged mid-fall and sent immediately Beneath."

Ashur let out a huffing sigh. He possessed divinity? Impossible. That would make him more divine than the fallen angels he stalked.

No. He could not— Perhaps, though, that was how he had been able to once love?

"Indeed. That was an oversight," Raphael added. "Love and demons don't mix. Yet it was a residual from your former divine nature. Unavoidable, really."

And this bastard had tortured the love from his flesh and steel bones with relish and a wicked smile.

"That was Ariel, not me."

"You made the command."

"And do you protest the punishment was unfitting?"

Ashur hung his head. "No."

"Damned right."

"So if twenty were taken and forged as Sinistari, then there have only ever been one hundred eighty Fallen?"

"Yes, well, forty-seven were extinguished before and during the flood. And eleven Sinistari remain."

"So that means there are more muses than Fallen," Ashur said, quickly working out the implications. "Unless there were only one hundred eighty muses?"

"Two hundred, actually. Which leaves extras. Some Fallen go after other muses after they've impregnated their own. When that happens, that means you guys haven't been doing your job. Sort of like Zaqiel. His muse was dead by the time the chap got to her, so he's been stalking others."

He knew that.

Ashur gripped the angel's shoulders. They transformed to molten heat under his fingers. Amidst the Arctic storm, he relished the heat, so did not let go. "What sigil am I?"

"You mean to ask," Raphael corrected slyly, "what sigil *were* you?"

"The sigil has never been replaced by another Fallen, so I still am." Ashur was not sure what he was saying but at the same time he knew it for truth. When he'd originally fallen— he could not remember that time—he must have been one of the two hundred destined to mate with mortal females.

"Yes, but it's not as though you can do the task a Fallen does—create a nephilim. The sigil is merely that. A forgotten design. A symbol of connection to a mortal muse."

"And?"

"Very well. You, Sinistari, are number six."

Chapter 24

Empty wine bottle in hand, Eden strolled down the hallway. The recycle bins sat outside the back door. There was an old man in the neighborhood who went around monthly and collected wine bottles from everyone. He crushed them and sold the tiny bits as mulch for gardens. Eden had noted a few gardens on the drive here that glittered under the sunlight.

She pressed a hand to the door, but stopped before the latch clicked open. She'd almost forgot. The wards. She was trapped inside until Ashur got home.

He'd left her bed so quickly, she would take it as rejection if she hadn't known what had been on his mind.

He suspected the same thing.

Setting the wine bottle on the laundry sink, she leaned over and toyed with the constant drip no amount of fussing with the handle would stop.

Ashur wasn't your standard guy who could do odd jobs

around the house, grill a burger and tinker with the car engine. Though after he'd walked the world to gain knowledge, he probably possessed those skills and more, Eden figured.

She needed to imagine him bent over the engine of her car, his jeans slipping low on his hips and a smudge of grease on his cheek. That picture fit into her idea of normal.

Okay, so normal for her was handing the driver the keys and sending him off to the shop to fix whatever was wrong with the vehicle, then signing the credit-card statement a month later.

All her life she'd never wished for more or less. Her father, while distant, had managed to keep her grounded. She didn't need fancy balls, though she did like to attend charity events. She didn't require bling or sports cars or a fifty-thousand-dollar platinum cell phone.

All she needed was someone with whom she could share her life. Someone normal. Someone who would not abandon her. Was that asking too much?

A bang toward the front of the house made Eden stand up and listen. Must have been the wind. It gushed across the lavender fields today, filling the house with the scent. Eden recognized the creak that followed.

The front door. He was back.

She skipped down the hallway and into the kitchen only to find it was not Ashur poking his head through the door, but a stranger—who had opened the door.

"Stop! Don't open the door!"

Her cry only succeeded in prompting him to step inside and quickly close the door behind him.

"Sorry, ma'am." He removed the black fedora from his head and nodded. "It wasn't locked and no one answered after I'd knocked a few times."

"So you just…" Eden touched the door, running her fingers over the wood and trying to determine if the ward was still activated. She couldn't sense it even if it was, but going through the motion stilled her raging need to beat him over the head.

Remembering a stranger stood behind her, she swung about, pressing her shoulders to the door. "Who are you? Did Mr. Cantello send you for the wine bottles?"

"I'm Michael Donovan." He offered a hand to shake, but she remained pinned to the door. Why had she decided to leave her little blade behind?

"What do you want?"

"I believe you and I have a common interest we should discuss."

"How did you find me here? Have we spoken online?"

She pressed a hand to the door. If he opened it to leave would the wards be further damaged? Would the signal to Zaqiel grow stronger? No, the signal was not activated as long as she didn't itch. The scarf around her neck protected the itch, but she felt it tingle now.

"My boyfriend is on his way," she said, hoping to make him leery, or flat out leave. "He'll be here any minute."

"I'm not going to harm you, Miss Campbell. And I apologize for walking in like that. It was rude. Please, relax."

"Yes, well, you can't imagine what harm you have done merely by opening my door."

"Is that so?" He tilted his head to study her. He was attractive and had narrow blue eyes, short dark hair and a scar at the corner of his eye. A kind face that she'd normally smile at if passing him in the street. Did she know him? "Tell me what I've done."

"Even if I could explain the intricacies, you wouldn't understand." She crossed her arms and paced toward the table. "By opening that door, you've broken wards meant to keep me safe."

"From the vampires?"

She turned swiftly, meeting his worried gaze. "Vampires? What in the world…"

He winced at her reaction. "So you don't know about them. Sorry. Didn't mean to toss that one out there. What else would you need protection from?"

"I still don't know who you are, and I'm worried a crazy man is in my house."

"I'm a halo hunter, Miss Campbell. I've come from your penthouse in Manhattan, and—"

"You were at my home?" She backed toward the counter where the knife rack sat. "Halo hunter?"

"I've been tracking you online for a few months. You buy halos, yes?"

"And what does a halo hunter do?" She didn't want to give him any information he might already know. "Were you *in* my house?"

"The construction crew was repairing a window. I admit I did slip in for a bit."

Turning and grabbing the only knife left in the wood block, she was disheartened when it turned out to be a small paring knife with only a three-inch blade.

"You don't need that." Donovan put up his hands in placation. "I said I'm not here to hurt you. I want to talk. We're on the same side, I promise you."

"Yeah?" She wielded the knife, point out, not about to drop the small piece of security. "What side is that?"

"The one opposite the vampires."

"I don't know how vampires play into all this. I think you're in the wrong movie, mister." Out of her peripheral vision she thought she saw the door open, and her eyes flew toward it. But the door remained closed.

"They're after the halos," her unwelcome visitor explained. "To lure the Fallen, and ultimately see them get a muse pregnant and give birth to a nephilim."

Eden dropped the hand she held the knife in to her side. Wow. He knew everything. But vampires? Ashur hadn't mentioned bloodsuckers were a part of the deal.

"You follow what I'm saying," he said. "I can tell by the fact that you're not calling the police and haven't tried to throw that little knife at me."

She set the paring knife on the counter. It could do little harm, and really, if she tried to attack him he could take it from her and turn the attack on her. "Fallen angels and nephilim I get. Vampires are new to me."

"Yeah, well, they were new to me only a few months ago. Now they seem to turn up everywhere I go. I confess I took the halos from your office. It was necessary," he said quickly as she started to protest. "The vampires are tracking them. I promise I will return them to you after...well, whatever the hell this is, is all over."

"You stole my..." He'd been in her home, had touched her things and had taken the halos, which meant so much to her. "I think you need to leave."

"That's another one." Ignoring her plea, he noted the halo stuck in the wall and approached it.

"Don't touch it!"

The halo glowed blue. Donovan retracted from his attempt to touch. He shot a wondrous look at her. "I've never seen one do that before."

The front door slammed inward, and Ashur's imposing dark figure filled the doorway. He took one look at Michael Donovan and crossed the room and slammed him against the wall.

Chapter 25

Zaqiel was crossing the street before the city's center fountain when the black SUV peeled around the corner and hit him. His body, though fashioned of metal and glass, was ultralight. He soared through the air and landed at the cement base of the fountain, which was forty feet in diameter. Cold water spit on his head.

The SUV stopped and out jumped a man in jeans and leather jacket. He rushed toward Zaqiel. "Dude, are you okay?" He knelt by Zaqiel and inspected him. "You look fine." He gripped Zaqiel's hair and smashed the back of his head against the stone fountain steps. "You feel fine? Yeah? I thought so. You angels are as hardheaded as they come."

Shaking off the bells jangling in his head, Zaqiel went for the man's throat, but a knee jammed him up under his chin, effectively pinning him.

"Ah, you're not going anywhere until we talk, you fallen piece of crap."

"Who the hell are you?"

The man smiled, revealing vamp fangs. "Name's Bruce. Not so pleased to meet you, Zaq. I've been tracking you for the days you've been on earth. You're not doing so hot, are you? Should have banged that muse days ago. What's the problem? Sinistari scare you away?"

Forcing the vampire from him with a sweep of his will, Zaqiel jumped to his feet and flashed to meet the flying vamp as he crashed against the side of his car. He gripped the vampire's throat. The vamp reciprocated.

"We can go at each other all day," Bruce said through the pinch on his throat. "You can't kill me without a stake, and I can't kill you—"

"At all," Zaqiel finished for him. "You want the hurt I can give you, bloodsucker?"

A fist smashed his nose. Zaqiel swallowed his own blood; it tasted like hot molasses. He returned a punch to the vamp's gut. The fang-face smiled and shook it off, bouncing on his feet and gesturing for another brutal fist.

"Come on! You want to do this? I welcome it."

"Why are you so concerned for what I do?" Zaqiel asked. "Why are you following me?"

"It's my job. I'm the head angel rustler, you might say. Hey, check this." The vampire twisted and swung up his leg, clocking Zaqiel in the face.

Zaqiel wavered, but didn't fall. In human form he wasn't as strong and couldn't spring back from attack as quickly as in his natural form. But he couldn't change here in the plaza where a crowd had begun to linger and observe their interaction. Hell, he could only change halfway anyway.

Zaqiel grabbed the gold chain from around the vampire's neck and ripped it off. "A cross?"

"I'm not baptized," the vampire confirmed with a sneer.

He slammed the gold cross against Zaqiel's forehead. "What about you? This do anything for you?"

Snarling, Zaqiel shoved the insipid vampire from him and stalked a few paces away. "It is but a symbol. It means nothing to me. What do you want from me? I tire of your infantile bully tactics."

"Yeah, I think it's time I cut to the point." Another fist to his jaw sent Zaqiel stumbling backward. He tripped on the fountain steps and toppled. The vampire gripped the back of his head and forced his head underwater.

Zaqiel swallowed water and choked. This was a bad situation. It didn't take long to drown an angel, and drowning was the only way to take him out without a poisoned blade.

This had happened once before. That damned flood had swept him from his feet and taken the breath from him. He'd come to in that blasted ninth void and had been imprisoned there far too long for any creature's sanity.

He wasn't about to go down a second time.

Pulled above the surface, Zaqiel sucked in air and sputtered water. The vampire turned him over and slammed his head against the step again. His skull vibrated nastily, and Zaqiel struggled to maintain consciousness.

"I need names," the vampire hissed. "Names of your fellow Fallen still bound in the ninth void."

"Fuck you!"

"Come on, dude, you don't care about the others. Why not give them up?"

And he knew then how he had come to ground. It made little sense. But how else could this asshole have such information, and be so hot to get it? "The *vampires* are summoning us?"

"You bet. So about those names." The vampire kneeled on his chest and bounced. A couple rib bones cracked. Zaqiel winced. "Just a couple will do."

"Why should I give you names?"

"Don't you want to spread the love around? I mean, the more of you walking the earth, the more the Sinistari have to track."

Made stupid sense. But Zaqiel was not stupid. "If I am the only Fallen then I've an entire hoard of muses to pick from."

"There is that. But, dude, I've seen you and the Sinistari. He's going to win, trust me on that one. And we'd appreciate it if you'd cough up some names so we can match them with the sigils from the paintings and have others to replace you when you've become angel toast."

"Why are you summoning us now?"

"Not your business."

Another brutal smash of his human skull against the hard stone pushed Zaqiel beyond anger and into rage. He let loose the ear-piercing scream that would shatter a mortal's eardrums—and quite possibly a vampire's, too—but a rag was stuffed in his mouth.

"That trick only works once, dude. I caught on with the last fallen angel." Bruce jammed his knee into Zaqiel's groin, and once again he cursed his human form. "Names."

Ashur charged the man standing next to the halo. Eden dashed out of the way to give him clear access. He slammed his hand against the man's throat and pinned him to the wall, his feet dangling.

"Do you know him?" he growled at Eden.

She shook her head and stepped farther away. "He followed me from New York. He was *in* my penthouse!"

He closed his fingers around the man's throat. The man yelped, but only briefly as Ashur could feel his throat muscles slacken.

"Don't kill him!" Eden yelled. "He's a halo hunter."

"A what?" The man's hand clambered to claw at Ashur's arm, but his efforts were ineffectual.

"He looks for halos to keep them away from vampires," Eden explained.

"Vampires?"

"Yes! And he broke the ward."

He had sensed the nonresistant wards as he'd entered the house. Dropping the man in a heap, Ashur did not relent. He jammed his boot against his shoulder, hard.

The man gasped, easing his fingers over his injured vocal muscles. That he had been here alone with Eden made Ashur want to reach in and rip out his throat through his mouth. And if he had touched her, he'd be seeing the psychopomp again soon because this asshole had but moments of breath remaining.

"Did he touch you?"

"No," Eden warbled. She was distraught, and Ashur sensed it might be more from his actions.

"I don't know who or what you are," Ashur said, leaning in close to the man's reddened face, "but I do know you broke in without permission and you were standing close to my woman. You've got five seconds to explain before I make you a choker of that halo."

"The vampires—" he gasped as he clasped his throat and heaved "—want the halo."

Eden bent over beside Ashur and put a hand on his shoulder. Her soft pear scent invaded his senses, which calmed him and shook him from the rage.

"He said vampires are looking for the halos to trap the Fallen. Something like that. Ashur?"

Ashur kicked away from the man, which allowed him to roll forward onto his elbows. Head bowed, the man choked. Ashur put an arm around Eden's shoulder. "Vampires exist," he muttered.

She chuffed out a breath.

"But I don't understand why they would be involved with angels." He stretched out an arm toward the halo, which flashed blue. He knew it best to leave that thing alone for now. "That still doesn't explain why he's here."

"I'm trying to keep the halos from the vampires," the man said, and followed with another cough.

"His name is Michael Donovan," Eden offered. "I think he's on our side. Even though he did admit to breaking into my penthouse."

"The door was ajar," Donovan said. He pushed himself up to sit against the wall. Head lolling, he heaved in breaths. "What is he?" he asked Eden.

Ashur again heeled the man's shoulder with his hard rubber-soled boot. "What do you think I am?"

"You can't be an angel. You could be. I don't know, man. I'm as new to this lexicon of mythological creatures walking the earth as she seems to be."

Eden's fingers clutched about Ashur's biceps. She did not hold him back, only tamed him enough to listen to what the intruder had to say.

"For ten years I've hunted halos," Donovan explained. "The angels fell to earth—they dropped their halos. I find them. It's a hobby. An expensive one, at times. At other times, adventurous. It's all good. But I never expected to learn about vampires—that they exist or that they want to capture an angel and force it to mate with a muse."

Ashur tugged his arm from Eden's grip and paced away to put distance between him and Donovan. The man knew much. Though how vampires fit into the Fallen's vile quest baffled him. Halo hunter? He'd never heard of it.

He regarded the fallen man from over his shoulder. His face was still red and he rubbed his throat. Anything was possible, Ashur told himself. Hell, Eden's small collection could qualify her as a halo hunter.

Eden poured a glass of water from the fridge and offered it to Donovan, who remained on the floor. He accepted with a nod and drank the whole thing in a slow, long swallow.

She returned to Ashur's side and whispered, "What did you find out? Are you?"

She wanted to know if he'd gone to Raphael and asked about his origins. She must have figured it out. Some of it. She could not know it all. That he had been one of the original fallen, and that he had joined in the vile pact to walk the earth and seek mortal muses to create the vampiric progeny—

"They want to control the nephilim," he suddenly said. It made sense to him now. Walking over to Donovan, he asked, "The vampires. Is that what you know?"

"Nephilim, yes," Donovan confirmed. "The child of an angel and his muse. Nephilim are like the original blood drinkers. They are cannibals who eat anything on four or two legs. They drink the blood of man and have no moral code. Supposedly they are the founding blood in a line of vampires I had the displeasure to meet a few months ago. It was a tribe, actually. Called themselves Anakim. The vampires believe if they can get their hands on a nephilim they can use it to strengthen their bloodlines."

Feeling Eden's fingers curl into his, Ashur closed his hand gently about them. She stood silent at his side. He could sense her fear; it was as strong as it had been that day Zaqiel had smashed through her bedroom window. He could imagine the bizarre images racing through her mind. He would not go there. He didn't need to.

It all made morbid sense to him.

"You think you can stop it from happening?" he asked.

"I'm going to try," Donovan said.

"Why you? You're a trinket collector. You have no reason to care. And beyond all that, you are but a common mortal. You cannot stand against the supernatural."

"I was nearly killed by the vampire leader not too many months ago," Donovan said. "He tried to kill my girlfriend, too. Well, she's my girlfriend now. We sort of bonded during the experience." He laughed. "She's a vamp. Didn't expect that one, but love comes in all sorts of packages, doesn't it?"

Ashur looked down at Eden, who smiled up at him.

"Listen," Donovan said as he bent his legs to push himself up against the wall. He winced and stroked his throat. "As long as I know the location of this halo, that's cool. I'll leave it with you because I have a feeling you won't let it fall into the wrong hands. But why does it glow?"

"We think it might belong to Zaqiel," Eden offered. "It must sense he is near."

"Is he the angel after you?" Donovan asked. "You're a muse, I suspect."

"I am, and he is," Eden confirmed. She revealed the sigil on her forearm to him. "But he's not my match." A glance to Ashur entreated for information, but he intended to keep any secrets close to his chest and away from this intruder.

"You can't let him get his hands on this halo," Donovan said.

"Not going to happen." Ashur reached behind him and unsheathed Dethnyht. He displayed it before him.

Donovan swallowed. "I'm a little weak on the whole hierarchy of angels, muses and vampires, but I'm guessing you're not in that league. A slayer?"

"Sinistari," Ashur said. "A demon who will not pause

to remove your head should you make one wrong step. Understand?"

Donovan nodded profusely. "Completely." Then he eyed Eden and Ashur. "Interesting pair."

"I am her protector," Ashur felt the need to say.

"Uh-huh. And more." Donovan clapped his hands together. "I should go."

"What did you do with the halos you took from my home?" Eden asked.

"They're safe. I promise I will return them to you when this is all over. I may look like a thief to you, but I'm not. I can't risk them falling into vampire hands. And if I got into your place so easily, nothing could have stopped a vampire. I hope you can understand."

"What means do you use to protect the halos from the vampires?" Ashur asked.

"I've a safe protected by a witch's spell. And garlic," he added with a shrug. "I know that stuff doesn't work, but it gives me strange comfort."

"You should take that one, as well." Ashur nodded toward the halo in the wall.

Donovan inspected the halo, which flashed blue intermittently. "Nope, I don't think so. That one needs to be here for reasons beyond my understanding. Just keep it safe, and if the angel should get his hands on it, run like hell. Oh, and if a vampire named Antonio comes near you…stake him."

"Antonio?"

Recognition tightened Eden's voice. Ashur reached for her hand, but she slipped away. "What is it?" he asked.

She shuffled through her purse on the table and drew out a slip of paper. "Antonio Del Gado?"

Donovan gaped. "How do you know his full name?" The halo hunter took the paper Eden offered him. "Is this his number?"

"Yes. Is he a vampire?" she asked. "He bought all my paintings from a gallery showing the other night. I paint angels. Real ones that I see in my dreams."

"Seriously? You see— Do you have examples?"

"Yes." She pulled her laptop from the case and powered it up on the table. Within moments, she and the halo hunter were staring at the angel paintings.

"Can I get a copy of these?" Donovan asked. "They are remarkable. Never seen an angel myself, but if that's what you've seen in your dreams—"

"You don't think I'm crazy?" Eden asked hastily.

"Nope. You dreamed these sigils, too?"

"Not exactly. Those just sort of drew themselves as I was creating the work," Eden added as she slipped a disk in the drive.

"Do not give him a copy." Ashur slammed his fist on the table. "You don't know this man. He could be working with the vampires. His girlfriend is a vampire!"

"We got together *after* I rescued her from Antonio," Michael said. "I know it sounds hypocritical, but she's not one of them. Antonio had enslaved her. You can trust me, Miss Campbell."

"I do." She handed him the disk with the copies of her paintings on it.

"Here's my card," he said. "I have a feeling you're in good hands, but if you get any leads on more halos, I'd appreciate you keeping me in the loop."

"I will." Eden tucked the card in her back pocket. "Thanks, Mr. Donovan."

Michael retrieved his fedora from the kitchen table and walked toward the door. "Can I open this now?"

"Yes, the wards have already been broken."

"Sorry about that. I hadn't a clue. Goodbye, Eden, Ashur. And good luck."

Ashur hugged Eden to him as the door closed. They clung to each other as the engine rumbled away down the road. Forgetting his quick anger and jealousy, Ashur squeezed her against him, wishing that one of their hugs would eventually imprint her upon his being so he would never forget her.

She smelled ethereal, like he imagined Above must smell. Could he ever touch those memories? Did he want to?

"Now, about us," she said.

Looking down into her eyes, he wished the world was different. That *he* was different. That he could change things with the snap of his fingers.

Impossible.

He needed to snap Eden's neck if he wished to please his archangel master.

Chapter 26

He pulled away from her when she most needed him to enfold her in his strong arms and reassure her that everything was going to be okay. That did not bode well for Eden's future.

Because somewhere in the past few days she'd forgotten that this relationship was just a muse and her demon protector. Eden had mistakenly fallen into the romance of it all. Yes, she had fallen, just like a wicked angel.

"You spoke to Raphael?" she prompted, hoping to win back his regard.

Ashur leaned in the front doorway, his back to her and his hands stuffed in his jeans pockets. All his trouble to set up the wards had been destroyed by one unknowing halo hunter. Donovan couldn't have known. He'd seemed genuinely apologetic.

A bird fluttered near the door, but with a swish of Ashur's hand, it was redirected away.

"Ashur, talk to me." She suspected he wasn't in the mood for touch, but he wasn't going to push her away. Not now. She knew what it was like to want to push away those who loved you. It was a mistake.

Eden wrapped her arms around him from behind and spread her palms across his chest. He was warm now, humanly warm. Was it because he'd raged earlier when the halo hunter was here? Or was he becoming more human the more time he spent on earth?

"You asked Raphael about the mark on the back of your head," she said. "Are we?"

He clasped one of her hands and kissed it. Then he held her fingers against his mouth and nodded.

His silent confirmation swept a giddy wave through her system. Eden smiled against his shoulder. Yet she suspected he was not so overjoyed. Of course, she knew he guarded his joy well.

"I am your muse? How can that be? You're...not an angel."

He turned and tugged her to stand between his legs. Adjusting his position against the door frame, he lowered himself to eye level with her. Caressing her hair, he stroked it for a while, drawing it down her chest and tracing the curling ends of it upon her breast.

Nothing else in this world distracted him. Just her.

Eden loved standing like this, against him, a part of him, so accepted, as if he couldn't imagine standing any other way. She dared to hope, because hope was all she had.

"I did speak to Raphael," he finally said. "The truth is remarkable. When two hundred angels fell, so many millennia ago, twenty were removed from the ranks before their feet could touch earth. From those twenty, angelic metal was drawn and twenty blades were created. Then the twenty fallen were forged into the Sinistari and matched to a blade. It was necessary, because only an angel can kill an angel."

"So you were once…an angel?"

He nodded. "Apparently one so willful and wicked as to participate in an evil pact to fall."

"Oh." She understood where his head was at. He considered the Fallen the most foul, evil things to walk the earth. And to discover he had actually been one of them…? "You are not what you were, but what you are now, Ashur. You're a good man."

He snorted a mirthless chuckle.

"Ashur, I know you." She pressed a hand over his chest, where his heart did not pulse. "You are not evil."

He grabbed her hand and held it against his heart. Nothing about his lacking pulse bothered her. She accepted him.

But could he accept her?

Eyes closed, Ashur said, "Do you not find it ironic that the one woman I fell to earth to claim—to rape and put a monster child in her belly—" he opened his eyes and pinned her with his mirthless gaze "—is the one woman who now makes me wish for a human soul?"

"You mean that? You would take a human soul?" His announcement quickened her pulse. That would mean they could really be together.

Now she felt him stiffen and their connection faded too quickly. "A human soul will never be mine."

"Yes, it can be. Ashur, don't you see? We were destined to be together."

"Not in any romantic or loving manner. Open your eyes, Eden. I am not like you. I never will be like you. How can you persist with this charade of caring about me?"

"Because I love you."

There, she'd said it. And she meant it. They had known

each other but a few days, but Eden's heart had been waiting for Ashur forever. He fit her soul.

But Ashur's reaction ripped out her heart and thrust it against the wall.

He tore away from her embrace and stalked off across the stone courtyard. He made haste down the road leading up to the house. How could he walk away from her after she'd put her heart out in the open?

"What have I done? Will I never learn? Even if he could love me, I can never give him the one thing he values most. Joy."

Which, as Ashur interpreted it, was actually a child.

Eden tucked her head against the door frame and sniffed tears.

Never in her life had she been so ready to fall into a man's arms and face together whatever life tossed at them. It felt right. She could think of spending time with no other man.

But he wasn't man. He wasn't even human.

"I don't care," she murmured. "I love you, Ashur."

Bruce laid the list of names on the black granite desktop. Antonio snatched it up. He always wore old stuff like frock coats and lace and weird shoes with buckles. Bruce had once thought him eccentric, a vampire stuck in a lost past, but lately he just thought him a nut.

Though his idea to capture a nephilim so they could strengthen the tribe's bloodline was genius. Bruce looked forward to the day when he could actually walk during the day, instead of lurking about in the shadows.

Not all vampires feared sunlight. Most had evolved over the centuries, and if you were created a vampire today you could walk in the daylight for a while without burning.

Bruce could walk the day because he'd been created by

a rogue vamp. Antonio's pockets were deep, and he required a day walker to do his dirty work, thus, this arrangement.

What kind of weirdness was it that Bruce's blood master was a frail old coffin-sleeper?

He edited the word *frail* from his thoughts. Antonio was strong and devious. Bruce wouldn't dream to question his authority.

"From the angel?" Antonio asked.

"Zaqiel."

"He still hasn't found his muse?" Antonio leaned back in the modern leather office chair and put up one buckle-shoed foot on the open desk drawer. "We need to become more involved. If the Fallen cannot find their muses…?"

"It's the Sinistari. He's scared the Fallen one off. What we should be doing is tracking them, both angels and muses. In fact, I think we should grab us a muse and lure the Fallen to us. You know, to make sure they find the correct match."

"It is a good idea."

"Really?" Bruce straightened and set back his shoulders. "Yeah, it is."

After lounging in bed for an hour, watching the full moon move across the sky, Eden realized Ashur might not return tonight. Had he walked out on her for good?

She should be used to it by now. But a girl never got used to being alone, whether by choice or force. What was it about her that forced people away? She had been doing well for years, not mentioning her dreams of angels to others. Yet if she could speak about them to anyone it was Ashur.

She honestly thought he cared about her. Was she fooling herself?

She slipped on her robe and strode downstairs for something to nibble on. As she walked through a swath of moonlight, she twanged the halo, still stuck in the plaster wall. They figured it had something to do with Zaqiel. Maybe, though, it simply liked the air here in Italy and glowed in response. Tonight, however, it wasn't glowing.

She was surprised Michael Donovan had left the halo here, given that he'd stolen the other three from her home. Something about it glowing had freaked him. She sensed he wasn't sure he wanted involvement in this game, but had been thrust into it. And he was in deep, what with his vampire girlfriend.

Angels and demons and vampires. It was a bizarre, impossible mix, but Eden wasn't up on supernatural creatures. Likely the juxtaposition of creatures worked just fine to them.

Unless you were a halo hunter being stalked by vampires.

And yet some vampire had purchased her paintings. And she could guess why. If Ashur's guess that she had innate knowledge of angel sigils was correct, then perhaps they were required by the vampires to summon Fallen.

"I should have asked Michael if crosses were good protection."

Down in the cellar sat dozens of jars of preserved garlic from the garden out back, but Michael had testified that garlic didn't work. So now where was the cross that Ashur had used for the warding? It had disappeared, or at least, she hadn't noticed it lying around. Eden felt sure she could rustle up a cross somewhere.

But what about a stake? She could fashion one from… a chair leg?

Maybe. She'd have to have Ashur help her with that.

She sliced a juicy peach and sprinkled cinnamon on it. The fruit satisfied what she suspected wasn't actually hunger but more longing for Ashur to return. But like the watched pot that doesn't boil, she knew he wasn't going to walk through the door if she sat and stared at it.

After eating, she decided to wash the dishes still sitting in the sink. The cataclysmic shaking the house had taking during the warding had left a coating of dust on them.

Her hands sloshed around in the dishwater, and she worked at the crusted food on a plate with her fingernail. The sensual feel of slick soap on her skin as it glided over the porcelain made her think of making love to Ashur.

Everything about Ashur was hard, save for his heart.

Yet that heart did not beat. It should bother her more, but she couldn't go there. Couldn't summon fear or loathing. He'd been so shocked when she'd told him she loved him.

But it was true. She had fallen for him, as he had fallen from heaven. The man had once been an angel. Now all he sought was joy.

Eden set the last plate aside on a towel she'd laid out for drying. She had to admit a strange sense of pride in this domestic chore. She had never washed a dish in her life. It was actually kind of rewarding to pull out a clean plate from the soapy water and admire her reflection in it. But it would be much more fulfilling if Ashur's smile were paired alongside hers.

Scratching her neck, Eden swore. "Stop it. Damn, it itches." She plunged her hand into the water and slopped it along her neck, but the soap irritated the angelkiss further.

Leaning forward and closing her eyes, she tried to focus her mind away from the burning desire to drag her finger-nails along her flesh.

"Where is he?" she muttered.

She decided to drain the sink and run clean, clear water

over her neck. Cool water did the trick as she leaned over the sink allowing it to trickle slowly over her flesh.

"Ashur, I need you," she said aloud. She didn't know if he could hear her, but she wasn't going to discount that wacky notion. "It's been four hours. Where are you?"

Suddenly the comforting warmth of strong hands slid about her waist and a hot kiss nestled against the back of her neck.

"Mmm…" She tilted her head against the crown of his head and slid her hands along his arms. "I've missed you."

"I've been missing you far too much. But finally I have you."

That voice. But even more, that scent. Sweet and subtle.

Spinning about and pressing her spine against the hard sink rim, Eden stared into the unnatural blue eyes of Zaqiel. The circle sigil about his left eye glowed.

Chapter 27

"It's about time he left you alone long enough for me to slip in." Zaqiel stood before her, less than a hands-width between them.

The disturbing lack of kindness in his voice only ratcheted up Eden's adrenaline. She gripped the sink behind her, her knuckles tightening. There were no knives in the sink; they were beneath the plates, drying on the towel.

Zaqiel was different now than when she'd seen him at the gallery. Now he looked only half human and half... She didn't know what.

Iron armor studded with spikes and gray feathers sat on his shoulders like football gear. Or maybe it *was* his shoulders. And the feathers weren't soft and fluffy, but rather fashioned of fine wire.

The iron swept down across his ribs in slashes that gave wonder if it were a part of his flesh. Tight steel abs were etched with a black tattoolike design Eden did not recognize, but she could guess it wasn't the Boy Scout emblem. It looked demonic with the five-pointed star in the circle. But how could that be?

His leather pants looked like some kind of liquid metal and resembled muscled sinews clamped together with strands of silver chain.

"Look all you like, Eden. You're mine."

"Don't say my name," she hissed. That she'd the audacity to speak to him bolstered her confidence. "I'm Six to you."

"Six, sex, it all sounds bloody delicious."

She realized with a gasp he was in the form Ashur had said was necessary to have sex with her. Half angel, half human.

"Pity your demon lover didn't refresh those wards. The fellow invited me to dinner with open arms, so to speak."

Eden swallowed and eyed the halo over Zaqiel's shoulder. If it could be used as a weapon, could she wield it?

He caught her focus and turned. "Ah! What in blazes are you doing with one of those? Such pretties are not for human consumption."

The halo didn't glow blue when he touched and sniffed it.

"Is it yours?" she asked. Slowly she walked her fingers along the countertop toward the drying dishes and knives.

"Mine? Hell no. It only glows for the one it loves, darling. I'll be damned if I can find mine. Would like to. It would serve as a nifty weapon. Not so sure I need the soul, though. Mortal death is so vulgar."

It glowed for the one it loved? Meaning…the one it belonged to. The few times Eden had seen it glow Ashur had also been present. Did it belong to him? If so, it held his earthbound soul.

"You know vampires are looking for these things? Bloody fang-faces." He twanged the halo with a snap of his finger, then danced back to her and stuck his face into her personal space. The spike piercing his lip wobbled as he spoke. "You know what I'm here for," he said matter-of-factly. "So let's get to it before loverboy returns, eh? It doesn't take long, and I promise I won't hurt you…too much." He preened the feathers on one shoulder; the fine black filaments glowed blue on the tips as his fingers stroked over them. "We can do it here where there's lots of room for my wings to stretch out. I think I'll pin you to that wall."

Eden whipped her arm about, slamming his head with the plate she'd grabbed. It shattered against his skull. Zaqiel yelled, which provided enough distraction for her to slip past him and run for the front door. If the wards were broken she wasn't about to stick around and trap herself inside with a horny angel.

The Fallen stood before the door. Her palms slapped his steel chest. The contact stung and reverberated up her arms.

A flick of his tongue snaked out at her. "I'm going to make you itch all over."

Clamping her head between his hands, he licked along her cheek and up across her forehead. A hot burn bloomed in his wake.

Eden kicked and struggled but he held her easily. His tongue traced her jaw. And then she was airborne, slung over his arms and cradled as he ran up the stairs and into her bedroom.

"Changed my mind. We're going to throw in some romance with the deal. Have you any rope?" he asked, tossing her onto the bed as if a discarded pillow.

Eden scrambled off, but again, he beat her to the door. "Ah, you should know I am quicker than air."

He slammed his forearm against her throat, pinning

her to the door. "Not funny, pretty one. And if you're not nice to me I think I will feed you to the vampires. I promise you're going to like angel sex much better than demon sex. You think he's got something you want? Wait until you see what I have for you."

"You have no feeling," she countered. "Sex is merely a task for you."

"Do you see me arguing? Feeling or not, I'm in for the prize. But oh, correction—I can get pleasure from a muse."

"I'm not your muse!"

"Doesn't matter. After I've done my match, the rest of you are up for grabs."

"What would He think of you?" she cried.

The statement stopped him momentarily. "No, no no, not going to get me with that one. I do miss Him. But He abandoned me."

"Because you fell."

"Because He was not as loving as you mortals would care to believe. Care to partake in holy ablutions with me, muse?"

"I can't carry a child to term!"

Zaqiel scoffed. "Certainly no mortal child. But my progeny? Oh, yes!"

One slash of his arm sent her soaring onto the bed where she fell onto her stomach and face. Eden struggled with what to do, how to flee. Where was Ashur? Before she could think, she was quickly wrangled and her wrists tied to the headboard with the belt Zaqiel drew out from his belt loops.

Ashur had promised to protect her. It was the only promise he had ever given her.

"I do love to play a bit before the holy event." Zaqiel tugged the belt tightening her hand securely to the iron bedpost. "You ever see an angel in all his glory? No, of course you haven't. It would render you senseless and you'd be dead, which would rule out any chance of you carrying my nephilim."

"You can't get all your glory up. You sacrificed that when you fell."

"My, my, aren't we a smarty-pants."

"You've no wings. You can't do this without them."

"Heh, heh." He stepped back and stretched out his arms. Tilting his head back, he then shrugged his shoulders.

Silver metal screamed out from his back and shoulders, stretching, growing, crashing through the window and tearing the plaster casements. The wings grew out thirty feet. Eden couldn't see where they ended. They moved fluidly, bending near his back thanks to gears that rolled on oiled cogs.

Zaqiel leaned over her. "How about these wings, bitch?"

"Is that any way to speak to the future mother of your child?"

"Oh, I do like you."

He twisted, and his wings, while folding, still cut through the wall as if a knife slicing through butter. The ceiling cracked and Eden worried more that she might be crushed by building materials than raped by an angel.

She screamed so loudly her voice cracked.

A dark figure landed crouched on the floor before the bed.

It straightened, flexing black steel arms bulging with smooth muscles forged of something dark and sinuous.

Ashur.

Chapter 28

The Fallen had the audacity to attempt his woman. *His* woman. The one female walking this earth who had been put here specifically for him. No matter the original intent when he'd fallen, he would not allow anyone else to touch her.

Ashuriel the Black snarled and smashed a steel fist into his palm. The sound clanged like iron against a rail tie. He charged the angel. They collided in the center of the bedroom. Like steel pummeling brick, the sound rang across the surrounding acres. The house timbers shook. Glass clattered throughout the adjoining rooms.

Eden screamed. Bound to the bed at her wrists, she struggled. A red robe covered her limbs, yet Ashur couldn't know if Zaqiel had been successful with his vicious deed.

"I will rip your head from your body," he growled as he fought the angel's supernatural strength. In his true form his voice bellowed.

"Fine with me, but that won't kill me, demon." He bashed a fist into Ashur's face, crushing the sinus cavity. Thick blood ran down his throat.

She witnessed it all. He'd never wanted Eden to see him in his true form. It could not be prevented.

Kicking high, he wedged a foot into the angel's gut and hiked him out the broken window. Ashur leaped. He landed on the ground with hooves, gouging out the soil and lifting a dusty cloud. The Fallen spread out his wings completely, an impressive span.

The wings were like additional arms to the angel. One bent forward, nearly stripping its gears, yet slashed Ashur across the chest. The razor-edged wingtip cut open Ashur's steel torso. Though he was made of the hardest substances from the earth, he still felt pain.

Blocking the other wing soaring toward his head, he gripped the bladed appendage and yanked, toppling the angel forward. He delivered an adamant hoof to Zaqiel's forehead, ripping it open to spill out glowing blue blood.

The Fallen flashed away. Ashur shook his head, feeling his left horn had loosened. Black blood oozed down his face and he licked at the hot substance. Dragging himself up from the pummeled grass and dirt, he shook like an animal, flinging dirt clods through the air.

The angel was nowhere in sight.

Eden's scream tightened every muscle strapping his form. Summoning Dethnyht to hand, he held it ready. Moonlight glinted on the tip. The poison stirred. Charging the villa and leaping, he crashed through the remainder of the bedroom window and landed on the floor.

The angel, in half form, looked up from where he knelt over Eden. Her robe was open down the middle, exposing her breasts and belly.

"Ashur!"

Half-human from the waist down, Zaqiel ripped open the front of his leather pants and gripped his shaft.

She must not know the horrors the angel could visit upon her. That thought steeled Ashur's determination.

But even more, she belonged to *him*.

"This is my destiny!" Zaqiel yelled.

"She is not yours!" Ashur argued.

"If I don't do her, then another Fallen will. You can't kill us all!"

"Oh, yes, I can."

"Thought you were supposed to kill this one?" Zaqiel growled. "You disobeying orders on behalf of a wishy-washy heart, Sinistari?"

"She's mine!" Ashur dodged the slash of the angel's wing.

"Is that so? If you're so lovey-dovey for the muse, then why not allow her the one thing she desperately wants? You know she wants a child. And who is the only one who can give her that desire?"

Ashur paused. Yes, a child. That was what Eden wanted most. It was what he wanted for her. She'd been right all along. The joy he'd thought he felt—it had been a deep and pure love.

Forced away from the bed by the angel's will, Ashur's body soared out the broken window and landed in the stone courtyard. He'd let down his guard. Zaqiel had taken advantage of that.

Eden's scream echoed across the countryside. It fixed into Ashur's skull and tore at his pulsing heart. Yes, it pulsed. He had a heartbeat.

Because of Eden.

Roaring and stomping the stones that cracked under his hooves, Ashur leaped for the window.

Crossing himself from shoulder to shoulder, and from

head to gut, Ashur then plunged Dethnyht into Zaqiel's back. The weapon did not go in easily. It was like pushing a steel rod through granite. The poison on the tip burned through angel flesh and made entry only a little easier as it chewed away at the seemingly impermeable metal bones and innards. It sought the light within. The solid glass heart that had once held grace and divinity.

Ashur's fists slapped against angel flesh. Dethnyht had pierced the heart.

Holding the dagger handle securely, Ashur lifted the flailing angel from the bed. He writhed and screamed in a high-pitched tone that shuddered the walls. Ceiling plaster crumbled to the floor and bed.

Ashur flung him to the floor before the window. Brilliant light burst from the entry wound in the angel's chest. Zaqiel struggled, his bent wings tearing across the ceiling. Plaster fell in chunks. Ashur leaped onto the bed and stood over Eden, protecting her from falling debris. A chunk hit his back, dented it and bounced onto the floor.

Death enveloped the Fallen in its bold and brilliant grip. Arms stretched across the floor, its chest spasmed and heaved and every pore opened and released the shimmery souls sacrificed upon Zaqiel's fall. The souls of those Zaqiel had taught the arts upon his fall, and then had stolen in payment.

Ashur glanced down at Eden. She lay motionless. Blood dribbled from her forehead. Had the angel harmed her? He moved to touch the wound, but recoiled. If he touched her in his natural form he might crush her skull, as heavy and powerful as he was like this.

Was she dead? He stared at her chest. It did not rise and fall with breath. No! She cannot—

"Ah, I knew I'd be seeing you sooner rather than later." Blackthorn toed the fallen angel dust on the floor then tapped his cane against the side of his shoe.

Ashur growled. He would rip the psychopomp's head from his neck—

"Not your call, Sinistari. Unless you're willing to make a trade?" He inclined his head to look over at the floor.

On the floor, amidst the plaster and rubble, the angel expired. Souls swirled up from Zaqiel's chest. The prize waited.

If Ashur did not move now, he would lose them. Yet Eden…

If she was dead, there was nothing he could do now. Raphael had gotten what he'd demanded. And once again the master of the Sinistari had completed his task. Blackthorn would take her soul Beneath— No!

"Take them," Ashur said, moving protectively before Eden's body. "Quickly and be done with it!"

Blackthorn posed over the Fallen, his arms extended and chest high. The thick cloud of glittering lost souls spun before him as if unsure, seeking. Gathering his arms slowly before him he collected the souls. They sparkled and clung to his body, hair and clothing, until he was amassed with them all.

"Ashur," cried a weak voice from the bed.

He cocked his head. A movement on the bed alerted him. She was alive? But the psychopomp would not have arrived if she hadn't been— The souls. Of course. Blackthorn had not come for Eden; he'd come for the abandoned souls.

"You trickster!" He lunged for the psychopomp.

"Please, Ashur, don't…"

She dared to tell him what to do?

Ashur gripped Blackthorn by the throat and began to shake him above the floor. Stealing souls was what he deserved. He was a demon. He always would be. He would never change. *She* could not change him.

"Let him have them!" Eden cried weakly.

The shimmering souls began to fall away from Blackthorn as Ashur shook him. He started to inhale, to selfishly consume the prize, but Eden's voice blocked his innate desire to possess.

"I love you."

The world stopped. Blackthorn hung limply in Ashur's grip. The souls shivered.

And Ashur's demonic heart pulsed. The black lump of metal had not been designed for love. Nothing could get inside unless he willed it.

Not even Eden.

And yet, he could not do it. These souls...

He flung Blackthorn away from him. The psychopomp flew out the window and dematerialized midair in a glimmer of souls.

Zaqiel's ashes gleamed upon the wooden floor as if fine glass crushed beneath a stampede.

Ashur bowed his head, closed his metal eyelids. A loosened horn dangled, but he was not broken. Far from it.

Yet he sensed something inside him cracked and broke in two pieces. He slapped a palm to his steel chest.

It was still beating. For her.

Impossible. He must not let her in, never again.

"Ashur?"

So soft her voice. Too soft for one so ugly and cruel as he.

He had not wanted her to see him in this form. His true form.

Yet are you not an angel in origin?

Angels can be far more wicked than demons.

He could not look at her for he was ashamed. It was the worst feeling he had known.

"You...I've...seen you before."

Her painting. She'd known him before he had known her. They'd been destined for each other.

Ridiculous.

He could never have her. Not like this. She deserved something human, someone real. Someone who could wrap her in mortal arms without crushing her. A man who could kiss her and mean it when he said he loved her. Not a beast blackened by innocent souls.

Yet she had tamed him briefly.

He'd prematurely declared that he cherished her. A roundabout means to confessing love. He knew it was love. She knew it. Surely Raphael knew as well.

He would take the punishment afforded the crime, deservingly.

Reaching back, Ashur flicked a taloned finger across the belt binding one of Eden's wrists to the bedpost. She could free herself now. But not before he made sure she would never suffer his presence again.

Turning to the shattered window, Ashur took a step away from all he desired. The one blessed piece of his heart that had opened to Eden's love now fell away. It broke upon the floor, and was crushed beneath his hooves.

"Wait, Ashur! I have your halo!"

He smirked. He had suspected that it might be his after learning his truth. Didn't do him any good now.

As the Stealer of Souls leaped out and high into the sky, the cries from the woman he loved fixed into the darkness in his chest, becoming a part of the faint pulse. But there was not room for such emotion. The imprisoned souls attempted to push her back out.

Chapter 29

Ashur had left—but he would return.

Eden repeated that thought like a mantra.

Hours later the bedroom had not changed. A corner of the plaster ceiling lay crumbled upon the bed. The window was shattered. Wood floorboards were crushed where the immense demon had stepped. Angel ash lay upon the floor glimmering like cut diamonds.

Eden sat on the floor by the door, her knees up and palms pressed to the wood. Shock had kept her there for the first hour. Disbelief, fear and yes, relief, had twisted her muscles, stretched and pulled them, and now they were so utterly weak, she simply could not move.

Much as she wished, pleaded and prayed, Ashur did not return.

And she knew in her heart he would not return. He'd turned a look over his shoulder at her before he'd leaped through the window. Shame had spotted two white pinpricks in his dark blue eyes. The demon had revealed his true form to her. And he dared not show himself to her any longer.

"It doesn't matter," she murmured. "I love him no matter his form."

The demon had not been vile or ghastly. He'd been beautiful. A black steel beast intent on her protection. Just like the angel she had painted. It had never been demonic, her work. She had known, somehow, of his angelic origins.

"Come back to me, Ashur."

She wept, releasing the fear and utter terror Zaqiel had infused into her soul. An angel had terrorized her.

And a demon had rescued her once again. For the final time.

Was she safe from other Fallen who thought to put a nephilim inside her? She stroked the mark on her forearm. The Roman numeral had not faded. It looked the same as it always had.

Tentatively she touched her forehead. A plaster chunk had fallen from the ceiling. She'd seen it drop toward her face and hadn't been able to struggle out of the way. The wound felt deep, but it no longer bled. Blood crusted down the side of her face and in her hair.

Stroking her palm down her cheek, where the angelkiss had abraded her skin, she found it did not itch. Perhaps it was only effective while the instigator was alive. Could it attract other Fallen?

She needed answers. Now. And if Ashur would not return, she'd give someone with a higher rank a call.

"Raphael!"

Eden had no idea if the angel would heed her summons a second time after he'd deemed the first unnecessary. But since an angel lay dead on her floor, she figured someone in the holy ranks must be paying attention.

"I demand an audience. Come to me. I…need you. Please. Don't you see? One of your own is dead!"

Nothing. Dust motes floated before the window, seeking the pale beams of moonlight. Below, on the ground, havoc had torn a hole in the earth where the two supernatural beings had battled.

Eden squeezed her hands into fists.

Maybe Michael Donovan could help? He'd left his business card. No, he was as confused by this situation as she was. And Ashur had not liked him being here. She would respect his dislike for the halo hunter.

"Please, Raphael. I don't know what to do."

She had felt Ashur's heart pulse beneath her palm. The heart he'd claimed hard and black and incapable of feeling had beat. For her. She knew it. She selfishly wanted it so.

A flash of white light prompted her to shield her eyes. Behind her a man spoke in a British accent. "What now?"

Eden reached back with an arm. "Can I look?"

"Yes, yes. I am in human form, not my dazzling cloak of divinity."

She turned to Raphael.

"What do you require, muse? Ah, I see Zaqiel has been dispatched. You mustn't label him one of my own. Egads. He left the ranks of his own free will. He ceased to possess divinity so long ago."

"Where is Ashur?"

"He's gone Beneath. You didn't know? Quite the sacrifice. Saves me the trouble of taking him there myself."

"You would have sent him Beneath? But he hasn't done anything wrong, except slay a wicked angel. And save me!"

"Bang-up job he did of that. You've a concussion. Avoid shut-eye for a while, if you don't want to slip into a coma."

Eden swallowed and touched the wound again. Really? She didn't feel light-headed or tired.

"They never do," Raphael said. "And then they die."

He toed the angel ash, which revealed a single white feather embedded within the diamond dust.

"What is that?" Eden lunged and grabbed the item before the archangel could. "A feather?"

Raphael snatched for the feather, but she clutched it to her chest. "No, this belongs to Ashur. For his crown. He said he claims them after he slays each angel."

Raphael crossed his arms. "Indeed? He's told you much."

"I love him. We share everything."

"Not everything, sweet peaches. He obviously didn't tell you about the deal we made."

"Deal?"

"Ashur has done his job, and he's done it well. He is highly revered by the Sinistari, by demons throughout Beneath, despite his infuriating tendency to fall in love with mortal women."

"He never admitted to love."

"Doesn't matter. I know him. He is in love." The angel sighed. "Again."

"Well, it's too late for you to banish him. I think he did it to himself. My God, why didn't he take the souls?"

"He was offered a soul for Zaqiel's death."

"What?"

"With a condition. Since he's refused so many times before, I had to add a proviso, you understand."

"He refused a soul again? But he could have been with me. What was the condition?"

"That he kill you." Raphael brushed his fingernails over his suit, polishing them with bored disdain. "He didn't even try. Idiot."

Eden hugged herself to prevent the shivers but still her body trembled. He'd made a deal with the archangel to kill her? "What would my death serve?"

"It would remove you from the running. As you've noticed, just because a Fallen one has mated with its muse doesn't stop it from seeking other muses."

"But that's not right. I'm not Zaqiel's muse. I'm Ashur's—"

Raphael tilted his head at her. "You know that? He's been exceedingly indiscreet with you."

"Ashur knew? That must be why he left me."

"He came to me recently. I told him what he suspected was truth. And then he ran home to tattle to you."

"No! I figured it out. He has a six on his neck. I'm a six. We're a pair, right? But I don't understand why. Ashur could have been a Fallen? He might have come after me to…"

"You got it. Wham, bam, start the apocalypse, ma'am."

"Why not kill all the muses? If you kill me, you must kill the rest. Or is it just me you've got a problem with?"

"Of course it's just you. Eden Campbell, painter of Fallen and Sinistari."

"But those images of angels came to me in my dreams. Maybe all muses are like that. Do you know? And what does it matter? No one will ever recognize the truth in my paintings."

"Someone already has."

"The vampire?"

Raphael nodded.

"Your artwork is insignificant in the greater scheme. Yet you've thrown a wrench into the workings of Sinistari versus Fallen. Ashuriel the Black fell in love. Again! One would have thought he'd learned the first time around. Torture and all that, don't you know."

"I love Ashur, and I know he loves me. It's wrong to punish someone for enjoying the most wondrous emotion on earth? Isn't God all about love?"

Raphael sighed. "Semantics. The Sinistari are not His subjects."

"They used to be! Ashur said his feet never touched the ground. He was still divine before he was made into a demon. That's got to count for something."

"I will not argue the rules, muse. Just be thankful you yet breathe. You got the feather. That will be your lovely parting gift. You can tuck it in your hair and forever remember your tragic hero."'

Just like that? Raphael would walk away and she'd never see Ashur again?

"What about the vampires?"

Raphael huffed out a sigh. "Insignificant to the greater order of things."

"Michael Donovan was pretty worried. They're after the halos."

"A halo is worthless in the hands of a vampire."

"They don't want to use them as weapons. Don't you know anything about the vampires?"

"Of course I do. I don't need to discuss them with a muse. Now…" Raphael lifted his arms, as if to lift into flight.

"Wait! I have to see him. I didn't get to say goodbye."

"He chose to part with you, Number Six. Accept that. Get on with your humdrum life."

"But I won't. I—I have to give him this feather. It belongs to him. Is he not the master of the Sinistari?"

"Ashuriel the Black, Stealer of Souls." Raphael angled a coy look at her. "You want to place that prize in his crown?"

Eden knew what that meant. Ashur had returned Beneath. A place she could only imagine must be hell. He wore his crown because he was master over all the Sinistari, and because with every innocent mortal soul he had stolen he had earned the right to sit upon a throne. A lonely, silent throne that annihilated his memory and battled to steal his joy.

Joy was his definition of love. She wouldn't let him lose it this time.

"Yes," she said softly. "I want to place this in his crown."

Raphael's eyes changed to an unnatural blue. They glowed like the halo in the kitchen. *It must be Ashur's*, she thought. *His halo*.

Raphael's smile carved into his face. "Indeed, it was."

"Can he wear it again? It's got his earthly soul in it!"

"Never. Once demon he can never return Above. Despite his divinity, his feet have touched earth, you see. But the feathers are his consolation."

"So the soul is in the halo?"

"It seeks Ashuriel, which is why it glows. The only way he could have possibly gained a human soul was through my mercy or if he committed a selfless act."

"But letting me live was selfless."

"Really?"

She thought about it. This was not the end. Just because Zaqiel had been dispatched didn't mean she was safe from other Fallen. And if she lived to then carry a Fallen's child, she would bring a wicked, evil creature into this world.

He should have let her die.

"Yes, well, you see what havoc love imposes?" Raphael extended a hand. "I suppose he believes he did the right thing."

The right thing.

Chris, her ex-fiancé, had used those same words when

he'd proposed to her. They were her least favorite words in the world.

"It wasn't the right thing. It was what Ashur's heart told him to do, and that's all that matters to me."

"If that is how you wish to term it. Shall we?"

Eden nodded. She reached out, expecting to take Raphael's hand, but he did not do the same.

And the world darkened. The floor fell away and rippled like obsidian lava beneath her feet. Eden's tattered red robe listed across her flesh but the breeze was so hot she felt the burn all the way to her bones.

The only sound was a steady pulse, a deep throb echoing from within her heart. She sensed no danger, yet she suspected this was not a place where she could survive for long.

"Beneath," she mouthed.

Striding forward, Eden stepped across the wavering black liquid. It was not deep. Each footstep sunk in up to her ankle, and when she pulled her foot out the black slipped away like oil. It was hot, but not oppressively so.

"Ashur?" she whispered, not daring to speak aloud for the silence possessed a soul of its own. A menacing presence tickled her soul and threatened it with dark seduction. *Come to me.*

No, she was imagining that, allowing her fear to get the better of her.

If Ashur had accepted a human soul for killing Zaqiel he would have had to kill her. And why not? Ashur deserved a soul. Had he not served as a Sinistari long enough? He was not beyond humanity; she knew that well. In fact, it was the one thing he clung to in an attempt to remain humane.

But knowing she would not have been around to watch him come into his own soul devastated her.

Clutching the angel feather as if a candle before her, she wandered toward a dark mass set on the horizon. It was miles away, and yet each footstep brought her closer as if a rocket had launched her the distance.

In three more steps she stood before a grand throne that grew out from the black liquid and pulsated as if alive. Upon the throne sat the demon master, his horned head bowed. The crown of feathers and bone clasped in one hand marked a bold, colorful gleam against the bleak landscape.

Eden stepped up and placed the feather in the crown. She palmed the feather tips and counted fifteen total. One was of amethyst, another of gold. One moved like green digital code against a black setting. Another wavered like seaweed yet was bright as a bluebird's egg.

Gorgeous, all of them. Yet they were prizes he'd claimed from fallen angels intent on spreading menace and chaos across the land.

Ashur had sacrificed so much to keep mortals safe from the nephilim. Sure, he had stolen souls, and she could not forgive him for that. But truly, this demon was kind beyond a measure that had any meaning to him. Because he had no means to measure kindness. Slaying the Fallen was his task, his life. He did it because he knew nothing else.

She prayed he would remember her love for him. That it would be the joy he would hold for centuries to come here in the Beneath.

"It belongs to you," she told him. She touched his hand, cold and hard, yet he flinched away. "Sorry."

She waited for him to lift his head and look at her. He did not, and instead glanced across the undulating ocean of darkness.

Eden could not stand this. She needed him to look at her. Did he not understand that she would never be the same without him? That if he did not regard her now, she would always wonder if she had imagined their closeness, the love they had shared?

Do not abandon me as the others have.

"I love you," Eden said, her voice wobbling.

"You cannot." His deep voice rumbled like gravel. Immense in depth, it echoed across the black sea, sending ripples fleeing in wide circles. "Don't look at me. Turn away. I am an abomination."

"You are my lover. I love you no matter what form."

"Go away from me, Six!"

"I am not a number!"

"You will always be just a number."

"Really? Then I am your number. We were destined for each other since before you fell from Above. I am your muse, and you have been my muse. I belong to you, Ashur. I am yours."

"And I will not have you!"

His bellow sent her stumbling away from the throne, but Eden did not cower. "You're just saying that. Raphael told me about your deal. You could have had freedom, a mortal soul."

He looked down, not meeting her eyes. One horn dangled at the back of his head, an injury from his battle with Zaqiel. Eden wanted to touch it, to soothe away the hurt.

"Thank you," she offered. "For my life. Many times over."

Exhaling, she set back her shoulders and wondered how soon Raphael would retrieve her. She wanted to stay, even if it meant suffocating in the oppressive atmosphere. Just to be in his company. He was not ugly to her. This man, this demon with the black heart, was the most beautiful sight she had ever seen.

"I painted you before I knew you existed."

"Means nothing."

"It means you've always been a part of me. In my soul. You, Ashur, were my muse."

It was incredible to say, and more incredible to believe. But she didn't have to believe. Eden *knew*. He had inspired her.

"Foolishness," he muttered.

She'd forgotten he could sense her moods and her thoughts.

He placed the crown upon his head. It hooked on a horn and tilted at a jaunty angle. The demon crowned in angel feathers and bone stood and towered over her. The black lake rippled silently around them. If he had sat here for a thousand years, he had suffered more than the souls he kept in his heart.

Eden could not fathom existing in nothingness for so long. He was her opposite in every way, for she had been tormented by images of angels always, while his mind must be void and black.

"I love you," she whispered. "Hold that in your heart, if you can."

Finally he looked into her eyes. The myriad colors of an angel's eyes looked back at her. Raphael had said Ashur had not lost his divinity; it had become tainted with the sins of mortals. Eden recognized that divine spark in his irises. Much as he believed he was evil, nothing could destroy his joy.

"There is something I must do," he said. What sounded like a sigh wavered in the air. "You have changed me. Made me…better."

"You've always been good, Ashur."

"Goodness does not steal life. The souls within me, I have greedily taken and relished their institution, no matter the pain."

"You knew nothing else. It's what you were made to do."

"I could have refused them and taken a mortal soul millennia ago." He looked across the undulating black sea. "I recall you asked if I could release them. There is a way."

"You would do that? That would be wonderful."

He walked around behind the throne, his hooves sinking into the oil-like surface. The throne began to melt before Eden, slipping into the black sea surrounding them. Ashur stalked away from her to the end of the island they stood upon.

Lifting his head, he declared, "I am Ashuriel the Black, Stealer of Souls, Master of Dethnyht!" He produced Dethnyht and lifted it above his chest.

He turned to her and said, "And I love the mortal, Eden Campbell."

She gasped. He admitted his love for her!

"This is for you, Eden."

He plunged Dethnyht into his demon chest. The steely black flesh opened wide spewing out the glinting souls of thousands.

A scream caught in Eden's throat.

Even while she was horrified Ashur may have killed himself, the beautiful souls swirling above stopped her outburst. So many of them, wispy and sprite. Dashing into a tornado of freedom and spinning deliriously. With one great burst, they were gone. Vanished. Returned to their rightful resting place, be it Above or Beneath. But at last they were free.

The demon dropped to his knees. It required monumental effort to lift his head and look to Eden. "I wish I could have given you more. A…child."

"No, it's not what I need from you. You've already given me—"

The demon began to fade.

Eden ran toward him, her steps splashing up viscous black oil. She would not let him die. He must not after such a sacrifice. He was hers. The world could not deny their love. "You've given me hope!"

Halfway across the sea that distanced them, her feet landed in wet grass and Eden plunged to the ground in daylight.

Chapter 30

It was the most extraordinary thing. He'd never expected the demon to give up the souls. And now that he had, Blackthorn had a lot of work to do. Souls to collect and ferry on to their final, much-awaited resting place.

He had no preference for either Beneath or Above. His job saw him visiting both places myriads of times daily. Each had its appeal. Neither would ever hold his bones when he was dead.

But first, he strode through the roiling black sea, jauntily kicking up the liquid and pausing to do a tap step. Swinging his cane, he ambled on toward the fallen Sinistari.

Approaching the hulking mass of demon sprawled at the sea's edge, Blackthorn slowed and bent over Ashuriel the Black. He tapped the demon's solid carapace. It clanked like a rusty old pickup truck.

Blackthorn smirked.

"When you're dead no one pays you the respect you deserve when you're alive. I did respect you, despite your penchant for theft. You made the world a little better—"

Struck by the sound echo of a pulse, the psychopomp leaned forward, putting his ear close to the demon's chest. Once again, the metal chest resounded with a clank, much like a heartbeat.

"No. This is not right."

Eden had witnessed the Sinistari master kill himself to release the souls he'd stolen. He'd taken his life to allow those souls to finally move on.

It had been beautiful to witness. And devastating.

He'd done it for her.

Still on the rain-slick grass before the decimated villa, Eden sat on her heels and shook her head. She'd never see him again. Never touch him. Never see his gorgeous multicolored eyes. Never know his kind regard. "Ashur!"

She didn't want to exist without Ashur. How could she walk through life without him at her side? How could he do that to her?

And yet she would not deny she had become so much stronger over this past year. After a devastating blow and losing her fiancé, Eden had begun again. She should not allow this blow to topple her.

She would not.

Truly, Ashur's sacrifice had been a selfless gift. Not a soul walking this earth could be so generous.

He'd given up his prizes so they could go on to their final rest.

A waver of brilliant light flashed behind her. The intensity of it stung her eyes. She did not turn around and closed her eyes because she knew who stood near.

"You are correct. It was the most selfless act I have witnessed in a long time. Especially from the Sinistari." The familiar angel's voice said from behind her, "No, don't turn around. I am in all my glory this time. Wouldn't want to burn your eyes out."

"Ashur sacrificed, and for what? He's dead now," she said.

"You would prefer he'd kept those souls prisoner for another thousand years?"

"No." And yes, if it would have given her one moment longer in his arms. Even if those arms were black steel. Because now she knew, had he held her once more, she would have felt his heart beat against hers. "He said he did it for me. But it doesn't feel like it. It hurts so badly, Raphael. I want him back."

"Just as you wanted to hold your baby in your arms?"

"That's not fair."

"It's the same kind of love. You and Ashuriel share the same obnoxious desire for love and family."

"Nothing wrong with that. It's something I could never give him, though." Her heart thudded against her rib cage and she sucked in her lower lip.

"I sense what you really need to know," the angel said. "The child would have been born afflicted with holes in its heart, and dependent upon life support for what would have been a short life."

She looked up. The sky was gray from the rain, but a beam of sun fought for exit between the thick clouds. It was stupid to question why God would let that happen. Eden was smarter than that.

"I wasn't meant to have a child. Not a human one, at least. I can accept that now."

"Can you? And what about letting Ashuriel go? It is the same kind of sacrifice."

"I'm thankful for the time I had with him," she managed, though the tears rolling down her face wet her lips, and her words wobbled. "But why do I have to make the same sacrifice twice? I love him."

"Love is exquisite, or so I've been told. And look at you. Able to see beyond the outer costume and into the demon's soft, black heart. Good on you, Eden. You've come a long way since the miscarriage."

"It happened for a purpose," she said. "I would have never been happy in that life."

"Your daughter's soul resides Above."

"A girl? I never knew. Truly? She's in Heaven?"

"She's there, Eden. Take peace in that knowing."

"I will. Thank you." Tears streamed freely down her cheeks. They were not sad tears, but more joyous than she could imagine. Something wondrous had come of her experience with Ashur. She could now fit that one missing piece from the puzzle into place. A daughter. "So what's next?"

The angel spoke. "You are still marked as Fallen bait. It may have been an oversight for me to request Ashuriel slay you. As you said, many more muses exist—killing one would have been fruitless. You have my apologies. Zaqiel may be gone, but others will follow."

"I'll face that hurdle when it arrives. And you needn't apologize. You're just trying to keep the entire world from falling apart."

"One does try. I must go then."

"That's it?"

"What more do you want? You've already received the greatest gift a Sinistari could ever grant—his very life!"

So she had been the selfish one. The realization pushed Eden forward onto her forearms, staring down at the grass. "I asked too much of him."

"Silly girl. Don't beat yourself up about it. Yesterday is the past. One minute ago is the past. You must learn from it, but not cling to it."

"I can do that," she said softly. "I will do that."

She had the picture she'd painted of Ashuriel. It was a pitiful replacement, but it would remind her of the wonderful days she'd learned to love and trust again.

"By the by," the archangel said, "you may like to know, since Ashur did commit such a selfless sacrifice he wins a human soul. Angel rules, and all that bother."

"What?" She almost spun about but stopped when a flash of brightness made her wince. "Does that mean…?"

"Yes. You'll be seeing him soon enough."

"He'll be human? Completely?"

"Yes, and wearing the same old costume that put your heels above your head the first time around. Only this time it'll be all human, no steel heart or talons and horns. But I thought you liked that look?"

"Will he know me?"

"He will. But he will quickly lose memory of his Sinistari service. As it should be for any former angel condemned to serve time as an earthwalker."

"Condemned? He won't think that, will he?"

"How can he? He'll have no memory of what he once was. Joy to you, Eden Campbell. See you when you arrive Above. That is, if you don't change that trajectory before your demise. Oh, and here."

Dethnyht appeared on the grass before her.

"The fact that Six still walks this earth is a tempting lure to the remaining Fallen. You might want to teach Ashur how to use that thing. Oh, and keep your distance from vampires."

"I will," she answered breathlessly. "If you could teach me how to recognize—"

The angel's presence receded like a warm sun slipping away.

Eden stood and scanned the vast grass field before the villa but saw no sign of Ashur. He'd won a soul, and he couldn't have been aware of the prize when he'd been determined to sacrifice for her and the souls.

"Ashur!"

No answer. Perhaps he was up at the house?

Clasping the huge weapon to her chest, Eden ran toward the villa. Only when the damaged walls reminded her of the battle earlier did she slow her approach. Instinctively she held the dagger with both fists wrapped about the hilt, prepared to stab.

A stone from the wall broke loose and clattered across the cobbled driveway. The entire north corner was a loss. She could see her bed from the ground.

Lowering the dagger, she sensed no others inside. She'd developed a weird sense for Fallen and their sweet scent. She prayed that sense only developed further if, as Raphael had alluded, others would be after her in the future.

"Eden!"

She spun about and dropped the dagger on the stones with a clank. There in the field stood Ashur. He wore only jeans. His arms were spread out to catch the light rain along his arms.

She ran, her bare feet slipping in the grass, and when she lost her balance, it was to fall into Ashur's arms. He spun her about and hugged her so tightly she thought he would break her.

"You're alive," she said.

He set her down and bracketed her face with his hands. "Of course I am. And you. Look at your eyes. They're so green."

"They've always been green."

"Not like this, Eden. They are like the grass, with depth and sparkle. Wow. I never realized before."

"When you were demon you could only see black and white and a little bit of color. The world must look incredible to you."

"My senses were not attuned for the earth," he answered, obviously still in grasp of his history. "I love you. I didn't want to die, but I wanted you to know the souls were free. I had to do it. Yet how am I here? I should be dead."

"You sacrificed selflessly. You won a human soul from Raphael. A soul that could have been yours so long ago."

"Maybe I was waiting for the right soul mate to come along to share it with me."

She beamed. "We can be together now. Forever. On this earth."

"Will you have me?"

"Yes, oh, yes."

"No matter my…" He paused, searching for something, then shook his head. "Not sure what I was going to say. Seems like I thought I had…horns, or something odd like that." He grinned a goofy, dismissive smile. "God, you're so beautiful. It's like I haven't seen you for a thousand years. What happened to the villa?"

"Lightning storm," Eden summoned quickly. He must have been thinking about his past. A past that was rushing away from him faster than the rain poured from the cloud.

"Hell. It did a number to the place."

"Don't worry. We can sleep in the downstairs bedroom tonight. Then fly back to New York tomorrow."

"Yeah, New York. I must have to return to work…"

"You don't have a job, lover. You'd been traveling the world when we met. I want to do more of that with you."

"A traveler, eh? Works for me. Do you think we need

to clean up that mess or can we go inside and find a dry place to make love first?"

"Mess? What mess? Let's go dry off, lover. And then we can start the first day of the rest of your life."

Epilogue

Antonio drew his finger down the list of fallen angel names the Fallen had provided to Bruce. Before him, lined along the wall, were the eight paintings Eden Campbell had created. He'd copied the sigils from each of the angels, and that paper sat beside the list of names.

He wasn't sure if any of the names would match the sigils, but he would try them all, in all combinations.

He tapped the first name. "Juphiel."

Dipping his finger in the ewer of blood near his elbow, he then began to trace the first sigil up the glass sheet he'd laid over the desk. A black candle flickered but did not snuff out.

The moon was full. The summer wormwood was in bloom. The blood had been provided courtesy of a virgin born on this very day eighteen years ago.

"I summon thee," he began to whisper in reverent tones. "Juphiel, the Fallen…."

* * * * *

*Juphiel has been summoned
to earth to search for his muse.
Read FALLEN, the next installment in the
Of Angels and Demons series
in bookstores February 2011*

*Read the prequel to the series and learn
how Michael Donovan got involved in
hunting more than just halos.
Find "Halo Hunter" at eHarlequin.com
or your favorite online retailer.*

*For more information on the
Of Angels and Demons series,
visit Michele Hauf's website at:
michelehauf.com*

nocturne™

COMING NEXT MONTH

Available June 29, 2010

#91 ZOMBIE MOON
Lori Devoti

#92 THE VAMPIRE'S KISS
Vivi Anna

HARLEQUIN®

A Romance

FOR EVERY MOOD™

Spotlight on

Heart & Home

Heartwarming romances
where love can happen
right when you least expect it.

See the next page to enjoy a sneak peek
from Silhouette Special Edition®,
a Heart and Home series.

Introducing McFARLANE'S PERFECT BRIDE
by USA TODAY bestselling author Christine Rimmer,
from Silhouette Special Edition®.

Entranced. Captivated. Enchanted.

Connor sat across the table from Tori Jones and
couldn't help thinking that those words exactly described
what effect the small-town schoolteacher had on him.
He might as well stop trying to tell himself he wasn't
interested. He was powerfully drawn to her.

Clearly, he should have dated more when he was
younger.

There had been a couple of other women since Jennifer
had walked out on him. But he had never been entranced.
Or captivated. Or enchanted.

Until now.

He wanted her—*her,* Tori Jones, in particular. Not just
someone suitably attractive and well-bred, as Jennifer had
been. Not just someone sophisticated, sexually exciting
and discreet, which pretty much described the two women
he'd dated after his marriage crashed and burned.

It came to him that he…he *liked* this woman. And that
was new to him. He liked her quick wit, her wisdom and
her big heart. He liked the passion in her voice when she
talked about things she believed in.

He liked *her.* And suddenly it mattered all out of
proportion that she might like him, too.

Was he losing it? He couldn't help but wonder. Was
he cracking under the strain—of the soured economy, the
McFarlane House setbacks, his divorce, the scary changes
in his son? Of the changes he'd decided he needed to make
in his life and himself?

Strangely, right then, on his first date with Tori Jones, he didn't care if he just might be going over the edge. He was having a great time—having *fun,* of all things—and he didn't want it to end.

Is Connor finally able to admit his feelings to Tori, and are they reciprocated?
Find out in McFARLANE'S PERFECT BRIDE
by USA TODAY bestselling author Christine Rimmer.
Available July 2010,
only from Silhouette Special Edition®.

HARLEQUIN *Presents*

Bestselling Harlequin Presents® author

Penny Jordan

brings you an exciting new trilogy…

Needed:
THE WORLD'S MOST
ELIGIBLE
BILLIONAIRES

Three penniless sisters:
how far will they go to save the ones they love?

Lizzie, Charley and Ruby refuse to drown in their debts.
And three of the richest, most ruthless men in the world
are about to enter their lives. Pure, proud but penniless,
how far will these sisters go to save the ones they love?

Look out for

Lizzie's story—**THE WEALTHY GREEK'S**
CONTRACT WIFE, July

Charley's story—**THE ITALIAN DUKE'S**
VIRGIN MISTRESS, August

Ruby's story—**MARRIAGE: TO CLAIM HIS TWINS,**
September

www.eHarlequin.com

HP12927

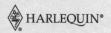

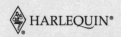
HARLEQUIN®

Showcase

LESLIE KELLY
Naturally Naughty

Wicked & Willing

On sale June 8

Reader favorites from the most talented voices in romance

Save $1.00 on the purchase of 1 or more Harlequin® Showcase books.

SAVE $1.00 on the purchase of 1 or more Harlequin® Showcase books.

Coupon expires November 30, 2010. Redeemable at participating retail outlets.
Limit one coupon per customer. Valid in the U.S.A. and Canada only.

52609057

Canadian Retailers: Harlequin Enterprises Limited will pay the face value of this coupon plus 10.25¢ if submitted by customer for this product only. Any other use constitutes fraud. Coupon is nonassignable. Void if taxed, prohibited or restricted by law. Consumer must pay any government taxes. Void if copied. Nielsen Clearing House ("NCH") customers submit coupons and proof of sales to Harlequin Enterprises Limited, P.O. Box 3000, Saint John, NB E2L 4L3, Canada. Non-NCH retailer—for reimbursement submit coupons and proof of sales directly to Harlequin Enterprises Limited, Retail Marketing Department, 225 Duncan Mill Rd., Don Mills, ON M3B 3K9, Canada.

5 65373 00076 2   (8100)0 11654

U.S. Retailers: Harlequin Enterprises Limited will pay the face value of this coupon plus 8¢ if submitted by customer for this product only. Any other use constitutes fraud. Coupon is nonassignable. Void if taxed, prohibited or restricted by law. Consumer must pay any government taxes. Void if copied. For reimbursement submit coupons and proof of sales directly to Harlequin Enterprises Limited, P.O. Box 880478, El Paso, TX 88588-0478, U.S.A. Cash value 1/100 cents.

® and TM are trademarks owned and used by the trademark owner and/or its licensee.
© 2010 Harlequin Enterprises Limited